BLACK
NIGHT

BLACK NIGHT

S.J. STRAYHORN

KENSINGTON BOOKS

KENSINGTON BOOKS are published by

Kensington Publishing Corp.
850 Third Avenue
New York, NY 10022

Library of Congress Card Catalog Number: 96-076019
ISBN 1-57566-051-2

First Printing: August, 1996
10 9 8 7 6 5 4 3 2 1

Printed in the United States of America

This book is dedicated to "Fogie," a most manly man, within whom burns the soul of a bard.

Acknowledgments

My special thanks and grateful acknowledgment go to Jo Ann and Walter Ahrens, who so graciously opened their home and their hearts, and remain unfailingly encouraging to me in my work.

No one lives [who is] without a crime.
(Nemo sine crimine vivit.)
Dionysius Cato, *Disticha de Moribus*

If you share your friend's crime, you make it your own.
(Amici vitia nisi feras, facis tua.)
Publilius Syrus, *Sententiae*. No. 10

For I must talk of murders, rapes, and massacres,
Acts of black night, abominable deeds.
Shakespeare, *Titus Andronicus*

ONE

L ENA and Eugenia had been in the Victorian house on the park for nearly a week before they noticed their neighbor to the south. The adjoining lot to the north was nothing but a pile of brick, wire, and rubble littering the ground. Much of the town of Fort Grant, they had come to discover, was in nearly the same condition, with crumbling older homes and buildings sitting vacant and idle beside newer, modern businesses and smaller, cheaper homes.

The house to the south of Lena and Eugenia was another Victorian home, though not nearly so well kept and ornate as the house the women inhabited. The morning they saw their temporary neighbor, mother and daughter blinked and looked at each other in surprise. The occupant was a man with long black hair, dark skin, and a blue bandanna tied about his head.

"Twentyish?" said Eugenia, and her twenty-five-year-old daughter shook her head.

"Older."

"How can you tell?"

"I don't know."

"I hope he's not thinking of mowing."

"So what if he does?"

"You promised you'd mow this lawn, but you haven't."

"It's been too hot. And the Lutzes' mower isn't self-propelled like ours. Besides, the grass is all brown and dying. It's not getting any taller."

"It was part of our agreement with the Lutzes that we would keep up on these things."

"Do you think they're back in Eugene mowing our lawn right now?" Lena asked.

"I doubt it," said her mother. "The weather channel says it's still raining in Oregon."

"I'm still wondering who got the worst of this trade," said Lena. "Them with the rain, or us with the heat."

"It's only for a few more weeks. You promised you wouldn't start carping at me."

"I'm not carping, Mom."

"You are. Do something nice and go introduce yourself to our neighbor. Tell him why we're here."

"How can I do that when I don't know?"

Her mother only looked at her.

Lena glanced next door again and filled her lungs with the heavy morning air. With purpose in her movements, she stepped off the porch and walked across the lawn.

The neighbor was sitting on his own porch and didn't look up until she was in his yard. When he did lift his head, his hard black glare brought Lena's feet to a halt. In the half second they stared at one another his eyes did a quick, insolent inspection of her bare legs and faded jeans shorts and traveled up her middle to her breasts, outlined against the loose T-shirt she wore. Lena blinked in angry surprise and stood back.

"Excuse me," she said stiffly. "I don't mean to disturb you."

"What do you want?" he asked.

"Nothing. I was going to introduce myself. We're staying temporarily in the Lutzes' home—"

"Temporarily?"

"That's what I said," Lena snapped, responding to his aggressive behavior. Her mouth was open to speak further, but he already looked bored. Without another word, she turned on her heel and walked away. She could feel him watching her as she went.

"Well?" said her mother when Lena returned to the porch.

"Guy's a jerk," Lena muttered.

"What did he say?"

"He asked me what I wanted. Really rude."

"He seems nice-looking."

"I was too busy being insulted to notice."

"Lena, I swear."

"What? You go talk to him if you're so interested. I'm not into this neighbor thing the way you are."

"It never hurts to know your neighbors," said Eugenia. "The better to safeguard against burglars or prowlers."

Lena's lip curled. "That asshole could be either one."

Eugenia rolled her eyes and gave a small wave to the man sitting on the porch of the house to the south. His dark brows met beneath his bandanna, and he stood up suddenly and went inside the house.

"What is his problem?" asked Lena.

Eugenia said nothing. She was staring in the direction of town and the fort again. Lena sighed after a moment and touched her arm.

"Let's go to the fort today."

"No. Not yet."

"Mom . . . we've been here for days already."

"I know. I'll go. I will. I have to."

"Please do, so you'll be able to sleep at night. You haven't slept at all since we've been here."

Eugenia looked at her daughter, dark-haired and dark-eyed like herself. "It's hard, Lena."

"I know, Mom. I mean, I don't know, but I do, just from watching you."

"I'm afraid the ghosts will come back. I'm afraid I'll see them and hear them and smell them all over again."

"Mom," Lena said gently, "you were a small girl when you lived in Vandegrift Hall. Kids in orphanages imagine all sorts of awful things."

Eugenia looked as if she were about to argue, then she changed her mind.

"I've said I'll go with you and I will," Lena told her. "I'll be right there with you the whole time."

"There were other bad things there," said Eugenia. "Things I've never spoken of."

The air felt much heavier suddenly as Lena sucked in her breath.

"You're not going to tell me something really awful, are you?" she asked.

Her mother shook her head. "No."

Lena exhaled. Then she frowned. "What was it? What was it you never talked about?"

"Things," Eugenia said, and she rose from her position on the porch. "I'm going to the store. Do you need anything?"

"Some raspberry juice. Or tea."

"Is it that time?"

"Yes, it is, and yes, I have pads."

Eugenia shook her head. "I've never understood that about you, Lena. Why do you use pads when every other young woman your age uses tampons? I use tampons."

Lena made a face. "I can't bear the thought of an alien presence inside my body."

"What did you call your last boyfriend's penis?" her mother asked, her look direct.

"Disappointing," said Lena with a grin.

Eugenia walked away and left her chuckling daughter on the porch as she walked inside the house to pick up her purse from the front hall.

Once behind the wheel of her Taurus and driving down the

tree-lined street, she allowed herself to smile at her daughter's joke. Lena was such a wit. As her mother, Eugenia had a hard time understanding why men weren't falling all over themselves for Lena. She was pretty and trim, with an athletic figure. She was bright and funny and warm. Her only flaw, that Eugenia could see, was her unwillingness to defer to any male at any time. Eugenia didn't know where the attitude and Lena's belief in female superiority came from, but it was something of a turnoff to most, if not all, of the men she encountered. At first amused by her daughter's predisposition, Eugenia was beginning to worry.

Still it was wonderful to be with Lena, and to have her there constantly. She made Eugenia laugh at the silliest things and actually made her feel stronger about coping with what she had been coping with since the death of her husband, Lena's father.

The ghosts came back to her when Leonard died. The ghosts she had known long, long ago, here in Fort Grant at the old officers' quarters that had been restructured into a home for destitute children. Vandegrift Hall, they had called it, named after a prominent citizen of the time.

Eugenia's innards still clinched and quivered at the memory of the fear she had known within the rooms of the Hall, the complete and utter desolation she had experienced during her time there.

But she had to come back. She had to look at the walls of the fort through adult eyes and try to rationalize her experiences there. It was the memory of the ghosts, she told herself, and not the actual ghosts themselves who had come to her after Leonard's death a year and a half ago.

She tortured herself until finally making arrangements to trade houses for five weeks with the Lutzes, a retired couple whose name she found in a travel magazine. They wanted to see the Pacific Northwest, and Eugenia wanted to return to Fort Grant, Kansas, and put an end to an ancient nightmare. Now all she needed was courage.

On the spur of the moment, Eugenia screwed up her face and

twisted the wheel of the Taurus in the direction of Fort Grant's leading tourist attraction.

Ross Schweig sat at one of his outdoor tables in front of the deli he owned and watched the woman in the blue Taurus while he sipped water from a paper cup. Twice in the last ten minutes she had gotten out of the car, and twice she had gotten back in again. His view of her was perfect, since his deli looked out over the parking lot of the fort. Her age was hard to guess, but her dark hair and toned figure made him place her somewhere in her early forties. He watched with interest as once again she threw open the door and forced herself out of the car. For several seconds she stood frozen on the sidewalk in front of her parking space. She appeared to be staring past the main entrance of the fort to some-where beyond. Suddenly she threw up her hands in what appeared to be frustrated resignation and slid behind the wheel of the car to start the engine.

One hand lifted the cup to his mouth, and Ross gave his head a brief shake. Whatever battle she was fighting, she had opted on retreat. He emptied the cup and crushed it in his hand before returning inside the deli. It was time to set up for the day. His was a small operation, run by only three people, Ross and two employees, even during the busy summer days when people from all places stopped to look at the refurbished fort and read about early Kansas. Ross's deli offered pop, chips, and sandwiches, simple fare for seasonal travelers. He wasn't rich, but he did all right. He paid his bills and had money left over at the end of the month.

Once or twice a year Ross himself liked to travel and get away. Earlier that summer he had gone to San Antonio, and farther south to Corpus Christi. He loved it. He wanted to pack up the bar in the Menger Hotel and take it home with him, the place had such character. It was purported to be the place Teddy Roosevelt had recruited his Rough Riders. Right next door to the Alamo.

Ross loved places with history. Corpus Christi didn't have much visible history since the city was wiped out by a hurricane every couple dozen years or so. Still he enjoyed the beach and the gulf. It was nice to leave home on occasion.

And good to get back, he thought, as he inhaled the aroma of the bread baking in his ovens. He stopped in front of a small mirror hanging on the wall behind the counter when he noticed a powdering of flour on his chin. He wiped it off and grimaced when he felt a slight soreness under the skin. He moved closer to the mirror and examined the sore spot. Ross grunted. Men over fifty-five weren't supposed to get pimples.

He thought about squeezing it, then forced himself away from the mirror when the phone rang.

"Schweig's Deli," he answered.

"Good morning," said Lorraine, a woman who worked at the *Fort Grant Tribune* as a staff writer. Ross had been dating her for over a year.

"What's up?" said Ross. He had left her only an hour or so ago, slipping out before her kids woke up.

"Rafael Chavez."

"Who?"

"The convict in our midst."

"Oh, yeah. What about him?"

"His mother died and left him her house, you know. The one near Nuss Park. I probably already told you about it, or you may have read it. Anyway, last night some people were out walking and they saw him skulking around the park."

"Skulking?" Ross repeated.

"Whatever. They said he looked like he was up to mischief."

"What exactly made them think so?" asked Ross, curious. "What was he doing?"

"Just walking . . . and looking."

"I do that all the time," said Ross.

"Yes, but you weren't convicted of killing two women."

"He served his time, Lorraine."

"He was paroled, Ross. There's a difference."

"I don't think so," said Ross. "He's still serving time because you people printed everything about him in the paper and because now he's suspected of every missing dog and pregnant cat that turns up.''

"You realize you're defending a heinous murderer," said Lorraine. "People have a right to know when someone like that moves into the neighborhood.''

"I can't argue with that," said Ross. "But don't sound an alarm just because the man takes a walk in the park.''

There was dead silence for a moment, and then Lorraine said, "You have a nice day, too.''

Then she hung up.

Ross muttered under his breath and replaced the receiver. He wasn't defending the man, he was only saying how ridiculous it was to judge a person's actions based on what you thought you knew about him. Ross remembered reading the stories about the case fifteen years ago. Every paper within three hundred miles carried pictures. Rafael Chavez did not confess to the killings, but he was guilty. Every piece of circumstantial evidence and two eyewitnesses who saw him enter the house and leave were responsible for his conviction.

It was true prison rarely rehabilitated anyone, but Ross felt it only fair to give the man an even break, at least until he proved he didn't deserve one. If he had been slipping around peeking in people's windows, or sitting near the playground and watching little girls, Ross would say there was cause for suspicion. But taking a walk in the park?

He couldn't believe the number of people driving down the street where Chavez lived in an attempt to get a glimpse of the man. Ross knew because he had done the same thing himself, cursing the impulse even as he followed it. He didn't see Chavez, and he didn't think anyone else did, either. He had heard the man's mother had left him some money along with the house, but he understood having a job was usually a condition of parole, so he assumed Chavez was working for someone somewhere. Probably nowhere close, Ross told himself. He doubted anyone in Fort Grant would give the man a job.

The timer on his ovens sounded and Ross grew busy taking out the bread and setting out the loaves to cool. His two employees arrived, high school sweethearts who couldn't keep their hands off one another behind the counter. Ross had threatened to fire the both of them after finding them messing around in his office the week before. He hadn't felt the same about his desk since.

Not that he couldn't remember what it felt like to be seventeen and horny all the time. He could. Sometimes he wondered if he would ever stop remembering.

Ross thought it must be their smell that affected him so. When Kim looked at Kevin and Kevin looked at Kim there was something almost palpable in the air between them. Many times he had to stop and wonder if any girl had ever done that for him. He didn't think so. Or maybe he just couldn't remember. Maybe it was something you didn't think about until you were sure it was never going to happen again. It made Ross irritable to think about it, and, to console himself, he thought he might just possibly ax the two lovebirds and hire himself a convicted killer in their stead. That would certainly make life interesting for a while, and who knew what it could do for his business, considering the number of people who were anxious to ogle the guy and get their first glimpse of a real live murderer. Ross might have to hire twice as much help just to handle all the business Chavez would bring to the deli.

The thought of the likely expression on Lorraine's face at finding Chavez wearing an apron and slinging meat behind the counter was enough to make Ross smile as he reached for a knife to begin slicing some ham.

Life would most definitely become more interesting.

TWO

L ENA forced herself to look with interest once more at the numerous photographs in the Lutzes' parlor, many of them depicting early denizens of Fort Grant, along with historic buildings and events. After five minutes her forced interest began to wane and she found herself walking to the window for the seventh time in half an hour and peering out at the house next door. She told herself she had no idea what she looking for, but it was a conscious evasion on her part. She knew exactly what, or who, she was looking for.

The way he had looked at Lena bugged the hell out of her. What gave him the right to look her up and down like that before even acknowledging her as a person?

The antipathy in his black glare disturbed her even more. She had done nothing to deserve such animosity.

Her eyes rounded and her breath caught when she saw a young woman approach the neighbor's house and walk up on the porch to ring the bell. Several seconds passed and she rang it again, her expression impatient. Her long blond hair swayed at the ends as she turned suddenly to look in Lena's direction. Lena fell back and away from the window, catching one fingernail in the delicate lace curtain and tearing it as she struggled to get away.

Her face hot, Lena cursed and picked up the curtain to look at the tear. Ruined. The thing was ruined, and it looked really expensive. Her mother was going to be upset.

Unable to help herself, she inched toward the window again and looked outside. There was no one on the porch.

She looked both directions down the street and saw a small red car sitting near the curb.

The girl had obviously gone inside the house.

A girlfriend? Lena wondered. She supposed it was possible her neighbor wasn't surly with everyone he met. But she hadn't noticed the girl coming by before. This was, in fact, the first time she had seen any activity around the house other than when she and her mother had seen him on the porch earlier.

Lena tried to recall if the Lutzes had mentioned anything about neighbors in their correspondence with her mother, but she couldn't remember any specifics. She was relatively sure she would have.

She would have to ask her mother when she came home. Lena probably should have gone with her to the store. Knowing her mother as she did, she could see her mom bolstering up her courage to drive by and look at the fort just long enough to give herself a case of the shakes.

It would be nice if her mother would talk more about her childhood. All Lena knew was that there were ghosts at the fort. She wasn't sure what that meant, even after asking a dozen different questions on numerous occasions.

"What do you mean when you say ghosts?" she would ask.

"I mean ghosts."

"What kind of ghosts?"

"The scary kind," her mother would reply, and quickly do her best to change the subject. It was frustrating beyond belief, and it was the main reason Lena had agreed to accompany her mother to the huge outdoor oven that was Kansas in September.

September wasn't supposed to be like this. It was supposed to be cool and brisk, with a bite to the air, not sweltering and muggy and miserable. Lena missed Oregon.

As she was looking out the window she saw her mother's blue Taurus pull into the drive. Lena walked outside to help with the groceries, and with one look at her mother's face she knew she had been right.

"You've been to the fort," said Lena.

Eugenia turned away to pull out a sack. "I went by, yes."

"You didn't stop?"

"No. Could you get the milk?"

Lena took the milk and reached for the other sack.

"Take me with you next time, Mom. It'll be easier. I've been there myself already, and—"

Eugenia's head came up. "You've been through the fort?"

Lena nodded. "The second day we were here, when you took a nap I went over there. I didn't see anything to be afraid of. It's an interesting place."

Still holding the sack, Eugenia stared at her daughter. "When you were in the building that used to be Vandegrift Hall . . . did you feel anything?"

"Curiosity," said Lena, with a shrug.

Eugenia released her breath and walked past her daughter to go inside the house. Lena followed, frowning at her mother's relieved expression.

"What was I supposed to feel?"

"Nothing."

Lena gritted her teeth and marched after her mother to slam the sack of groceries onto the kitchen counter.

"Don't do that to me, Mother."

Eugenia turned away to begin unloading the sacks and putting things in the refrigerator. When she made no response, Lena muttered under her breath and left the kitchen. It was no use. Once her mother clammed up she stayed that way, and the more Lena pried, the more wrong she felt. She didn't want to cause any pain.

She walked onto the front porch in time to see the blonde leaving the house next door. The visitor was hiking up her panty hose and trying to count some money in her hand at the same time. Lena stared at the woman's rumpled appearance, much different than when she had arrived, and came to an unsettling conclusion.

If that girl wasn't a hooker, then she had done some pretty swift housecleaning. And most housekeepers didn't wear dresses, panty hose, and heels to work.

Strange hours for a hooker, though, Lena told herself, as if she knew much about the business practices of such people.

She watched the woman saunter out to her car, and then she looked at the house again. Her neighbor was at his door, looking not at his departing guest, but at Lena.

Once again she felt herself being thoroughly inspected visually, from the tops of her toes to the crown of her head, his gaze lingering on the curving places in between.

Prepared this time, Lena stared right back, giving him the same insolent once-over he had given her. Beyond a brief, noticeable blink, there was nothing to indicate he was surprised at her boldness. In fact he stepped even farther out of his door and stood holding it open while he looked at her looking at him.

Unwilling to back down, Lena stood her ground. At least until her mother called her name. Eugenia's strident tone told Lena the torn lace curtain had been discovered. Fighting the urge to cringe, Lena gave a visible sniff and turned her back on her neighbor to go inside the house.

She felt better after that, after showing him she wasn't intimidated by his juvenile tactics. Her mother managed to make her feel like dirt about the curtain, however, so she was forced to scour the phonebook and later take the curtain into town with her to see if she could find the address of the one seamstress whose ad mentioned lace.

After a small amount of wandering she managed to locate the shop and she took the curtain inside to place it on the counter.

There was no one in attendance, and she looked for a bell to ring. The counter was empty but for a cash register.

"Hello?" she said several times, and waited.

Nothing.

Lena was tempted to leave. If she were at home she might have, but this appeared to be the only place capable of repairing torn lace, and she was stuck. After knocking hard on the counter and saying another loud hello, she walked over to part a curtain behind the counter and looked around. Boxes. Lots of boxes and lots of garments hanging on hangers. Looked like the back room of a dry cleaners.

"Hello?" she said again, and went on walking. Finally she heard the sound of someone crying. Someone else was talking in low, soothing tones as if to console.

"I don't know what he wants or needs from me," said the woman with the weepy voice. "This morning when I called to tell him about Rafael Chavez he acted as if I was a nuisance of some sort and shouldn't waste his precious time with such trivial nonsense."

"I would hardly call Rafael Chavez trivial nonsense," said the other woman. "It's not every day we have someone of his ilk move into the community."

"All I did was repeat what I heard, that Chavez was skulking around in the park last night. Ross made me into some kind of small-town harridan on a witch-hunt."

"Why don't you dump him, Lorraine? I've told you all along he's not interested in anything permanent with you. He's just not the type."

Lena cleared her throat and stepped into the back room. "Excuse me? No one was out front, and I heard voices back here."

A woman with bright, dark eyes and smooth Asian features jumped off a stool and gave a pat to the back of the crying woman, who looked at Lena with red, mascara-smeared eyes and then turned her head to blow her nose.

"I'm terribly sorry, I didn't hear you come in," said the woman standing. She extended a hand and waited for Lena to precede her to the front of the shop. "Tell me what I can do for you."

"A torn lace curtain," said Lena, walking ahead. Once in the front of the shop at the counter, she presented the tear and asked, "Can you fix it?"

The woman frowned. "Ouch. That's a bad one. I can't make you any promises, but I will try."

"I appreciate it," said Lena.

"Name, phone, and address, please," asked the woman, and Lena told her.

The dark head lifted. "You live right beside him."

"Who?" asked Lena.

The woman smiled. "Never mind. I was just thinking aloud to myself. Do it all the time. I'll try to have this by next Friday, but if I don't, I'll call you."

"Thanks," said Lena, and her brows were pinched as she left the store.

Live right beside whom? The Rafael Chavez they were talking about?

What on earth had the man done?

On the way home Lena chewed on her lip and allowed her imagination to run wild. She knew there was something about him that wasn't quite right, something sinister in those black eyes and dark, winged brows that made her skin crawl.

Worst of all, she was more excited than she had been in a long time. She hated herself for it, for being intrigued by him and made curious by the comments of the women in the seamstress shop. All the same, she knew she was going to return to the Victorian home on the park and set her mind and body on permanent surveillance of the man in the house to the south. She couldn't resist.

Besides, she was already bored. If she were back home in Eugene she would be busy at work, testing and evaluating children for everything from speech problems to learning disabilities. Her mother was a speech pathologist and they worked together as a team, traveling from school to school and offering their services to parents for sliding scale fees. Lena had approached her mother about visiting some of the schools in Fort Grant, but Eugenia wasn't interested. She hadn't come here to work, she said.

Back at the Lutzes, Lena found Eugenia lying on the long, richly patterned sofa in the parlor, her eyes closed. Lena crept over to listen to her breathing, and the sound of it said her mother was dozing.

Lena stepped back and watched her a moment. Her mother had done just that, dozed, since they had arrived in Fort Grant. At night Lena would awaken to hear her prowling the floors and turning on faucets and doing everything in the world but sleeping. This dozing state she was in now was only the first or second stage of sleep, a hypna-something state, Lena guessed or thought she remembered. It wasn't the deep, refreshing sleep a person needed six to ten hours a night. If her mother didn't sleep soon, she would be overcome with exhaustion.

Somehow, Lena told herself, she would have to get her mother to that fort and get this business over with.

Ross stood behind the counter of the deli with Kim and Kevin and eyed the smirks on their faces. Then he surprised all of three of them by saying, "Out. Both of you. Last week I warned you. This time you're gone."

The smirks changed to openmouthed stares of disbelief.

"You're firing us?" said Kim.

"Both of you," repeated Ross.

On Kevin's young face the disbelief became petulant anger. "Over a little thing like a hair?"

"Pubic hair is no little thing in the food service business. That woman was so ill she threw up."

Kevin's mouth twitched like he wanted to smile; then he thought better of it.

"Hey," he said, "I didn't make the sandwich."

Kim stared at her boyfriend. "You did so, you liar. I stood right there and watched you."

Kevin got in his girlfriend's face. "Well let's take the hair down to the police lab and find out who it belongs to, little miss-help-me-masturbate."

"Shut up," said Ross, and he lightly cuffed Kevin on the shoulder. "Get your things and get out. I'll mail your checks to you."

Kim started crying. "This isn't fair. I shouldn't get fired. I didn't do anything."

"Oh, but I should?" said Kevin. "God, listen to you, you little baby. Cry and maybe he'll feel sorry for you, huh?"

Kim cried harder. Ross ignored both of them and went into his office, closing the door behind him.

For the next twenty minutes he heard loud, long recriminations and angry invective, and then things became quiet. He put his hands on his desk, wondering what he was going to do, and then he heard the bell on his counter. He walked out to find an attractive young woman standing at the counter. She wore a vexed expression, and when she saw Ross she placed her hands on her hips.

"Does everyone in town conduct business this way?"

Ross ignored the question. "I'm sorry. I just lost my two employees. What can I get for you?"

She exhaled. "Two turkey sandwiches on wheat bread with mozzarella cheese."

"Special sauce on that?"

"What's in the sauce?"

"Fat-free everything."

The woman hesitated, then nodded. "Okay."

"Anything to drink?"

"No, thanks."

Ross rang up the amount, took her money, gave her change, and told her he'd have her order right up. She nodded and walked to the front of the deli to look out the window. Something about her jangled a few bells in Ross's memory, but he couldn't put his finger on it.

As he worked he kept an eye on her, and he noted that she hadn't relaxed any. Stiff as a board.

Ross shook his head. Women like that bothered him. Women who thought everyone wanted something from them, walking around with an attitude and just daring some man to come up and breathe near them.

The second he finished the thought, the woman surprised him by whirling and asking if he was going to be hiring anyone else.

Ross blinked. "I . . . yeah, I have to. You know somebody who'd be interested?"

"I am," she said. "But only for the next four weeks or so. I don't live here, I live in Oregon, and I'll be going back there sometime in October. I can help you out until then."

"I don't know," said Ross. "I was hoping to find someone permanent."

"You still can," she said. She turned back to the window again. "I need to be close to that fort."

"The fort?"

"Yes."

"Mind if I ask why?"

"It's a long story. Do you need me or don't you?"

Ross inhaled and held his breath several seconds before answering. "I need *some*one, and no one else has come in to volunteer, so I guess you're it. When can you start?"

"Today," she said. "How late are you open?"

"Until eight."

"Okay, great. I'll take my sandwiches home and be back in an hour."

She came forward to take the completed sandwiches from him, and he suddenly thought to ask her name.

"Lena Fairfax," she answered. "I'll fill out an application when I come back, whatever you need."

"All right. I'll see you later."

Ross shook his head again as he watched her go. When she was out of his sight he asked himself what the hell he had just done. Hired someone for four weeks. So she could be close to the fort.

"Great," he muttered to himself.

Lorraine was going to love this state of affairs, particularly once she got a look at the new help.

THREE

RAFAEL Chavez had worked in the barber shop in Lansing for a time, so it was no problem for him to cut his own hair. It was a spur of the moment impulse, not something he had been planning since his release. He simply looked at himself in the mirror that afternoon and decided the hair had to go. Without the hair he wouldn't need the bandanna to keep it out of his eyes. And maybe he wouldn't be so recognizable around town.

He was ready to get out. He was tired of being cooped up inside, which was almost worse than Lansing, since he had at least gotten time in the exercise yard and the weight pit while incarcerated. Already he could feel his muscles growing flaccid and losing tone. He did what he could around his mom's house, repairing screens and fixing whatever looked broken, but now he was ready to go outside.

The rotted lattice beneath the porch had snagged his attention that morning, at least until the neighbor woman came over. Rafael had been prepared for the worst; he had been ready to hear whatever abuse she cared to heap on him and remain unmoved. He had listened to plenty of it already, most of it behind his back in the form of whispers at the grocers and jeers at the hardware store. He had expected nothing less.

What he didn't expect was the shapely, haughty female with the arching eyebrows and the lively, snapping eyes that tried so very hard to put him in his place.

He drank in the sight of her like a man on the brink of dehydration; and paid for it later when he couldn't stop thinking about her mouth, and her hips, or the way her breasts jutted out from beneath her T-shirt.

Rafael had a girlfriend when he went into prison at the age of eighteen. Now he was thirty-three, and he had had sex with only two females in his life, one of them that day.

The neighbor obviously knew nothing about him, had been told nothing by the Lutzes, who surely had been eager to get out of town once they heard Rafael was coming home.

Maybe they were hoping he would be arrested again before their return, or that someone in town would take out a gun and shoot him. Several such promises had come to him through the mail in the last two weeks. Scared people using cowardly tactics to make themselves feel better.

Rafael wished he could leave. He wished he had been paroled out to anywhere but Fort Grant. The job he had been promised by a local contractor fell through just two days after his release. No one on the crew wanted to work with him, and everyone threatened to quit unless he was let go. The boss said he was sorry and claimed he was left no choice, leaving the newly paroled and already-apprehensive Rafael to live off the meager amount his mother had left him when she died. In prison he had earned a degree in communications, but he wasn't likely to find anything in that line, he knew. He would probably end up taking something for minimum wage, if he was even that lucky.

He thanked God he had no rent payment and blessed his recently departed mother for being so good to him, the son who had done so much to disappoint her and made her time on earth so miserable.

Rafael couldn't think about his mother without becoming angry at himself, without wanting to smash his fist into something or beat his head against a wall until he drove the thoughts of her away. He couldn't bear it.

He had never known his father. All he knew of the man was his name, and that he had left before Rafael was born. A disgrace to her family, his mother had gone off on her own in search of his father and ended up in Fort Grant as a waitress and later the owner of her own restaurant. His mother never returned to her relatives, never wrote to them or called, and she never looked back. Rafael had to learn to do the same.

Restless at his thoughts and unwilling to continue, he forced himself outside to look once more at the rotted lattice. The heat was still oppressive, but showed signs of letting up as the sun neared the tops of the trees in its descent. An old man sitting on the porch of the house to Rafael's south had his eyes closed, his hands on a cane. He was nearly deaf, pretty much blind, and a hospice worker came to check on him regularly, Rafael's mother had said.

As Rafael stood outside he saw his other neighbor bound out of the Lutzes' house and hurry toward the blue Taurus parked in the drive. The older woman, with darker hair and skin more olive in tone, walked out after, her expression pinched and seemingly worried. The younger woman gestured impatiently for her companion to come on.

Then the younger woman turned and saw Rafael.

Her eyes registered first confusion and then surprise at sight of his haircut. Then her spine stiffened. From where he stood, Rafael could see the flare of her nostrils and the thinning of her lips. Her body was poised as if for flight, and she forcibly lowered her hand to open the passenger door of the Taurus.

"Mother, come on," she called, her voice sharp.

"I still don't understand why you did this," said the mother as she climbed down the steps.

The daughter made no reply, only went on matching stares with Rafael.

He enjoyed that about her, the fact that she wasn't in any way cowed or intimidated by his overtness.

Most women couldn't handle being stared at in such a fashion. They either pretended to look for something in their bag, acted like they didn't see, or lowered their heads and stared at their fronts, to see if everything was in order.

Not this woman.

Rafael dropped his gaze finally as the car left the drive. He filled his chest with air and then released it through his nostrils.

Too bad. It was too bad he couldn't do anything about her. He sure as hell wanted to.

Once someone decided to fill her in about him she'd start looking in her bag, acting like she didn't see, or glancing at all her buttons.

He wondered where she lived, and why she and her mother were staying temporarily in the Lutzes' home. He'd never heard of anything like that before, people swapping houses. Maybe people from different countries, but these women were obviously Americans. He wondered what she did for a living, and decided it had to be something good, since she had the money to leave her job for an extended period of time. She could be anything with those legs of hers.

Rafael clamped down on the direction of his thoughts. No need to start thinking about that again. He didn't have any more money to spare, and he didn't necessarily want to spend any more time with Ruanda. She was okay, but she had a funny smell. Still, he would have to thank his old friend, Bob Pena, for giving him her number. Pena was one of the few friends Rafael possessed in Fort Grant. They had known each other since high school, and Pena had stood by Rafael through the worst of everything. It was Pena who talked the construction foreman into giving Rafael a job to get out on parole. It wasn't Pena's fault the job had fallen through.

Pena would come around, but he had a wife and kids and a lot of responsibility on his shoulders. Rafael understood.

What Pena was doing with Ruanda's phone number was the part Rafael didn't understand. He thought if he had a wife, kids, and a good job, he would have everything.

Fifteen years of incarceration had led him to such a belief.

It wasn't something he thought was going to happen for him anytime soon. Someday, maybe. Probably somewhere else.

He walked around the house to the detached garage to look and see if there was any paint stored anywhere, something to match the lattice in front.

Besides his mother's old Ford Escort, there were lawn chairs, a lawn mower, various boards, boxes, a few tools, and other assorted clutter. There was no paint.

The lattice wasn't going to cost much, Rafael knew, but the paint would cost more than he could comfortably afford for simple house repair.

He threw a screwdriver into a box, frustrated. If he couldn't do it right, he wouldn't do it at all. He walked back into the house and pulled off his clothes to put on a T-shirt and a pair of running shorts.

It was time to let everyone in Fort Grant have a good look at Rafael Chavez.

As they approached the deli Lena looked at her mother and saw that her gaze was fixed across the parking lot, on the entrance to the fort.

Lena said, "We can go in now if you like. I told him I'd be an hour."

Eugenia looked at her. "You did this on purpose. You took this job so I would have to bring you here every day and pick you up every evening."

"I took this job because I'm already bored senseless and I could use some extra bucks. It's not like I signed on as a tour guide for the fort itself."

"I never realized you could be so calculating, Lena."

"And I never realized you could be such a coward, Mother."

The two women stared at one another.

"You don't know what you're talking about," said Eugenia after a moment.

"Maybe not," Lena agreed, "but I know you can't keep putting off the inevitable. This is why we came here, isn't it?"

Eugenia gripped the wheel. "I didn't realize how difficult it would be. I didn't anticipate the fear."

"Fear of what?" asked Lena in frustration.

"The past, Lena."

"Your past?"

"The past."

Lena shook her head. "I'm sorry, Mother. That makes no sense to me."

Eugenia drew in breath and sighed. "You'd better get in there if he's expecting you. What did you say his name was?"

"I didn't ask."

"He probably thinks you're something of a fruitcake."

"He's probably right. Come in and meet him, so he can see the fruit that made the fruitcake."

"Not tonight, honey. Maybe next time."

"Are you sure? He's a nice man. And good-looking, in a rough way. He has really nice, gentle eyes."

Eugenia was surprised. "You met him for only ten minutes."

"So?"

"Nothing. I've never heard you say such a thing about a man."

"Don't start with that again, Mother. I'm not the wicked manbasher you make me out to be." Lena sighed and reached for the door handle. "I'll call you when it's time to come and get me."

"I can let you have the car, Lena."

"No, you can't. For crying out loud, I'm trying to help you. Let me, okay?"

Eugenia gave a brief nod. "I'll see you later."

Lena got out of the car and went inside the deli. Eugenia

turned in front of the shop and then went back to the parking lot of the fort to sit behind the wheel of her car and stare at the fort entrance.

Her daughter's heart was in the right place, but she had no idea what Eugenia was dealing with and no conception of what she was about to face.

Coward, Lena had called her.

She couldn't know what Eugenia experienced, couldn't even guess. Lena was obviously not like her mother in that particular area.

But then Eugenia wasn't *that way* anywhere else. Just here in Kansas. Here at the fort.

Nowhere else was she a coward. Or at least she hadn't been until Leonard died. Until the ghosts came back.

With a sudden burst of effort and energy, Eugenia threw open the door of the car and dashed up the walk to the entrance of the fort. In seconds her breathing grew tortured, but she did not allow herself to stop. Using her momentum she reached for the heavy entry door and jerked it back with both arms to go inside.

A man dressed in the uniform of state park personnel looked up from behind a long counter in the immediate room to her right.

"I'm afraid it's a little late to tour the fort today, ma'am. We were just about to close."

A tremendous surge of relief, quickly followed by angry disappointment, passed through Eugenia. She had made it all this way, come this incredible distance, only to be sent home again.

"Ma'am?" said the man again. "Are you all right?"

"I . . . yes," Eugenia answered. "Would you mind if I used the rest room?"

The man hesitated, then nodded. "Straight down the hall and to your left, past the stairs."

Eugenia thanked him and walked toward the stairs. As she neared the opposite end of the building she could see large windows in the wall. Beyond the windows she would be able to see the restored officers' quarters that had been the site of Vandegrift Hall.

Her footsteps slowed until it felt as though she were trudging through thick black mud instead of walking on a polished and gleaming hardwood floor. Her hands reached instinctively out before her, as if to ward off whatever she was about to see. It was already too late; she could hear their voices.

Trembling fingers touched the panes of the windows and she looked outside with eyes that did not blink. Directly across the parade ground from Eugenia was Vandegrift Hall. There were children on the steps, little boys in long pants, woolen shirts, and suspenders, and little girls in worn dresses. These children were not playing, they were working. They were scrubbing the steps. As Eugenia stared, one little girl looked over her shoulder and seemed to spy Eugenia behind the glass of the window. She stood up and pointed. Soon the other children were standing up and pointing, and Eugenia squeezed her eyes shut.

Please no, she prayed. *Not again.*

The little ones broke her heart.

When Eugenia opened her eyes she saw one small boy, aged four or five, with an open, trusting face and hopeful eyes, stumble down the steep steps and begin to run in her direction. Other children made similar motions, but a large white-haired woman in a dull gray dress appeared at the top of the steps with a wooden bucket in each hand, and in a deep, almost-masculine voice began to shout at them to halt. The children immediately stopped—all but the boy, who fell down and tore his trousers, but picked himself up again to continue, his eyes now round and terrified. The woman at the top of the steps made a noise of fury and hurled one of the buckets at the running child.

Her aim was perfect.

Eugenia squeezed her eyes shut again and felt her throat begin to hitch. She couldn't open them again. She couldn't. There was so much blood.

"Ma'am?" said a voice behind her. "Ma'am? We're closing now. You'll have to go."

A hand at her arm made her turn. The man's face was concerned, but also impatient.

"I'm going," she said.

"You can come back tomorrow if you like. We open at nine."

"Thank you," Eugenia whispered, and walked unsteadily down the hall away from him. Once outside she drew in air and willed her limbs not to wobble. She made it to the car, and after three attempts managed to find the strength to open the door.

As she sat down behind the wheel, a sudden rush of nausea forced its way up into her throat. Eugenia turned her head to the side and let the vomit pour out of her mouth into the passenger seat.

She wasn't going back to that fort.

Not ever.

FOUR

R OSS was just putting the Help Wanted sign in the window when he saw a lean, muscular young man run by. The young man saw the sign, stopped, then jogged back. He wiped beads of sweat from his forehead with his T-shirt and then wiped the palms of his hands on his shorts before opening the door. Ross glanced over his shoulder to look for the stuffy Lena and saw her slicing pickles with her back to the door. She had told Ross to go on looking for permanent help, and that's just what he was doing.

The young man followed Ross's glance and came to a stop when he saw Lena. His limbs went motionless.

"What can I do for you?" asked Ross.

"Nothing," said the perspiring jogger, and he started out again.

"Did you come about the job?" Ross asked, and the question made Lena turn to see whom he was addressing.

When she saw who was with Ross, her mouth tightened. The man in question locked gazes with her and didn't even look at Ross as he answered.

"Yes, I came about the job."

"Mr. Schweig," said Lena. "May I speak to you a moment?"

"Hold on," Ross told her. The guy was older than Ross had at first believed, and Ross was having a hard time trying to understand what someone his age was doing applying for work in a sandwich shop, when suddenly he recognized the infamous dark-skinned face.

"Mr. Schweig," Lena said again, and he glanced over his shoulder at her.

"What is it, Lena?"

"May I please speak to you in private?"

Ross looked at the man in front of him again and asked him to stay put while he got an application from the office.

Still looking at Lena, the man nodded. Ross walked back to his office and beckoned for Lena to follow. For a brief moment he wondered if he should leave Chavez alone in the deli with the cash register, then he chastised himself for the paranoid thought and went to his file for an application.

Lena followed him in and said, "I can't work with that man."

Ross paused and turned to look at her. "Are you telling me you're a bigot, Miss Fairfax?"

"I'm no such thing," said Lena, her voice sharp. "It's bad enough I have to live next door to him while I'm here; I'd prefer it if I didn't have to work with him, too."

"Next door, you say?"

"That's right. My mother and I are staying in the Lutzes' home while they stay in our house back in Oregon."

"Just what is it you find so offensive about him?" Ross had to ask. "His prison record? Or his sweat?"

Lena blinked. "Prison record. I knew it had to be something like that."

Ross was surprised. His mouth opened to tell her the rest, what everyone else in town was talking about, but something made him shut it again. Chavez didn't look like a hardened criminal. He didn't have any tattoos and his hair wasn't crusted and greasy. He looked like a guy just desperate enough to apply for a minimum wage job.

"If he wants the job, he's got it," Ross said, surprising himself for the third time that day. "Next weekend is the Mountain Man/ Indian Rendezvous at and around the fort, and I'm going to need the help. You don't want to work with him, don't."

With that, Ross slipped an application from the file and strode out of the office, leaving Lena to stand with her jaw muscles clenched.

Chavez looked surprised to see him back so quickly. Ross handed him the application and grabbed a pencil from the counter.

"This is just a formality of sorts. Have you ever worked in food service before?"

"Yes," said Chavez, his voice even. "In prison."

"Uh-huh. Well, things move a little faster here. We take the order and get it out as quickly as possible, with a good, quality sandwich. Nothing sloppy. Would you mind if I ask to see your hands?"

Chavez hesitated, then he presented his hands.

Ross nodded. Clean, trimmed nails with no dirt underneath.

"Good," he said, and though his stomach was jumping nervously, Ross asked the convicted murderer when he could start.

"Tomorrow?" said Chavez, a question.

"That's great," Ross told him. "Be here at nine-thirty so I can start training you."

Chavez nodded and went on filling out the application. When he was finished he handed it to Ross and waited for a reaction. Ross reached for his hand.

"Mr. Chavez, my name is Ross Schweig. You can call me Ross."

Chavez shook his hand and slowly nodded again. "Thank you. Thank you for hiring me."

"I can't pay you much, but if you do right by me, I'll do right by you."

"You know who I am," said Chavez, his voice uncertain.

"I do. I'll see you in the morning, Rafael."

He breathed out in relief. "Thanks. Thanks again. See you tomorrow.'' He went to the door, then he paused and turned back. ''Is she going to quit?'' he asked of Lena, who had yet to come out of the office.

Ross shrugged and lifted his hands. Chavez inclined his head and went out the door to resume his run. When he had gone, Ross went in to find Lena. She was waiting just behind the door.

''Are you going to quit?'' Ross asked.

Her sable eyes flashed as she looked at him. ''You mean am I going to let him run me off?''

''Yeah, that's what I mean.''

''No,'' she said, and she went back to her pickles.

Ross smiled and shook his head, wondering if he had decided in his sleep last night to get up and rearrange his life that day.

He must have.

Rafael enjoyed an extra spurt of energy as he ran away from the deli. He felt good inside. The job wasn't much, but it was a job, and it meant there was one person in Fort Grant who didn't believe he was a monster and wasn't afraid to associate himself with an ex-con. Ross Schweig seemed like a genuinely nice guy, honest and nonjudgmental.

As Rafael ran he thought of his neighbor. He had heard Ross call her Lena.

Lena wasn't happy.

Tough, thought Rafael. At first he had thought to back out and leave, forget he ever saw the sign in the window. Then she had turned and stabbed him with those eyes of hers, daring him to look at her.

Sassy, snotty little princess.

It was likely to be nothing short of torture working behind a counter with that body in close proximity to his own, but he thought he could manage.

He was smiling at the thought when he rounded the corner and saw the police cars in front of his house.

Rafael cursed under his breath and slowed to a walk, thinking to himself, *and so it begins.*

The policemen knocking on his door turned in unison when Rafael spoke to them.

"May I help you?"

"Rafael Chavez?" the man on the right asked, his voice flat and unemotional.

"Yes," said Rafael, knowing the guy knew damned good and well who he was.

"We have instructions to bring you in for questioning."

"Pertaining to what?"

"Can't say."

"Am I being arrested?"

"No, you are not. If you wish to contact a lawyer before you answer any questions, that's fine."

"I don't have to do that," said Rafael. "I haven't done anything."

"Then you'll have no objections to coming with us."

"None whatsoever," said Rafael, and he walked toward the nearest police car.

On the way to the station, the policeman driving the car looked Rafael up and down and said, "You talk pretty good for someone locked up fifteen years."

"Thanks," said Rafael.

"You go to school while you were there?"

"Yes."

"It shows. I think it's great when a man uses time like that to better himself."

Was this a compliment? Rafael wondered. Then he saw the tiny smirk on the man's face. He didn't know what else he expected. He had attempted to educate himself in prison. Lots of guys did. Some gave up and some didn't. Rafael was one of the few who didn't.

Not that educating himself had done him much good, seeing

as how once again he was in the back of a police car after only two weeks of freedom.

He linked his hands together in front of him and remained silent for the rest of the drive. At the station he was led past the desk to a room down a hall with a table and chairs. Rafael knew the routine. The officers left him in the room by himself, where he was supposedly going to grow agitated and anxious and uncomfortable and ultimately be a nervous wreck by the time someone came to talk to him. Rafael sat down to wait.

An hour and a half later, a detective came into the room. The man was Hispanic, like Rafael, but his hair was thinning and his stomach was so large it strained the buttons on his shirt. He sat down across from Rafael and said two words: "Ruanda Beker."

Rafael's pulse jumped, but he allowed his face to reveal nothing.

"I saw her this morning," he said.

"Saw her?"

"Had sexual relations with her."

"Did you pay her?"

"That would be illegal, wouldn't it?"

"What else did you do?"

"What do you mean?"

"With Ruanda."

"Nothing."

"You sure? You sure you didn't take her over to the park and bash in her brains with a rock? I mean, it's good she had your address in her purse, otherwise we wouldn't have had a clue."

"I've already admitted I saw her this morning," said Rafael. "Are you telling me she's been killed?"

"Couple kids found her not too long ago. Who told you about Ruanda Beker? How did you get her number?"

"A friend gave it to me."

"Who?"

"A friend."

"Roberto Pena? He's the only friend you got around here, ain't he?"

Rafael said nothing. The detective sat back in his chair and eyed him.

"My name is Morales. What do you think I should do with you, Chavez? You're out for two weeks and a prostitute fertilizes the park with her brains."

Rafael remained silent.

"You know what I oughta do? I oughta get your parole revoked. I can't prove you did Ruanda, but I hear you got fired from your job already, and one of the conditions of your parole was gainful employment, am I correct?"

"I have a job," said Rafael.

"Yeah? Where?"

"Schweig's Deli. I start tomorrow."

"Ross Schweig hired you?"

"Yes."

"Where were you today?"

"At home."

"Can you prove it?"

"My neighbors saw me."

"Did they see Ruanda leave?"

"Yes, as a matter of fact, the daughter did."

"Got in the car and everything? Drove away from your house and you weren't anywhere near her when she left? See, I figure you could've followed Ruanda when she left."

"I didn't."

"We'll see."

"Talk to my neighbors."

"Okay. I'll ask them. Which ones?"

"The women staying in the Lutzes' home."

Morales looked up. "What happened to the Lutzes?"

"I think they swapped houses for a month."

"Huh. Probably heard you were moving in. Okay, Chavez, I'm going to call Ross Schweig and talk to your neighbors. Don't think about going anywhere, because I'm going to have someone watching you. Now get out of here.''

Rafael got up and walked out of the room. The officer waiting outside didn't offer him a ride, and Rafael didn't ask. He left the police station and started walking, trying to ignore the image in his mind of Ruanda Beker lying dead in the park.

Halfway home he saw a blue Taurus pull up behind him. The driver lightly touched her horn and gave a small wave. It was the mother. She pulled alongside Rafael and rolled down her window.

"If you're going home I can give you a lift."

Rafael opened his mouth to tell her no thanks, but the weariness in her liquid brown eyes made him hesitate. She looked really wiped out, but not too wiped out to be kind to a stranger. He smiled briefly at her and reached for the passenger door.

"I'm afraid you'll have to ride in back," she told him. "I had a mess to clean up off the passenger seat earlier and it's still wet."

The smell of sickness mingled with detergent filled Rafael's nostrils as he climbed into the backseat. He wondered who had vomited.

"Are you all right?" he asked as he settled into the back and closed the door.

"I am, yes." She made a face. "It still smells, doesn't it? Lena's going to have a fit."

"Your daughter," said Rafael.

"Yes."

"I saw her at Schweig's Deli a while ago. I'm going to be working there starting tomorrow."

The woman turned her head in surprise. "That must be a popular place. Lena started there only today."

Rafael wanted to tell her he wasn't sure Lena would still be working there after tomorrow, but he decided to keep his mouth shut. The woman didn't look at all well.

"My name is Eugenia Fairfax," she said from the front.

"Rafael Chavez."

"It's nice to meet you, Rafael. Have you lived beside the Lutzes very long?"

"No, I haven't. The house where I'm staying used to belong to my mother. When she died she left it to me."

"I notice you've been doing some work on it."

"Trying to. My funds are limited."

"I can sympathize with you. May I ask you something, Rafael?"

"Sure."

"Why did you cut your hair?"

"It was time," was all he said.

Eugenia nodded.

When they reached their block she slowed down and came to a stop in front of his house so Rafael could get out. He thanked her for the ride and she told him it was nice to meet him. Rafael told her the same, thinking to himself that her tune would change once the papers came out the next day. The news of Ruanda Beker's death was sure to be accompanied by a mention of one ex-convict taken in for questioning. As he closed the car door he noticed she looked a little better. Her face had more color.

Lena looked like her mother, he found himself thinking as he watched her drive away.

Too bad Lena wasn't as nice.

FIVE

WHEN Lorraine entered the deli she stared first at Ross and then at Lena, who was busy sweeping the floor. The blue eyes behind Lorraine's glasses narrowed.

"What's this?" she asked.

"I had to let Kim and Kevin go," said Ross. "They weren't working out."

"Ross, Kevin is my nephew. You could at least have given me some warning."

"I'm sorry, Lorraine. It was an impulse on my part. I got angry and lost my temper."

"What happened?"

"Pubic hair in a sandwich, that's what happened."

Lorraine blanched. "You're saying it was Kevin's fault? You're saying he did it deliberately?"

"I'm saying he wasn't working out."

"You never liked him," accused Lorraine. Then she turned to Lena. "You were in my friend's shop today. You came into the back room."

Lena gave her a brief smile. "I thought I recognized you from somewhere."

Lorraine didn't return the smile. "Times must be tougher than I thought if work in a deli is the best job available for a girl your age."

"Lena is here only temporarily," put in Ross. "She lives in Oregon and wanted to pick up some extra money before she goes back."

"A student?" Lorraine inquired, tilting her auburn head.

"No, I've already graduated. I'm here with my mother. She used to live here a long time ago."

"Really? What's her name?"

"Eugenia Fairfax. Used to be Eugenia Scavino."

Lorraine shook her head. "The name isn't familiar. Where did she attend school?"

Lena stopped sweeping. "I'm not exactly sure. She lived in a place called Vandegrift Hall."

Lorraine's face changed. Her nose wrinkled slightly, and a look of distaste crossed her features.

"I see," she said. Then she dismissed Lena and returned to Ross. "What time will you be finished here?"

Ross looked at his watch. "Another thirty minutes. You want a sandwich?"

"No. I'm going. See you later?"

Ross hesitated only a fraction of a second before saying okay. Lorraine was giving him one of her looks that said, *don't you dare embarrass me in front of this woman by saying no.*

Lena lowered her head and swept with increased energy, showing no interest in the conversation and paying little attention to the woman's parting glance at her. She was still wondering at the change in the redhead's expression when she'd mentioned Vandegrift Hall, as if the entire subject was somehow objectionable.

When the bell on the door stopped tinkling, she stopped sweeping again and looked at Ross.

"Why did her face turn all sharp and pointy when I mentioned the orphanage?"

Ross snorted with laughter. Then he sobered and said, "I'm

sure it was an okay place, really, but we heard a lot of bad stories about it when we were growing up. Poor trash lived there. Kids nobody wanted. Abandoned kids and juvenile delinquents. Our parents used to scare us with the threat of sending us to Vandegrift Hall to live. The town would have fund-raisers for the place, and it was the one time of the year we were scolded for telling bad jokes and making fun of the kids there.''

Lena was staring at him in horror. "You people made fun of destitute children?''

Ross shook his head. "You have to understand, Lena. Society's attitude back then was much different from now. If a child was homeless, it was because his parents were either drunks or dead-beats, and the sins of the fathers and mothers were visited upon the sons and daughters. I'm not saying it was right, I'm just saying it's the way things were. Poor white trash begat poor white trash. We weren't taught any different.''

"Obviously your girlfriend never changed her attitude about the place," said Lena, smarting with anger.

"Lots of people probably haven't," admitted Ross. "It all depends on what you grew up with. Most of us don't even think about Vandegrift Hall anymore. It never occurs to us to think about it.''

"Because you didn't live there," muttered Lena, and she gave one last vicious swipe with the broom.

The idea that people had ever thought of her mother as "poor white trash" infuriated Lena. It was no wonder she could never get her mom to talk about the place. How horrible it must have been to be raised in such a cruel, small-minded town.

"I apologize if Lorraine offended you," said Ross, and Lena turned to look at him.

"You're not the one who should be apologizing. But thank you. I was just thinking how much it explains about my mother. How she ever turned out so good and patient and kind is beyond me, knowing she faced such ridicule while living here.''

"You're making me ashamed of myself, Lena.'' Ross slammed

the drawer of the cash register. "And I probably should apologize, but to her, not to you."

Lena gazed out the window. "I've been trying to get her into that fort, the reason we came here, but she says the ghosts there are too scary for her yet."

Ross nodded, his face thoughtful. He was remembering the woman he had seen earlier that day.

"She drive a blue Taurus?"

"Yes," said Lena.

"I saw her this morning. She jumped in and out of the car several times before giving up."

Lena stared at him and then heaved a huge sigh.

"That's why I took this job, so she'd at least have to drive by it every day. She wasn't fooled for a minute. She knew what I was up to."

"Give her room," suggested Ross. "If what I saw this morning is any indication, then she's working on it."

Lena drew in breath again and nodded. "I guess I'll see you tomorrow. What time should I be here?"

"I told Rafael to come in at nine-thirty. You want to come in earlier or later, I'll leave it up to you. I do need you here by at least eleven."

"Fine," said Lena. "May I use the phone?"

"Sure."

Lena went behind the counter and lifted the phone to call her mother. The phone rang six times before it was picked up. Her mother's voice sounded groggy when she said hello.

"Were you asleep already?" asked Lena.

"I dozed off on the sofa again," her mother admitted.

"In that case, I'm sorry I woke you. I'm off work now."

She felt a finger in her back and saw Ross mouthing that he would take her home.

"Really?" said Lena.

"What?" asked her mother.

"Nothing. Mr. Schweig just offered to bring me home. Do you think you can go back to sleep?"

"I don't know. Is he sure? I can come and get you."

"He's sure, Mom. Try to go back to sleep. I'll be home in a few minutes."

"Tell him thank you, Lena."

"I will. See you soon."

She got into a white Toyota pickup and nodded absently when her new boss asked her to call him Ross. He knew the way to her house without her telling him, and when they rolled down the street she saw Rafael Chavez sitting on his front porch drinking a can of soda. Ross waved and Rafael inclined his head. He was shirtless, wearing nothing but his jogging shorts, and Lena found herself looking at his muscled chest and long brown legs and thinking that he must have worked out daily while in prison. She worked out daily herself—running, walking, and bicycling back in Oregon. She hadn't done much here but trot around the park a few times. She needed to do more, before her thighs turned to cottage cheese.

Ross let her out in the driveway and she turned to wave as he backed out and sped down the street. She looked deliberately at Rafael Chavez and found him looking at her.

Lena tossed her purse onto the porch and strode across the lawn. Chavez put down his soda and linked his hands together in front of him. His face was expressionless as she approached. She stopped before him and said, "I'm not quitting."

"Good," he said.

"Is that the only place in town you could get a job?"

"Yes."

Lena put her hands on her lips. She didn't believe him. "Why do you keep staring at me?"

His dark eyes flickered. "Why do you keep staring at me?"

"Because you're staring at me. And you're not even looking at me, you're looking at my body. You have no idea how aggravating that is."

"Admiration aggravates you?"

"Overt *staring* and slavering like some hungry dog aggravates me. Will you please stop?"

He gave a brief shake of his head. "I can't say that I will, no."

Lena pushed air out through her nostrils. "Just what did you do to get sent to prison? Rape someone?"

He lifted one brow, and said, "Is that what you think?"

"I have no idea. What did you do?"

He chose not to answer the question. Instead he looked away from her and said, "Go and take care of your mother, Lena. She threw up in her car today."

"What?" Lena's mouth fell open. "How do you know?"

"She was kind enough to offer me a ride earlier." He stood and picked up the can of soda before turning his back on her and reaching for his door. "See you tomorrow."

He went inside and left Lena standing before the porch. Abruptly she turned and walked quickly toward the house she shared with her mother. Eugenia was awake and waiting for her. Lena asked if what Rafael Chavez had said was true, and her mother admitted that yes, she had gotten sick in the car that day.

"Why?" asked Lena.

"It was nothing. I'm fine now. You were talking to Rafael outside?"

"Yes."

"He has a nice voice, doesn't he? A hint of an accent, just enough to tell you English wasn't his first language."

"Mother, please. What made you ill?"

Eugenia swallowed and the smile on her face faltered as she looked at her daughter.

"I went inside the fort today."

Lena blinked. "You did? After you dropped me off?"

"Yes. They were just closing, and I didn't make it past the old hospital, where you go in, before they came to me again."

"Before *who* came to you?"

"Them, Lena. The ghosts."

Lena blinked again. Something in the way her mother was looking at her, the complete and utter conviction in her gaze, set off warning bells.

"Mother . . . are you talking about real ghosts? I mean, really real ghosts?"

Eugenia nodded. "What did you think?"

"Holy shit," said Lena. Then she apologized. "All this time I thought you meant ghosts in the figurative sense, not the literal."

"They're real to me," said Eugenia, and Lena could see her mother's face growing pale just talking about it.

"What do they look like?" Lena asked.

"Like you and me. Dressed differently, from another time."

Lena plopped down on the sofa. "Why haven't you ever talked to me about this before?"

"Because talking can make things happen."

"Okay," said Lena, and she thought for a moment before speaking again. "You say they 'came to you.' How do you mean that?"

"I'm not sure I know," her mother told her. "All I know is that I walked down the hall to the back of the building, toward the bathroom, and I was drawn to the windows. When I looked out the windows I was there again, with them, in their time. Or, rather, I was *seeing* them in their time. And they could see me, too. At least I think it's me they see."

"They could see you?"

Eugenia lifted a shoulder. "I see them, they see me, and that's when it happens."

"What?"

Her mother told her.

When Eugenia finished, Lena's arms were crossed over her chest and her face was pinched with discomfort.

"How awful," she said, and then she repeated herself.

"Yes," Eugenia agreed.

"You never see anything else? I mean, does it always end at the same place?"

"No," her mother answered. "But I don't want to talk about it anymore."

"Because talking about it makes things happen?"

"Yes."

"All right, all right. We won't talk about it again." Lena looked at her mother then. "I do have to ask one more question, though."

"What?"

"Are you going back? Are you even going to try?"

Eugenia's answer was firm. "No."

Lena nodded, and after a moment she asked, "Do you suppose you were the only one who ever saw them?"

"You said just one more question, Lena."

"Sorry."

They looked at each other.

"Well?" said Lena.

"Well what?"

"Aren't you going to answer me?"

"Yes, I think I'm the only one who ever saw them. No one else appeared to notice. Now stop, or I'll leave the room."

Lena's mouth stopped, but her mind was in a whirling frenzy of wondering and worrying.

Soon she said, "Maybe you're one of those children reincarnated, and you're seeing it happen all over again."

"Oh, for heaven's sake," said her mother, and she followed through on her promise to leave the room, muttering to herself about how she shouldn't have told Lena anything.

Wounded, Lena watched her go. She was tempted to follow and apologize again, but she didn't want to aggravate her mother further.

"Damn," she whispered to herself, and though she hated herself for doing it, she wondered suddenly if her mother hadn't made up this whole thing about the ghosts because she didn't want to go inside the fort and face her past.

Maybe something terrible really had happened to her mother

at Vandegrift Hall, something her conscious mind was unwilling to accept, thus the story of the ghosts.

If that were indeed the case, then this entire trip was about to be rendered totally useless and ineffectual, since her mother was unwilling to go back.

Lena squeezed her lids shut and rubbed at her eyes. She was torn now between the desire to go home to Oregon and wanting to see her mother's problem resolve itself. If her mother wasn't going back to the fort, then what was the point of staying?

Of course the Lutzes might not appreciate having their rainy vacation cut short.

Lena decided she would ask her mother to call the Lutzes the next day and sound them out. She had no desire to stay and be ogled day in and day out by the ex-con next door, even if he did claim to be admiring her shape. Lena didn't go around staring at his crotch or his pecs all the time. She thought of giving him twenty dollars and telling him to call his female friend in the red car again. She would be happy to help him out, Lena was sure.

In her room Eugenia fell into an uneasy doze, her conscious mind struggling to keep her from slipping any further. Eventually her will weakened and exhaustion overcame the need for constant awareness. Soon she was deeply asleep, and within minutes she was dreaming.

She was following two women in long dresses across a dusty road. The woman in front held her golden head high and carried a fat purse in her gloved hands. Her dress was clean and pretty and made a rustling sound as she walked. The woman walking behind her was clean, but not nearly so well kept. Her brown hair swung in a messy braid, and her dress was tattered and stained at the hem. She carried an armful of parcels and packages.

The brown-haired woman stumbled on a stone in the road and dropped the load she was carrying. The blonde turned and heaved an irritated sigh at the other's clumsiness. Then her finely drawn features changed when an Indian in a cavalry jacket stepped from the shadows of a nearby building to help retrieve the packages. The blonde spoke sharply to him, but he ignored her and continued to pick up parcels. When they were all off the ground and safely in the arms of the brown-haired woman again, the Indian nodded to her and walked away.

The blonde looked coldly after the departing Indian; then she turned and said something with a curled lip to her companion. The woman with the messy braid looked at the ground and made no reply.

In her sleep, Eugenia frowned. This was no ordinary dream, she knew, even in her unconscious state. She had seen these ghosts before, had met them on numerous previous occasions as a child. Details were too clear for this to be just an ordinary dream. Her senses were too acutely aware.

She followed the women to their quarters within the fort and watched as the blonde dismissed the servant and went into another room to speak to her husband. The husband shook his head vehemently at first, and then he acquiesced to his wife's demands. The husband disappeared and soon returned with a Negro soldier, and Eugenia clearly heard the man say, "I'm to be your striker, ma'am."

The blond wife smiled at him and promptly left the room to go and tell the woman with the braid she would no longer be employed in her household. The brown-haired woman looked up with a stricken expression that brought a gleam of triumph to the face of the blonde.

"Go and make your bed with that heathen. It's what you've been doing for months anyway."

Eugenia's throat muscles tightened and she swallowed in her sleep as she watched the woman with the braid gather her meager belongings and depart the house. Outside she looked around herself with a lost expression, and then a measure of resolve seemed to take over her features. She moved down the road with her spine straight and her walk determined.

From a window in the house, Eugenia saw the husband of the

blonde, an officer at the fort, watch the departure of the servant woman. His jaw was taut, his facial muscles strained. The lip beneath his mustache was quivering.

The naked emotion on his face caused Eugenia to moan in her sleep and shift her position on the bed enough to wake herself.

Her eyes came open and she lay staring into the dark.

She wasn't at the fort, wasn't anywhere near it, and they had come to her anyway.

Had her visit to the grounds that day opened the door to them? Why start at the beginning of the story all over again, when she already knew what happened?

She had seen this particular tale's conclusion years ago. Knew it by heart.

Eugenia didn't want to watch it again.

Worse, she had the feeling that even if she left right now and went home to Oregon, the nightmare wouldn't stop. They would still be with her. The laundress, the scout, the children, all of them.

She rolled over in bed and pressed her face into the softly scented pillow. How she wished Leonard were here. Leonard had been her protector, her kind and gentle buffer against the hurts and haunts she suffered. Through him Eugenia had been able to reclaim some semblance of sanity and live life as a normal person.

"Help," she whispered against the fabric of the pillowcase. "Dear Lord, please help me. Tell me what it is I need to do."

The last word was punctuated by a silent sob. Before the tears could roll down her cheeks, Eugenia heard her door open. She lifted her head and saw her daughter peering in at her. "What is it, Lena?"

"I didn't want to wake you," Lena said, "but something is going on next door. About eight carloads of people just showed up, and they're all getting out."

"What?" Eugenia sat up. "What are they doing?"

"I'm not sure. Do you think I should call the police?"

"Wait," said her mother, and she left the bed and reached for a robe.

"I don't think I should wait," Lena told her. "I wasn't going to tell you, but Rafael Chavez is an ex-con. He's been in prison and I think he just got out."

"Then by all means call the police," said Eugenia, and she shoved her feet into slippers before racing out of the room.

Lena ran after her and watched in surprise as her mother charged out the door without even waiting for her. Lena hurriedly called the police, told them what was happening, then slammed the phone down to go after her mother.

She was further surprised to see her mother pushing past the crowd on the lawn to go and stand on Rafael Chavez's front porch. Rafael was nowhere to be seen. Lena moved to stand just in front of the porch and she turned to look at the people behind her.

Not the usual angry mob, she told herself as she spied the luxury cars and expensive clothes of the crowd littering the lawn.

"What are you people doing here?" Eugenia demanded in a strident voice.

"Looking for Chavez," someone yelled, and the person held up a large poster painted with bold black letters:

CBFG = Citizens for a Better Fort Grant

"Why?" asked Eugenia. "Why do you want to see him?"

"Because of Ruanda Beker, that's why," a woman in front yelled, and Lena blinked as she recognized Ross Schweig's snooty lady friend.

"Ruanda Beker was murdered earlier today, and we know she was here with Rafael Chavez this morning."

The girl in the red car, Lena told herself as she listened to the crowd.

"My neighbor was home nearly all day," Eugenia informed the people.

"Get him out here," snarled a man holding another large sign. "We want to talk to him."

"And tell him what?" asked Eugenia, her voice cracking.

"That you don't want his kind around here? That serving time for his crime wasn't enough?"

"Why are you defending him?" asked Lorraine. "Do you even know what he was convicted of?"

"No, and I don't—"

Before Eugenia could finish, the door opened behind her and Rafael stepped outside. He was dressed in a white T-shirt and jeans and he was barefoot. He moved beside Eugenia and looked out at the throng on his lawn.

"I've already been questioned by the police," he said, and Lena noticed that his accent was heavier in his agitated state. "I'm being watched by them every second. I didn't kill Ruanda Beker, and I want you people to leave."

"We want *you* to leave," barked someone in the crowd.

"I can't," he said. "I have to stay here until I'm off parole."

"And kill how many more women?" asked Lorraine. She looked at Eugenia, and then turned her head to look at Lena. "Fifteen years ago he savagely killed a woman and her daughter. Today he killed a prostitute. I'd watch myself if I were you, ladies."

Eugenia surprised Lena further by stepping forward and pointing aggressively. "You people go home to your families and leave this matter to the police. You're nothing but a Saab- and Lexus-driving lynch mob masquerading as a civic improvement group. You make up maybe two percent of the population of this town and yet you appoint yourselves moral guardians for the rest of the citizens."

"We've done more to clean up this town than anyone has for centuries," said Lorraine, her nostrils quivering. "Who are you to come here and behave as if you're better than us, when we're the ones who care about this community and you're just here for a nostalgic spit at the old Vandegrift Hall?"

Faces in the throng looked at each other, and then at Eugenia, who had visibly flinched at mention of Vandegrift Hall.

Lena went up on the porch beside her mother and looked Lorraine in the eye. "Ross didn't show up?" she asked.

Lorraine's quivering nostrils flared. She ignored Lena and looked at Rafael. "The police aren't the only ones who'll be watching you. We're not going to stop until you're out of our town and back in a cage."

A few of the men in the crowd had parting shots as well, threats and promises that made Rafael's back stiffen, but the majority were moving back to their cars, satisfied they had been heard and made their wishes known.

"Asses," muttered Eugenia, and Lena looked at her and blinked.

"These are the same people I grew up with," Eugenia explained. "The same bigots, racists, and rich, snobbish boors who made life miserable for us every chance they got."

"Mom," said Lena, and she reached for her mother's arm, but Eugenia moved away and proceeded to shock her daughter by placing her arms around Rafael Chavez and clutching him tightly to her.

Rafael was obviously startled at the contact: his skin jumped and the muscles in his arms twitched, but he made no move to pull away.

"I'm sorry," said Eugenia. "I'm sorry they did this to you. You have to understand who they are, Rafael, and know how much you frighten them."

She went on talking, using soothing, comforting tones, and Lena stared as she saw Rafael's head lower. When Eugenia fell silent he gently extricated himself and turned his face from them as he strode into the house.

Eugenia wiped moisture from her cheeks and walked past Lena to leave the porch and go next door. Struck completely dumb, Lena followed.

SIX

RAFAEL showed up minutes before nine-thirty, and Ross looked around outside for a car.

"How did you get here?" he asked.

"Lena brought me. My car wouldn't start."

"Lena?" said Ross in surprise.

Rafael nodded. "Her mother was still sleeping this morning and she thought my grinding the starter was going to wake her. So she brought me."

"Any idea what's wrong with the car?"

"None. I'll look at it later."

"Heard you had visitors last night. Maybe one of them is responsible."

Rafael lifted a shoulder. "Could be."

"Is Lena coming in?"

"She said she be in later. She wanted to run in the park first."

"You should run together," said Ross. "Keep an eye on her."

He felt Rafael look at him, and Ross said, "Yes, I read the paper this morning. Yes, I realize it was you the police questioned. No, I'm not worried about it. Okay?"

Rafael nodded.

"All right. First thing you do is scrub your hands real good. Always important in food preparation. Wash them every time you turn around, if you think of it. Next most important is quality. No thin slices, no skimping on the sauce. That's what keeps people coming back. Now, I'm going to show you how to use the slicer and how to make the sauce and where I store everything, so let's get started."

For the next hour Ross taught Rafael everything he would need to know, and at a quarter to eleven Lena came in the door, her wet hair tied back and her cheeks glowing. She brushed past both of them and went in the back to tie on an apron. Ross noticed Rafael look at her only once, and then struggle to keep from looking at her. Ross was having a bit of a problem himself. Lena was a good-looking girl, and having come fresh from the shower, as she obviously had, she made it difficult to rein in the imagination.

They worked silently for the next half hour, slicing and baking and cleaning the pop machine, and when the first customer came in, Ross told Lena to let Rafael handle it. She did.

Something Ross noticed as they worked was that Lena looked at Rafael almost as much as Rafael looked at Lena. Her look was different, of course—wary and almost bellicose—and once again Ross had to wonder about her.

Was she a lesbian? A misanthrope?

Maybe some guy back in Oregon had dumped on her and made her bitter. Probably about as bitter as Lorraine was going to be once Ross dumped her.

It was time, he was thinking. He hadn't enjoyed that little visual ultimatum she had given him yesterday, so he simply hadn't shown up at her place. When she called him, as he had known she would, he pleaded a killer headache and told her he was going to lie on the sofa and watch ESPN, something he knew Lorraine would have no interest in doing with him.

Later she called to tell him about her visit to Rafael's house, and how his new employee and her mother had defended the murdering bastard.

Ross had news for her. That murdering bastard was now his other new employee.

Lorraine hung up and Ross hadn't heard from her since. He fully expected to. He expected her to come marching into his deli any moment with her BMW brigade and picket the place.

He didn't underestimate the power of her little group.

But neither was he worried.

Most of his customers drove Fords, Chevys and an occasional Hyundai.

Business was slow for the next hour or so but picked up at noon. Ross and Rafael had their hands full making sandwiches while Lena took orders and worked the register.

Ross had to look up when he heard Lena say hi to her mom. Rafael looked up as well, and he greeted Lena's mother with a brief nod. Ross smiled and inclined his head when Lena made a hurried introduction. Eugenia smiled back at him, and Ross found himself thinking how much mother and daughter looked alike, and how pretty Lena would be if she would only smile like her mother.

Eugenia was a pretty woman, period. Ross felt himself sucking in his stomach as he worked and looking down at intervals to see how much of it still showed. He glanced at Rafael once and noticed the color in his cheeks was higher since Eugenia Fairfax's arrival.

Probably about last night, Ross decided, remembering how Lorraine said the women had defended the convict.

I'd be a little embarrassed, too, Ross thought to himself.

Then Lorraine came in. The narrowed orbs behind her glasses took in everyone at a glance. She put her purse on her shoulder and allowed herself a false smile.

"Well, aren't we just one big happy family?"

Ross wiped his hands on his apron and told Rafael he was on his own for a few minutes.

"We need to talk," he said to Lorraine as he came around the counter to guide her to his office.

She halted and refused to budge.

"Quite unnecessary. There is nothing that needs to be made clearer than it is right now."

"Okay, fine," said Ross. "Let's not have a scene in front of the customers, all right?"

"Oooh, no, I wouldn't dream of it," said Lorraine. "Seems to me you're going to have enough problems to deal with in the near future, and I will be the first in line to say I told you so."

"Great, Lorraine, you told me so." Ross let go of her and waited for her to make a move.

She stayed put. Her face sagged a little and she said, "You know I never thought it would end this way with us. I thought it would be different."

"I'm sorry," said Ross. "I really am."

"Are you?" she asked, and she looked at Lena and Eugenia. "Or did something better come along?"

Ross shook his head. He wasn't up for this. He returned behind the counter and went back to work, leaving Lorraine simply standing there. Not at all embarrassed, Lorraine lifted her chin and turned on her heel to leave. At the door she said, "One thing you can be sure of, Ross, is that all of you will get what you deserve. Don't say I didn't warn you."

Rafael hated that woman. There was a coldness and a cunning in her blue eyes that engendered a fear in him like no other person on earth; not even the worst of the murderous assholes in Lansing inspired the fear she did.

The place was dead silent for several minutes after she left, then bit by bit people started talking to each other again. Soon Eugenia stood and came to ask how he was getting along on his first day.

If Rafael hated Lorraine, he loved Eugenia. She was so kind and gentle and reminded him so much of his own mother his eyes threatened to water just thinking about it. But he wouldn't do that again, not after last night. He wouldn't let her do it to him again, just because she was nice to him when no one had been nice to him in a long, long time. He couldn't believe he had almost cried in front of her. And Lena.

His nostrils widened as he caught the scent of Lena passing close to him again. She smelled like perfumed soap of some kind; it was knocking him out the way she smelled.

"Is Mom's sandwich ready?" Lena stopped to ask, and Rafael hurried to put on the finishing touches and wrap it up. He handed it to Lena, and she mumbled a thank you before giving the sandwich to her mother. Eugenia told Rafael good luck and returned to her table to sit down.

Rafael turned to wash his hands again and came into full contact with Lena, who was once more passing behind him. Their two bodies sprang apart, but not before flesh became infused with heat at the accidental meeting of chests and pelvises. Rafael took a long, deep breath and willed away the instant arousal he experienced. Lena jerked around and looked at him as if he had collided with her on purpose.

"Sorry," he muttered.

"Don't let it happen again," she said.

Rafael turned away from her before the angry retort at his lips could could come out. From the pinkness in her cheeks and the breathlessness of her voice, he knew she was every bit as affected by the contact as he was.

The tension was broken as Eugenia stood once more and announced her intention to eat at one of the tables outside. Lena went out with her, and Rafael moved to wait on the customer at the counter. It was Morales, the detective, and he smiled as Rafael recognized him.

"Nah, I don't want anything. Just checking out your story. I went by your neighbors' house but couldn't find anyone home. Any idea where they might be?"

Rafael pointed to the two dark-haired women outside the deli.

Morales looked and said, "Imagine that. Okay. What did you say their name was?"

"Fairfax." Rafael had seen it on Lena's time card that morning. Her name was the same as her mother's, so he guessed it meant Lena had not yet married.

Big surprise.

"Be seeing you," said Morales, and he waved at Ross before sauntering out of the deli.

"What did he want?" Ross came to ask.

"To see if I really work here. And to talk to Lena."

Ross lifted a brow. "Are you sure you want him to?"

The question struck Rafael. One way or another he would soon find out. Unconsciously he held his breath and watched through the window as Morales approached the women. Lena looked up and went into her usual aggressive stance, while Eugenia appeared only curious.

Morales made a brief introduction, then he gestured behind himself with his thumb, toward the window and the deli. Ross and Rafael watched as both women turned instinctively to look.

Rafael stiffened as Lena's eyes met his through the glass. Her look for him was cold.

"Shit," he whispered.

Then he looked at Eugenia and saw her nodding. Her brows were pinched, and she had the same feisty expression she had worn the evening before while facing down the crowd on his lawn.

"Looks like Mama's going to bat for you," said Ross.

"She's a nice lady," answered Rafael.

"What happened to Lena, huh?" Ross said with a smile, and he winked to show Rafael he was teasing.

Rafael didn't return the smile. He himself had shared the same thought, but hearing it from someone else irritated him. He didn't know why.

He saw Morales address Lena and he saw Lena answer in reply to some question posed. Her slender arms spread and her hands went to her hips as she spoke. Her back was straight as an arrow.

She didn't look down or around or anywhere but directly at Morales as she spoke, and just by watching her Rafael knew her tone would be firm and her speech clipped. She wasn't taking any shit from any man, not even a man with a badge.

A customer came in and Ross gave Rafael a nudge, forcing him to look away from the people outside. This time the customer was Bob Pena. He stuck his hand across the counter and greeted Rafael with a huge smile. Rafael shook the hand and released it, his glance returning to what was happening beyond the window.

"When did you start working here?" the handsome, dark-suited Pena asked.

"This morning. What can I get for you?"

"Same as always, the Deli Special. Damn, I'm glad you finally found something."

"Yeah, me too. How you been?"

"Good. Just found out yesterday Marta's pregnant again."

Rafael lifted his brows. "What does that make, four?"

"Five," said Pena, and he looked heavenward. Then he cleared his throat and leaned close. "Were you questioned about Ruanda Beker?"

"Yeah, I was. By that guy standing right outside."

Pena turned to look. He clicked his teeth when he saw Lena. "So that's Morales. Who's the centerfold with him?"

"Morales called you?" asked Rafael, ignoring his reference to Lena.

"Yesterday. Asked me how I knew about Ruanda, and I asked him how he thought I knew about her. Hell, every guy over twelve knew about her. She moved here with her family last November and took over the town's trade. I just find out my wife's going to have another kid, and this guy wants to talk about a dead whore."

Pena paused and cleared his throat again. "Anyway, just your bad luck she happened to get killed the same day you gave her a call."

"Yeah," said Rafael. "I'll get that sandwich for you now."

He turned and nearly collided with Ross, who had the sandwich already made and was ready to ring it up.

"Pena's a regular," he said in explanation, and he moved to the cash register.

Rafael told his friend good-bye and looked outside again. Lena was just coming in. Morales was gone, and Eugenia was eating her sandwich.

Bob Pena held the door open for Lena and gave her a long, lingering once-over that made her mouth snap shut and her spine stiffen. For a moment Rafael actually felt embarrassed and ashamed of his friend—until he remembered he was guilty of the same behavior.

Lena's eyes met his as she approached, and Rafael was tempted to look away, but he did not.

"Well?" she said. "Don't you want to know what he asked me?"

"I think I know."

"Do you?"

"Ruanda Beker. The woman who was at my house."

"He wanted to know if I saw her leave."

"You did," said Rafael, and he waited for her either to confirm or deny the statement.

Lena did neither; she turned and greeted the customer who came in the door and moved behind the counter to wait on her.

Behind him, Rafael heard Ross give a grunt.

"Woman is just plain mean."

That woman is, Rafael silently agreed.

He filled the order Lena gave him and tried not to pay too much attention to her otherwise. He glanced outside at Eugenia once and saw her sitting with the sandwich poised in front of her mouth, as if ready to take a bite. He looked at her again five minutes later and found her still in the same position. When there was a lull in the customers, he asked Ross if he could take a break. Ross told him he could have ten minutes. Rafael thanked him and went outside to see Eugenia.

She didn't look at him when he spoke to her. He touched her on the arm and she didn't move. Her unblinking eyes were fixed on the distant fort, and her mouth was half-open, her hand still holding the sandwich in front of her.

Rafael spoke to her again and still received no response. He went back inside the deli.

"Lena, come out here please."

"Why?" Lena asked, her tone belligerent, and Ross looked up.

Not wanting to alarm the customers, Rafael moved to the counter and in a low voice said, "It's your mother. Come now."

Lena's face went white, and she rushed around the counter to shove past Rafael and hurry out the door. She dropped to her knees beside the frozen Eugenia and reached for her hand. "Mother? Mother, what is it? What's wrong?"

"I've already tried to speak to her. I'm not sure she can hear us."

Rafael moved to the other side and gently pried the sandwich from her fingers. Still she did not blink, did not appear even to be breathing.

"Oh, no." Lena was beginning to panic. "It's because of the fort. Oh, God, what do I do?"

Rafael looked at Lena. "The fort?"

"The ghosts." As if realizing suddenly that what she was saying sounded crazy, Lena glanced up and said, "Don't just stand there, dammit, get an ambulance."

"Don't call yet," said Ross, who came out the door with a container of ice-cold water and tossed it directly into Eugenia's face.

The effect was immediate: she gasped and choked and her hands went to her face as if for protection. Lena put her arms around her mother and Eugenia stared wildly about herself for several moments, her pupils large and dark. When her eyes landed on Rafael she seemed to calm somewhat and grasped for control. He moved forward to touch her shoulder, and she extended a hand to him. He clasped it in his own and Lena leaned away to look at her mother.

"I'm sorry," Eugenia said softly, water dripping down her cheeks. "I'm very sorry."

"Where were you?" asked Lena.

Eugenia looked at her daughter and shook her head. Ross stepped forward and said, "Years ago I was an orderly at the state hospital. Ice water didn't usually work, but it was the first thing we used to try. Do you have a family history of catatonia, Mrs. Fairfax?"

"No, I don't, Mr. Schweig. Thank you for your assistance. Lena, I think I'll go home now."

"I'll take you," said Lena, and without even looking at Ross she removed her apron and handed it to Rafael, who released Eugenia's hand to take it.

"Good," said Ross. "That's a good idea. Take her home. And you might think about calling your doctor."

"Back in Oregon?" said Lena, and Ross lifted his shoulders in a helpless shrug.

"Thank you again, Mr. Schweig," said Eugenia, and she asked Rafael to walk her to the car while Lena went back inside the deli to get her purse. Rafael took her by the arm and steadied her as she walked. She smiled gratefully at him and he said, "Lena seemed to think the ghosts at the fort had you."

Eugenia blinked and looked away from him. She made no comment, only continued to walk beside him. Rafael's curiosity grew as the silence lengthened.

"My mother used to talk about the fort," he said. "She'd say there were people in town who wouldn't go near the place. People who had good reason."

"I wonder what she meant," said Eugenia, feigning disinterest.

Rafael looked at her. "I don't know."

They reached the car and Rafael turned to see Lena coming after them, her expression worried, but still wary and slightly contemptuous. It made Rafael want to take her by the arms and shake her until she bit off that acid tongue of hers.

Eugenia patted Rafael's arm and slipped into the passenger seat after he opened the door for her. He closed the door firmly and nodded to her before turning and walking back to the deli. He didn't look at Lena. Of the two of them, and after everything he had seen that day, he thought Lena was the one who needed a doctor's help.

SEVEN

"W HAT happened?" asked Lena. "Was it them? Was it the children?"

Eugenia closed her eyes. "No," she murmured. "It was the blonde. Such a devious creature. I saw things today I've never seen before."

"The blonde?"

"Never mind, Lena."

"Mother, please don't keep this to yourself. Let me try and help you."

Eugenia opened her eyes and looked at her daughter. "What did you say to Rafael?"

"I . . . nothing. I was upset and started babbling. Why? What did he say to you?"

"He asked me about ghosts. He must think I'm insane."

"Is that what you're worried about?" asked Lena. "That people—even me—will think you're crazy if you open up and talk about it?"

"Lena, this is just too difficult a subject to expect understanding from any quarter."

"Even from your own daughter?" asked Lena.

"You're all I have left," Eugenia tried to explain. "I couldn't bear it if you turned away from me."

Lena's hands tightened on the wheel. "Mother, I admit I have had my doubts. I admit to wondering if you've told me or even yourself the whole truth about what happened to you at Vande-grift Hall as a child. But you must know that I will never, never turn away from you. Please believe me."

Eugenia looked at her. "Thank you for being honest with me."

"You're welcome. Now return the favor and tell me about this blonde."

Her mother sucked in breath and gave her head a fierce shake. After a moment she said, "The woman is a ruthless, conniving schemer. I'm seeing things I never saw all those years ago, things I wouldn't have understood then, but I understand now. The entire social life of the fort was under this woman's rule. She was the commanding officer's wife."

"You mean, back when the fort was still a functioning fort?" asked Lena.

"Yes, of course."

"So, that was when, during the 1850s?"

"I have no way of knowing, but I believe so. The men all wear those horribly heavy wool uniforms, and the women are still in whalebone and dozens upon dozens of buttons everywhere."

"You're actually seeing things that happened in that time period?"

"I believe they did happen, yes. Events we won't find anything written about in any history of the fort."

"What did this woman do? The blonde?"

"Because of her, a laundress and a scout were murdered."

"A fort laundress?"

"Yes. She began as a servant for the blonde, but when her relationship with the fort's Indian scout became known, the blonde threw her out."

"God," said Lena, "is this tawdry and twisted, or what?"

Immediately she knew she had said the wrong thing. Her mother's mouth closed into a thin, firm line, and no amount of coaxing could get her to begin talking again.

"I'm tired," she said, and that was all she said.

"I'm sorry," Lena adjured. "I truly am. I wasn't making light of anything, I swear I wasn't."

"You'd better get back to work," her mother said finally. "You don't want to leave Rafael all alone on his first day."

"Ross is there with him," argued Lena. "It isn't like he's learning acupuncture or anything."

Eugenia was finished discussing the matter. When Lena stopped the car in the drive, her mother opened the door and got out without looking at her daughter.

"I'll see you later," Lena said, but Eugenia pretended not to hear her and marched up to the house.

Lena had never seen her mother so touchy. These dreams or ghosts or whatever they were apparently held a great deal of importance.

She shook her head in wonder as she drove back to the deli, imagining what it would be like to witness events that happened almost 150 years ago. Was it possible? she asked herself, and then consciously bit her tongue. She had to stop doubting her mother. Her mom was no fruitcake, and she would have to remember to chastise Ross for even intimating that Eugenia had a family history of mental illness. An orderly in a state hospital indeed.

The men seemed surprised to see Lena come back. She answered both their inquiring gazes with a "She's fine," and went back to work.

One thing she noticed as the day wore on, and it did make her curious, was that Rafael was no longer staring at her at every opportunity.

He's using reverse psychology on me, Lena intuited, and she was disgusted to find herself suddenly looking for him at each available moment. Off and on throughout the day she caught herself eyeing the line of his thighs and the firmness of his buttocks inside the jeans he wore. Her gaze returned again and again to his well-formed biceps and pectorals, and to the flatness of his stomach. Against her will she pictured him minus his clothes, with his hair still long, and then sucked in her breath at her body's reaction to such imaginings.

As if sensing her thoughts, Rafael's gaze lifted to meet hers at that moment. This once, Lena let her eyes drop before his did, so he wouldn't see the fire in her cheeks.

He murdered two women, she reminded herself, and she had to wonder if there was some perverse streak in her that actually got off on the idea of getting naked with a convicted killer.

Savagely killed, she remembered Lorraine saying.

Then she had to look at his eyes again. She thought she should be able to tell something from his eyes.

She couldn't.

They were dark and deep-set, with long black lashes and irises so brown they were nearly black. They could very well be the eyes of a man with no regard for human life.

Lena forced herself to look away.

At five o'clock she volunteered to stay until closing at eight. Ross looked at Rafael. "You want me to take you home?"

"I'll walk," said Rafael.

"No, no, I'll take you," Ross told him. "Lena will be all right by herself. Save your energy for that run in the morning." Ross turned to Lena. "I told him he should run with you, keep you safe."

Lena surprised Rafael by asking, "What time do you run?"

He hesitated, then said, "About seven."

"I'll meet you outside," she said.

She wanted to watch him run.

Ross dropped Rafael at home and was tempted to go and knock on Eugenia Fairfax's door to see how she was doing—and to apologize for his apparent insult earlier, when he had asked his question about catatonia. He hadn't meant anything by it, of course, but Lena seemed to take it that he thought her mother was a crackpot. Ross thought the combative Lena was the crackpot, but he would never say so.

After arguing with himself for several minutes, he drove away from the house. He was attracted to the pretty Eugenia, but it was too soon to do anything about it. Particularly after everything that had happened that day. A woman like her wouldn't exactly jump at the chance to go out with a guy who dumped his current girl-friend in front of a dozen customers and then took it upon himself to throw freezing ice water in a seemingly catatonic woman's face. And there was the added fact that she would soon be returning to her home in Oregon.

Again, Ross had to wonder what kind of battle Eugenia Fairfax was fighting. Had she been mistreated at the orphanage? Beaten, perhaps? Molested?

Ross remembered tales of such happenings. He also remembered seeing groups of children leave each morning and return to the orphanage at night. These were the kids who got farmed out to work at local businesses. The businesses made donations to the orphanage, and the orphanage supplied the businesses with employees. The arrangement kept the streets free of human detritus and made the do-gooders happy. Ross had never before considered how the children must have felt.

He wondered if Eugenia had been one of the kids sent out as slave labor; and then realized he would feel like a complete idiot ever discussing Vandegrift Hall with her, since it was obviously a painful part of her past. It was painful for him, too, remembering how badly he had treated the kids there.

It had been a Halloween ritual to run and soap the windows and write all sorts of nasty things on the glass panes.

The words *bastard* and *slut* were used most often.

Every boy in town dreamed of catching a Vandegrift Hall girl out alone at night. Everyone knew they put out for just about any-one who asked.

Ross had never been out with a Vandegrift girl, but he knew guys who said they had.

Now he wondered why he had ever believed them.

Some of the girls at the home were wild, it was true, but the truly wild ones never stayed. They left Fort Grant in the middle of the night and didn't come back.

Just like anyone else with any sense.

Ross snorted to himself in discomfort with the last thought and drove back to the deli. He didn't exchange more than five words with Lena until closing, when he asked if she was still coming in to work the next day.

"Why wouldn't I?" she asked.

He shrugged. "I think I figured out why you want to be close to the fort."

"That hasn't changed," she said, and she told him good-night.

Ross sighed and locked up after her. At home he found paper grocery sacks full of his clothes and other items, and a letter from Lorraine stuck inside his storm door.

"Great," muttered Ross, and he took out the letter and opened it.

Ross:

> *I can't say I haven't known this was coming, but the way you handled it is inexcusable. I will never forgive you. I credited you with being a true gentleman, and now realize my mistake. Don't try to make me responsible for all that will befall you. Remember, I was the one who cared.*

> *Lorraine*

"Yeah, right," said Ross, and he couldn't help sticking out his tongue at the note. It was an instinctive reaction to everything she had written.

Still, he supposed Lorraine did have her good points.

At the moment he couldn't think of any, but he was sure he had seen some at one time.

She used her friends well, he knew that. Right now she would be at Ellen Li's seamstress shop pouring her heart out and sticking a hundred straight pins into the picture she carried of him in her purse.

He was okay with that. It wasn't like he had never dumped anyone before, or no one had ever dumped him. Ross knew the routine. His only real worry was what she might do to the other people who had entered his life during the last forty-eight hours. Rafael was a good guy; Ross felt it, saw it, and knew in his bones that the man's heart was good. He didn't know what had happened all those years ago, though he thought he remembered a heavy drug involvement, but he would say now that Rafael definitely had his act together.

The jury was still out on Lena, though Ross sensed that she, too, was a good kid, just a little misguided. Eugenia had spunk, but Lena had fire, and she was breathing it in all the wrong directions.

Ross found he was excited just to know all these new people and be involved in their lives. Nothing exciting had happened in Fort Grant for a long time, and suddenly here he was in the thick of things and actually a part of what the community was buzzing about.

It felt pretty good, really.

EIGHT

MORALES walked around the table and stared at the two young men slouched in their seats. They were sullen and bitchy and had spent the better part of two hours sniping at each other.

"Who threw the rock?" Morales asked again, and the boy on the left lifted a finger. Then he looked at his partner and said, "But he told me to throw it."

"You said that already. You do everything this guy tells you to do?"

"No."

"So what was the plan, guys? Huh? You told her you found her brother passed out in the park, and then what?"

The one on the left shrugged. "We were going to say he must've gotten up and gone home."

"And then you were going to ask her for a freebie, right? Was that the plan before you flagged down her car?"

"Yeah. She was drivin' real slow, puttin' on her makeup, and we decided to stop her."

"Just to see if she'd give you a freebie? Or maybe to take one. A whore would be the last person in the world to cry rape, now wouldn't she?''

The boys looked at each other.

Morales sighed. "So, she tells you both to go jerk off and starts walking away. You don't have the balls you thought you'd have, she's got a mouth on her and makes you feel about as big as your dick, which ain't too big, and you see a rock on the ground, a big rock, and being the stupid shits that you are . . .''

The boy on the left covered his eyes with one hand. The smart-ass on the right only smirked.

Morales looked at the smart-ass. "Your buddy here screwed up by coming down and confessing to me. See, he may have thrown the rock, but you are an accomplice from the word go. Both your asses are in for some serious cell time.''

"Maybe, maybe not," said the smart-ass. "I was going to come in, same as him. We didn't mean to kill her. We just got mad at what she said to us. We didn't call anyone because we got scared. No one in this town gave a shit about her.''

"Oh, but they give a shit about you, is that it?" said Morales. "Couple of baseball jocks, one of you with a deadly pitching arm, right? That rock was quite a bit bigger than a baseball there, Stretch. Feel like a fastball to you when you beaned Ruanda?''

The boy on the left started to cry. The boy on the right exhaled through his nose and shook his head.

"We ain't sayin' nothin' else. We want a lawyer.''

"That's the smartest thing you've said all day," said Morales, and he got up to leave the room.

Outside he ran into a member of the team assigned to keep an eye on Rafael Chavez. Morales told him to find something else to do. "Chavez didn't do Ruanda.''

"Maybe I should stick with him anyway," suggested the officer. "You didn't see the crowd at his place the other night. All that was missing was a rope and a buckboard.''

Morales shrugged. "I'll call the paper, give 'em the news.''

"Chavez'll be happy," said the officer.

"A lot happier than Lorraine Lake. That kid on the right in there is her oldest boy."

The officer frowned. "Lorraine who?"

"The leader of the CBFG."

"Damn. Good luck on that one, Morales."

Morales waved him on and walked away. He was going to need luck getting a conviction on that smartass son of a bitch. Lorraine Lake had a lot of rich friends, not a few judges among them. The kid with the pitching arm was going down for sure, but Morales could see the Lake kid getting off with a few years probation.

He smiled in bitter amusement as he thought of the way Lorraine Lake had gone after Rafael Chavez's blood, when it was her own stinking brat who had orchestrated the murder of the prostitute.

Not that he was going to apologize to Chavez anytime soon. Fifteen years ago Morales had been a rookie and the first officer at the scene when the two Montcalm women were discovered murdered in their home. A baseball bat had been the instrument of death, splintered and stained crimson with the blood of the two women whose skulls had been shattered and whose faces had nearly been obliterated. Chavez's prints were all over the bat handle, and one of his bloody handprints was on the wall. Morales still saw the two dead women and that handprint in his sleep sometimes.

Rafael Chavez might be straight now and chemical-free, but he was still a convicted murderer, and in Morales's book, that's all he would ever be. Morales knew that, and he knew Chavez knew that.

Morales nodded to a passing lieutenant and proceeded down the hall to his office, where he sat behind his desk and picked up the phone. He flipped through his addresses until he found the number of the paper, and then he punched in the number and sat back, ready to relish the conversation he was about to have.

Rafael spotted Ross Schweig's ex-girlfriend, Lorraine, observing him and wondered if she had drawn the short straw for the first watch. He matched her stare and she looked immediately away, as if she were sitting there on the street in front of his house doing something besides watching him.

The problem with his mother's car had been easily fixed, a clogged fuel filter, and after jogging home from the parts store he had gone to purchase some paint, convinced that Ross Schweig might actually keep him on longer than a week or two. Rafael bought a length of lattice as well and was working on ripping out the old lattice when he felt himself being watched.

The cops were definitely better at it. You felt something, but you weren't really sure. Lorraine was more obvious, sitting across the street in her car and making sure he saw her. She reminded him of a teacher he'd had in high school, an old gray horse who suspected anyone who wasn't white and nearly popped her veins trying to give Rafael the evil eye. Every day she counted the pennies in her desk drawer, as if Rafael was going to steal them from her. Lorraine could have been her daughter.

When Lena came home Rafael stopped and went in the house to get himself something to drink. He didn't want to look at her any more than he had to. He didn't know how he could still want her after knowing what a bitch she was, but he did. He was still thinking about what had happened after he bumped into her, and the way he caught her looking at him later. Her consent to go running with him the next morning was confusing as hell. He had to wonder what she thought she was up to.

After drinking a large glass of water he walked outside again and saw Lena sitting on her front porch and staring hard at a distinctly uncomfortable Lorraine.

Rafael's face creased into a smile and he had to go back inside before either woman saw it.

God, she was tough. He'd never known a woman as tough as Lena Fairfax.

She acted as if she hated his guts, but there she was out there throwing daggers at the limpid-eyed Lorraine.

He wanted to go over and kiss Lena.

Rafael had to sit down suddenly. The thought of kissing her, actually placing his mouth against hers, had not occurred to him before that moment. The image sent a jolt through his system and flushed him with a need so fierce it made him dizzy. There had been no kissing with Ruanda. He had not kissed a woman in over fifteen years, and the idea of kissing Lena Fairfax held him virtually paralyzed with wanting.

"Shit," he whispered.

His counselor had warned him about this, about falling hard for the first free and single female he encountered. Lena was it. He hadn't been around any others yet.

Ruanda Beker didn't count.

Just as abruptly, Rafael sobered and his senses returned to normal. Ruanda was dead, which was why Lorraine Lake was sitting out there in her expensive-looking car. Rafael didn't know what kind of car it was. He hadn't paid much attention to such things in prison, and every car on the road looked the same to him now. Her car was pricey, he knew that, and all the other cars sitting out in front of the house last night had looked every bit as expensive as Lorraine's, which meant money, which meant that regardless of whether he had actually killed Ruanda Beker, eventually these people would win, Fairfax women or no. Money always won.

He had no idea where Eugenia's faith in him came from, or Ross Schweig's, for that matter, but he was glad to have it. Their instinctive trust meant a great deal to him, particularly in the face of the CBFG's aggression, and especially since he had been prepared to live a long time without anyone he could call a friend.

He went to a window in his bedroom and looked out at Lena's porch. She was still there. Rafael wished it was Lena who would look at him as if she knew in her heart he was good. First free and single female aside, he wanted her approval and admiration, and not just the admiration for his body he had witnessed earlier. He wanted her to think he was a good person and not some hardened con topping the list for recidivism.

Which wasn't to say that while incarcerated he hadn't played the role expected of him by guards and other cons. For the first seven years he had been in a gang and enjoyed it. Until it got old. Until even the highs and the hooch didn't assuage the emptiness, and one friend after another was either released, moved, or put away by an enemy gang. When Rafael realized he was the oldest member of his gang, his eyes began to see things differently. For the first time in his life, he began to think about the future. The next few years were spent in torture both physical and mental as he attempted to break away from the all-too-available desensitizers and the *Grande Cojones* gang who called him brother. Neither let go of Rafael easily.

But he did it, and the fact that he had done it by himself was a source of great pride for him. His reward, he had frequently told himself during times of struggle, would be to have a normal life. A good job. A woman who loved him. A family.

His chest filled as he peered out the window at Lena, and his breath came out in a sigh. Looking at her, Rafael considered calling his counselor. A little wisdom at this point might go a long way toward redirecting the fantasies he was beginning to entertain.

Not that fantasy was anything new to him.

He just never imagined falling for such a cold-hearted bitch.

He reached for the phone and heard a peculiar ring from what sounded like outside. He peered out the window again and saw Lorraine put a cellular phone to her ear.

Rafael shook his head and was about to turn away again when he noticed Lorraine drop the phone and hurriedly turn the ignition on her car. The engine roared into life and in seconds Lorraine was speeding down the street. Rafael looked to see if Lena had witnessed the abrupt departure.

She had.

The hint of a smile curved her lips as she left the porch and opened the door to go inside.

Rafael watched until he could no longer see her, then he let the curtain fall and picked up the phone again to call his counselor.

He got an answering machine.

"Damn." Rafael left no message. Instead he replaced the receiver and went outside to finish tearing out the lattice, hoping the physical exertion would keep his mind off Lena.

He spent the rest of the evening trying not to think about kissing her.

NINE

THE blonde's name was Annabeth De Peyster Dixon, and she had left her very comfortable home in New York to follow her husband west to the untamed wilds in the middle of the continent. A descendant of one of the very oldest Dutch families, she despised living at the fort, where there were still Cherokee walking about, sometimes accompanied by their slaves, who didn't act like slaves at all, but behaved as if they were members of the same tribe as their Indian owners. Such matters disturbed Annabeth, who had enjoyed the presence of servants all her life, but never suffered any servant of color to do her bidding. She much preferred lower-class whites, who at least knew how to speak English, even if it was poor English. Annabeth also enjoyed being able to handpick her servants, and the fact that she had to choose between two bedraggled white women and a host of unclean soldiers set her teeth on edge.

She chose the younger of the two women and pulled her away from the job of fort laundress to function as housemaid and general servant girl.

The young woman's name was Audrey, and while her appearance caused Annabeth's lip to curl, she was sound enough and knew how to work. It was explained to Annabeth that Audrey was a widow whose husband had died of snakebite during his first year at the fort, leaving Audrey at the mercy of the then commanding officer, who promptly sent her to the fort laundress and told her to put Audrey to work.

A week after Audrey went into Annabeth's employ, Annabeth was to hear disturbing information from another officer's wife. It seemed that Audrey herself, the pale, thin waif with the scraggly, unkempt hair, had once been the mistress of the house she now cleaned for Annabeth. Her husband had been a brash young officer with a fiery temper who fell into disagreement with his superior when it became his superior's wish to move into the warm and comfortable house Audrey and her husband inhabited, leaving them to make do with his own musty, cramped, one-room abode. The young officer was incensed, stating that the commander had watched his wife make every improvement upon their place, turning it into a cozy, charming home, before deciding he would have the house for himself.

In punishment for the angry refusal and obvious insubordination, the commanding officer sent the young man away on an off-post detail far from the fort for an unspecified amount of time.

The young officer never returned.

There were rumors, the officer's wife explained, that it was not in fact a snakebite that had killed Audrey's husband. There was no way to prove it, however, since the man was purported to have been buried where he fell.

When the conversation with the officer's wife ended, Annabeth looked at her servant Audrey with different eyes.

No longer did she think of her as some dull-witted fool with only the most rudimentary skills. No longer did she think of her as harmless, inane, and uneducated. Annabeth saw her as a liar and a pretender. She saw deceit in its most fraudulent form.

At the first opportunity, she accosted the young woman and demanded to know if all she had heard was true.

Audrey said yes, it was all true.

"Have you been playing me for a fool?" asked Annabeth. "I would say you have. I would say you've been laughing at me."

"I don't know what you mean," Audrey protested. "I've done no such thing."

"Of course you have. Laughing and keeping your own counsel about all you know while I go blithely along in my ignorance. I won't stand for it, do you hear? I simply won't stand for it. I am the wife of the commanding officer, and I will not allow such dissimulation to occur in my presence."

Audrey lifted her head and looked at her with large brown eyes. "I'm sorry, Mrs. Dixon. I never considered such a thing. Truly, I didn't."

"You thought simply to go on working here for me, knowing this house better than I and pretending you did not?"

"I pretended nothing. I did the work you asked me to do."

Annabeth was made even angrier by the younger woman's submissiveness.

"Get out of my sight. I'll discuss with my husband what to do with you. For now, just go."

Audrey clearly didn't understand what she had done wrong, but she went.

Annabeth was trembling with indignation at having been duped by the cow-eyed girl. She realized she should take some satisfaction out of knowing the former mistress of the house was now its maid, but never again would Annabeth look at her home in the same way, knowing that each sweet improvement had been due to the former mistress and no one else. She didn't see how she could go on living there.

Her husband had a different idea. His dark brows lifted above his cool blue eyes and he said, "There is nowhere else, Annabeth. I will build nothing else. Satisfy yourself with a few changes if you like, but realize it is here we shall stay."

"You don't know what you're asking of me," said Annabeth.

"You don't know what you're asking of me," her husband replied. "I have had my say on the matter."

"I want her out."

"Who?"

"Audrey. I want the other woman. The old one. I should have chosen her to begin with."

"Nonsense. You chose Audrey, now keep her."

"I cannot. She is sneering at me, John. I know she is."

Her husband looked sternly at Annabeth. "We will have no further discussion on the matter. Is that clear?"

Annabeth stormed from the room, the fabric of her skirts swishing angrily against her legs. John Dixon watched her, and after a moment he got up from his chair and went to look for Audrey.

He found her in the kitchen, her hands covered with flour as she worked at preparing a meal. Her eyes lifted to his face and then just as quickly lowered again.

Dixon approached her and said, "I've told her you're staying. Do your best to avoid incurring her wrath. She is a headstrong woman with a streak of wickedness I once thought amusing but now find sickening. If she ever lifts a finger to you, tell me at once."

"Thank you," Audrey mumbled.

"It's nothing." Dixon moved closer and lifted a hand to touch her thin shoulder. "You poor, gentle creature. I would do more for you if I could."

"Don't," she whispered. Then, louder, "Please, don't."

Dixon stiffened, and finally nodded. "Yes, you're right, of course. If she were ever to guess, both our lives would be made miserable. I apologize most humbly and beg your forgiveness if I have offended."

Audrey said nothing, only gave a small shake of her head.

John Dixon drew in breath and let it out in a long, trembling sigh. He had never been so drawn to anyone, so inexorably pulled by the sweetness of cheek or the curve of jaw. He thought he could lose his soul to her eyes. The impulse to draw her against his chest and crush her to him was so strong he was almost overwhelmed by its intensity.

As if sensing his struggle, Audrey moved away from him and went into the pantry, watching him carefully over her shoulder as she went, as if afraid he might follow and trap her inside.

Dixon forced himself to turn on his heel and walk away, back to the sitting room, where he picked up the book of poems by Longfellow and struggled to make sense of what was on the page.

From the first moment he saw her, Audrey had this effect on him. Only a month ago he had arrived to take the place of the former commander, who was unexpectedly called back East. Dixon noticed Audrey the day he arrived as he inspected the fort and all its outlying buildings. She was in the laundry, her hair steamed into loose curls by the hot water, her face heated by exertion. He thought he had never seen a more beautiful woman.

He hoped desperately Annabeth would choose her for a servant, so he could be near her on a daily basis. The last week had been one of joy for him, being able to view her at his leisure, smiling at her, passing words with her.

And now Annabeth wanted to be rid of her, all because she was the widow of a young officer and had lived in the house before them. It was really quite ridiculous the way Annabeth behaved. Dixon could see he had indulged her for far too long. She was not going to ruin this for him. She was not going to take away the one small measure of happiness he enjoyed.

God knew he was disappointed enough in their childless marriage. For nine years they had been wed, and Dixon saw no hope of Annabeth ever conceiving. She claimed it was just as well, since she considered herself too fragile for childbearing and thought it might be dangerous for a woman with such a small frame. Dixon considered this so much hogwash. He had seen much smaller, more petite women than Annabeth have dozens of children and survive. He was convinced his wife did not wish to be a mother, and as a result her womb rejected his seed.

He should have known better than to marry money. Her good name had meant something to him in the beginning. He had been honored by her very presence and proud to show her off to his fellow officers. It was as if she were some enormous jewel attached to his arm that everyone turned to stare at in admiration. In her younger years she was truly golden.

She was still a beautiful woman, but her beauty was of the sort never meant to be touched or enjoyed, indeed like that priceless, enormous jewel, never meant to be worn, only to be uncovered and admired on occasion.

True to her breeding, she never gave any indication of enjoying marital relations with him. Annabeth had been reared a proper lady, and proper ladies did not experience passion. But the older John Dixon grew, the more he thought of enjoying a woman's arms around him. The more he thought of feeling a woman move beneath him again. He had known one or two such experiences in his time, before his marriage, of course. He thought of them constantly now, but not in relation to Annabeth, who would sooner drown herself in the nearby river as show an ounce of ardor in the bedroom.

No, he was thinking of Audrey, whom he could see dressed in fine gowns and fulfilling every aspect of her role as a dutiful officer's wife, and still allowing herself to unleash her emotions at night in the marriage bed. Dixon could see it all too clearly, with her thick brown hair tumbling loose around her face, her chest heaving, her breath warm . . .

Such thoughts brought him actual pain. He closed the book in his lap and clutched at his forehead with his fingers, as if to assuage the sudden ache.

Eugenia awakened with her fingers clutching her forehead in the same fashion.

Both her nightgown and the sheets were drenched with perspiration.

"I don't believe this," she whispered to nothing and no one in particular.

No longer content with just showing her what happened *after* Audrey left Annabeth's employ, she was seeing what had happened before, and she was now one with the ghosts themselves, sharing their thoughts, feelings, and witnessing firsthand what occurred at the fort all those years ago.

First she had been Annabeth De Peyster Dixon, and then her husband, John Dixon.

Eugenia closed her eyes again and moved her head back and forth.

"Why is this happening to me? Why me?"

Being inside the man, *being a man,* had been the strangest, most awkward sensation.

He wanted so much. His lust was incredible, literally humming through his veins with the intensity of sustained electrical surges.

Eugenia had to wonder if all men felt that way. Or if they only felt that way when they wanted someone they couldn't have.

She could still feel traces of him inside her.

On impulse she got off the bed, turned on the light, and went to look in the mirror, wondering if she would see a pair of bright blue eyes peering out of her face.

Her reflection was her own, very pale, a little uneasy, but still her own.

She turned off the light and opened the door to go into the hall. There would be no more sleep that night.

TEN

RAFAEL came to a stop in the middle of an intersection and turned to look at Lena, who ran past him to the curb and then stopped.

"Can't keep up?" he asked.

"I can keep up," she assured him, and she pushed a tendril of damp hair out of her eyes.

"Then why run behind me?"

"I'm looking at you," she said.

"Looking at me?" He lifted his T-shirt to wipe the sweat from his brow.

"What's wrong?" she asked as she eyed the dark line of hair beneath his navel. "Does admiration aggravate you?"

Rafael inhaled. "Let's just run, Lena, all right?"

She smiled tightly and took off, forcing him to hurry to keep up with her. A mile later she stopped again, this time in front of the public library. Rafael stopped and looked at her as she began to walk around and cool down.

"What?" he said.

"Is this place open?"

"I think it's too early. Why?"

"I want to look for something."

"About the fort," Rafael said intuitively, and she looked archly at him. Then her shoulders dropped.

"I have to do something about Mom. She can't sleep, she's losing weight, and she won't even talk to me. I have to find out what's going on."

She walked up to the door and read a notice that said the library didn't open until nine.

"Excuse me," said a voice behind her, and Lena turned to see a woman with a key in her hand waiting to get inside.

"Do you work here?" Lena asked.

"I do. The library opens at nine."

"Yes, I know, but I was wondering if you would consider letting me in early. I don't have a card, I'm not even from here, but I really need to look for something and I would be so grateful if you would allow me to come in now instead of waiting around outside for the next hour."

The woman looked over her shoulder at Rafael. "What about him?"

"I'm going to help her look," he said, before Lena could open her mouth.

Lena glared at him before turning back to the woman. "I promise we'll be no trouble, and we'll be out as soon as we can."

The woman stood in indecision and finally nodded her white head. "Don't tell anyone else. I'll have half the town in here at eight o'clock if they think they can get away with it."

"We won't tell anyone," Lena assured her.

"What exactly are you looking for?" the librarian asked.

"Old newspaper articles about Vandegrift Hall."

The woman paused. "You want to know about the Hall?"

"Yes."

"May I ask why?"

Lena's lips parted, and Rafael stepped forward to say, "It's personal."

"I see. Well, everything we have is on microfilm upstairs. I'll show you."

She led the way to the second floor and Lena and Rafael followed her. Halfway up, Lena turned to scowl at Rafael.

"You don't have to come," she said.

"It'll go faster with two of us looking," he told her.

The librarian took them to a long table and showed them how to operate the machines, then she wrinkled her nose and left them to return to the first floor.

"One of us must smell," said Lena.

"I'd say it's both of us."

"You definitely need a shower," she told him, eyeing his damp T-shirt and glistening flesh.

"So do you."

"You don't like a woman who sweats?"

"Men sweat. Women perspire."

Lena leaned back and gave a genuine belly laugh.

Rafael smiled at her, revealing white though slightly uneven teeth. "I knew that one would get you."

"You pig," she said, and, still smiling, she turned to the dozens of rolls of microfilm and plucked out the earliest date she could find. She handed the next one to Rafael and each of them sat down behind a machine to begin their search for material on Vandegrift Hall.

Only minutes later Lena shoved away from the machine and got up. Rafael glanced at her. "Find anything?"

"Sickening," said Lena. "How could they write such sickening things in the paper?"

Rafael leaned over to look at the page lit up on her screen. There were several stories and advertisements, but the most prominent article concerned the murder of an elderly woman who lived with her daughter on a farm. The daughter had gone off to market and left her mother to watch the place when a thieving neighbor boy showed up looking for things to steal. The mother tried to stop him and was hit over the head with a shovel. To cover the crime, the boy dragged the old woman into the hog pen. When the daughter returned she found her mother's half-eaten body still being torn and chewed by the hogs. Something of the boy's was left behind, and he was soon hunted down and hanged for the murder of the old woman, who because of her numerous infirmities made it a point never to go near the hog pen.

It *was* sickening. Every lurid detail was in the article, including the more grisly features of the hanging.

Rafael thought this explained why horror novels hadn't become popular until the twentieth century; before then people got their morbid chills and thrills from the daily newspaper.

"It's pretty bad," he commented for Lena's sake, and turned back to his own machine. A glimmer of a memory had come to him while thinking about the boy with the shovel. For just a moment he had seen another boy, this one with a bloody baseball bat in his hands. Rafael was tempted to shove away from the machine and get up as Lena had, but he forced himself to stay seated and keep reading.

Lena came back to sit down again, and as she eased into her chair their naked thighs came into contact. Rafael inhaled, but didn't allow himself to look at her. He concentrated hard on what he was reading; still he could feel Lena looking at him.

She eased her chair away from his and wordlessly went back to her own screen. For the next hour they sat and looked, going through only two more spools and finding nothing of interest concerning the Hall. It was time-consuming work, and the novelty of reading ads and editorials over a century old soon wore off and left both bored.

"You ready?" Rafael asked after he finished his spool.

Lena nodded. "Mom was probably right when she said nothing would have been written down."

"What's going on with her?" Rafael asked.

"It's personal, remember?" said Lena.

Rafael replaced his spool and was silent a moment before speaking. "My mother had a friend here who used to talk about the fort. This friend couldn't walk through the place without getting chills and hair standing up on her arms. Is that how it is with your mom?''

"Something like that," Lena answered as she left her chair and headed down the stairs.

She thanked the woman at the main desk, and the old librarian looked at her with raised brows.

"Did you find what you were looking for?''

"No."

"Doesn't surprise me," said the woman.

"Why?"

"Just doesn't, that's all. Lock the door again on your way out. It's still five minutes before nine."

Lena locked the door and Rafael followed her outside.

"Wanna run some more?"

"No," she said. "You can if you want to."

"Are you going in today?"

"Why wouldn't I?"

He lifted a shoulder. "Thought you might stay and keep an eye on Eugenia."

"She doesn't want me to keep an eye on her. It would drive her nuts if she thought I was hanging around to keep an eye on her."

"Maybe you should take her home," Rafael suggested, and Lena looked at him in surprise.

"You mean back to Oregon?"

Rafael faced her squarely, looked meaningfully into her eyes and said, "I don't want *you* to go back to Oregon, no. But I'm thinking of your mother."

Lena blinked, as if made uncomfortable by his directness. Then her shoulders stiffened and she quickened her pace. "I'm sure it's a possibility. In fact I've already mentioned it to her. She doesn't seem to think it would do any good."

"Why?"

"I have no idea. She believes time and space make no difference. It's happening because it's happening, and that's all there is to it. She doesn't think it will stop just because she moves to another location.''

"Why did she come here then?''

"I don't know, Rafael. Because she's human. Because like all of us, she still wants to believe in free will. Now stop asking questions. I told you she asked me not to discuss it.''

Rafael lifted his hands and fell silent. They walked quietly along for several minutes before he felt Lena look at him again. He glanced at her, and she said, "You worked out with weights in prison.''

"Yeah.''

"Do you miss it?''

"Sure.''

"Can't afford the gym?''

"No.''

"You've got great definition,'' she said. "It would be a shame to lose it.''

Rafael only nodded, confused by her rapid turnaround. Part of him reveled in the way she looked at him, and the other part didn't. She was looking only at his deltoids, biceps, and pectorals; she wasn't looking at him.

"I don't like guys who get too big,'' she went on. "You're just the right size.''

"Yeah, well you look pretty good to me, too, Lena. It's all I can do to keep my hands off you.''

He didn't know what made him say it. It just came out. He tried smiling after he said it, but it was too late. Her eyes went cold and she looked at him and called him a pig again.

"Bitch,'' he responded, and she bristled even further.

"Is fucking someone all you ever think about?'' she asked.

"Don't use that language,'' he said to her. Then, "Fucking *you* is all I ever think about.''

"Don't you dare tell me what kind of language to use,'' she spit at him, and drops of saliva flew from her mouth and spattered his cheek.

"Just say it, Lena, don't spray it." He wiped his cheek with a finger, and a sudden deviant urge made him stick the finger in his mouth and look at her.

Lena's nostrils flared, but she calmed suddenly and formed an icy smile. "Nice to know my initial impression was on target. For about three seconds there I wondered."

"I won't apologize," Rafael told her. "You know what you do to me and you enjoy it."

"Please."

"You get off on knowing how much I want you."

"Shut up."

"Give me a clue here, Lena. Is my skin too brown for you, or are your own testosterone levels too far up there?"

"You bastard." Lena spun away from him and opened up her stride.

"See?" he said, walking after her. "See how you treat me? Do us both a favor and come sleep with me tonight. I know I'll stop wanting you once we do it, and you probably know it too, you cold-eyed bitch. That's why you fight so hard to keep me coming on to you. That's how you get off."

A noise of fury came from her and she broke into a run, using all her speed. Rafael let her go. He wiped his face with his hands and kicked the ground with his running shoe while he mentally kicked himself in the rear.

He felt like shit. He felt worse than shit. He wanted to run after her, catch her, and tell her he didn't mean any of it. He wanted to tell her he was sorry and let her know how much he had enjoyed just being with her that morning, running with her and sitting beside her in the stuffy library. He thought she enjoyed herself, too. There was a sense of companionship between them he knew he hadn't imagined.

But he had blown it, and blown it badly.

"Goddammit." He kicked the ground again and then broke into a trot for home. Maybe he could talk to her at work.

If she let him.

ELEVEN

ROSS was losing just as much sweat as Lena and Rafael, but he was still asleep. He was cutting meat behind the counter when the bell on the door rang. He looked up and thought at first it was Lena coming in to work. A second glance told him this woman's hair was redder, her figure rounder—what people always called buxom. A longer look made his throat close and his heart begin to pound. His hands started to shake.

"Hello," said the woman as she came to stand at the counter. She was smiling at him—not a woman at all, but a girl approaching womanhood with an already-mature shape and figure.

"Hello, Martha," Ross croaked, and in the dream he was already beginning to wonder why she still looked young when he was so much older. Then it hit him, and when it did it came with such force he was brought immediately awake. He sat up in bed with a jolt and felt his stomach begin to roll. He swung his legs over the side of the mattress and stared with unblinking eyes at the bare wall beside the bed.

Ross found himself wishing away the same people he had welcomed into his life just a few days ago. They brought Martha Box with them, he was sure of it. Eugenia Fairfax and her problems, and Lena and her problems, and all of it having to do with that goddammed orphanage nobody liked to think about because it brought back long-buried memories shoved so deep inside only brain surgery with a laser could reach them, and most of the time they came out resembling only smarmy little references to the bad girls at the orphanage and how no boys ever really got it on with those girls—they just said they did.

"I never touched you," Ross said to the wall. "I never laid a hand on you, Martha."

He cringed to think how just a day or so ago he had been excited at everything going on around him and happy to be free of Lorraine and her constant connivery. One glimpse of Martha Box's face in a dream was enough to make him wish Superman would come and spin the world around in the opposite direction so he could go back to being as comfortably bored and secretly contemptuous as he was a week ago.

Ross groaned and forced himself out of bed. He went to the bathroom and uttered another long groan at the sight of his face. He looked like the cartoon dog Droopy, he decided, with his red, sagging eyes and saddlebag cheeks. All he needed was a little black nose.

For just an instant he saw Martha's face again, superimposed over his own; her sweet brown eyes in a pale, freckled complexion and her perfect even teeth revealed in an all-too-rare smile.

Unusual for such a pretty girl to be so painfully shy.

Ross swallowed and jerked away from the mirror. He was going to make himself late if he kept standing around. He turned on the shower and put himself through the motions until he was in his small truck and headed for the deli. He met Rafael at the door and nodded briefly in response to his greeting. He couldn't blame Rafael, he supposed. He didn't have anything to do with anything.

When Lena arrived he mumbled something to her and proceeded to ignore both his employees while he set about making the bread.

Soon he noticed that not only was he ignoring them, but they were ignoring each other.

Great, he thought. *Kim and Kevin, ten years later.*

That was just fine with Ross. He didn't need the aggravation of another workplace romance taking place under his nose.

The deli was ominously quiet for the next few hours and Ross was deep in his thoughts until the first customer arrived. Lena was slicing the fresh-baked bread and Rafael was busy mopping the floor, so Ross waited on the man and barked out his sandwich order to Lena. The caustic tone of his voice took her by surprise and she jumped, slicing open her hand with the bread knife. Ross watched in dismay as blood spurted over three perfectly formed loaves.

"Dammit, Lena," he complained, and Rafael looked to see what was happening. The younger man frowned and hurried behind the counter to help.

"Get her out of here," Ross snapped. "She's bleeding all over everything."

Lena blinked and stared. Rafael was still frowning at Ross as he took her by the elbow and guided her toward the sole bathroom.

"Sorry," Ross said to the customer. "Let me get that sandwich for you."

When the customer was gone, Ross went to the bathroom and looked inside. Lena was holding her head between her knees while Rafael held up her arm. A bloody towel was wrapped around her hand.

"What's wrong?" Ross asked.

"She's nauseous," said Rafael. "The cut went to the bone. She needs stitches."

Ross grunted and reached in his pocket for his keys. "Take her and get back here as soon as you can."

Rafael frowned at him again, and Ross wanted to tell him it was none of his goddamn business what was wrong, just do as he said.

He felt mean and ugly and he wasn't going to get over it anytime soon. He wanted them both to just go away.

"What did I do?" Lena asked once she was seated beside Rafael in the truck. She still felt so sick she could barely speak. He fastened her seat belt, put on his own, then started the truck.

"I don't know, Lena. Maybe he's having a bad day."

"Yeah, well, mine ain't been too great either."

Rafael pulled out onto the street, then he looked at her. "I'm sorry. I'm sorry for everything I said to you this morning."

She glanced over at the sincerity in his voice. His dark eyes were just as sincere.

"How far is the hospital?"

"Not far. Will you forgive me?"

"There's nothing to forgive, Rafael."

"There is. Lena, a chance with you is all I'm asking. Don't judge me based on where I've been, just look at who I am now."

"I am," she said, not looking at him.

She felt his gaze focus on her.

"I told you before I won't apologize for wanting you, or for letting you see how I feel. I've caught you looking at me, too."

"Because you keep looking at me," Lena said, her voice weak but stubborn.

His expression filled with concern suddenly. "You just went about three shades paler. Are you okay?"

"I feel sick again," she admitted.

He took a hand off the wheel and reached over to touch the back of her neck. "Bend over just like before until it goes away."

The feel of his hand on the back of her neck sent a shiver down her spine and her flesh began to goose-pimple. She put her head between her knees again and rode that way to the hospital. When Rafael stopped the truck and got out she undid her seat belt and opened her door. He came around and hesitated while he watched her get out.

"It's the blood," she explained. "It always gets me."

She held up the bloody towel around her hand and felt her

head begin to swim once she saw the darkness of its color; not just red, or crimson, but nearly black.

"Holy shit," she mumbled, and she felt her knees weaken.

Rafael was there to hold her up. His arm went around her shoulders and he held her against him as he walked her to the hospital entrance.

"Come on, baby, it's not far."

Lena gathered her wits enough to tell him not to call her baby. He gave her a squeeze and placed a tender kiss on her temple as they walked. She couldn't believe the comfort it gave her, or the warm feeling it engendered in her middle. She had the sudden urge to stop in the middle of the sidewalk and cling to him. Instead she reached up and held on to his shirt with her uninjured right hand.

He patted her hand and reached for the heavy glass door at the hospital entrance.

Two hours later she let her head loll on the seat once he got her in the small truck. The pill they had given her for the pain made her lids heavy and left her decidedly woozy. When Rafael got in the truck she slid sideways down the seat and put her head on his thigh.

His start of surprise made her groan.

"Take me home," she said.

"I will," he answered. "Do you . . . I don't think you should ride like that."

"Why not?"

"If you move, I'll probably have a wreck."

"I won't move," she said. And then she added, "This doesn't mean a thing."

"Lena . . ."

She closed her eyes. He said something else but she wasn't paying attention; she was listening to the sound of his voice through the denim of his jeans.

Abruptly a question came to her, the question that had grown in importance to Lena, and before she realized what she was doing, she heard a faraway voice speaking.

"Did you kill that woman and her daughter? Did you murder them?"

The muscles beneath the denim under her cheek tensed and then began to twitch. He said nothing.

"Rafael? Will you answer me?"

"No," he said. "Not now. We'll talk about it later."

"You did, didn't you?" she said. "I know you did, and because of that I could never . . ."

"Never what?" he asked. "Never have feelings for me? Never treat me like a human being? I was a different person then, Lena. I was so fucked-up most the time I didn't know who I was. I used whatever I could get my hands on and didn't give a living shit about anything or anyone but myself."

His accent was thick now, and in her stuporous state, Lena began to frown as she listened.

"I've been clean for years now and I've done everything I can to say I'm sorry to the family of those women. It doesn't change anything, I know, because I'm here and they're not, but I have to go on living, Lena. I have to go on trying and hoping I'll be forgiven for being so lost and stupid and addicted. I don't know what else I can do."

He fell into frustrated silence. Then he said, "To tell you the truth, I never remembered doing it. I only assumed I did it because all the evidence said I did."

"Do you think you did it?" Lena asked, her voice quiet in the cab of the truck.

There was a pause, then Rafael said, "Yeah. I have flashes sometimes. Just flashes, but it's there. Let's not talk about it anymore, okay?"

"How did you do it?"

"Please, Lena. Let's talk about something else."

He dropped a hand to smooth her hair away from her face, and she responded by turning away from his hand.

Rafael sighed and placed his palm back on the wheel.

The next thing Lena knew he was easing himself out from under her and lifting her up to a sitting position. Her mother opened her door and looked worriedly at her.

"She cut herself," Rafael said, and he reached in to pull her out. Lena allowed herself to be led into the house and guided to the same elegant sofa her mother often napped on. Rafael stood over her a moment, his expression unreadable, and he haltingly touched her cheek before moving away.

Lena said, "I got seventeen stitches, Mom."

Then she fell asleep.

When she awakened she heard her mother speaking on the phone to someone. ". . . still asleep. I'm sure she's fine. She never has been able to stomach the sight of blood. You tell Ross I said thank you for paying the hospital bill. Yes, I'm sure he's insured and he'll be reimbursed, but say thank you anyway. All right, I will. Good-bye."

"Who was that?" Lena asked when her mother came in to look at her.

"He wanted to know how you were doing. I'm not supposed to tell you he called."

Lena rolled her eyes the way her mother did.

"Tell me," said Eugenia. "Why would Rafael not want you to know he called?"

"Ask him," Lena answered.

"I'm asking you."

"Well how do you like not having your questions answered? I'm pretty used to it, myself."

"I want you to try harder with him, Lena."

"He's a convicted murderer, Mother, and today he told me he didn't even remember killing those women."

"Was it drugs?"

"He says it was."

"You don't believe him? Lena, I don't have to lecture you on the difficulties of the disenfranchised. Rafael served fifteen years for his crime. He went to jail a mere boy and has grown up a part of our penal system. Considering all he's been through, I'd say he's emerged intact."

"You don't know that. You've known him only a short time."

Eugenia turned her back and left the room, unwilling to engage in an argument. Lena held up her aching hand and wondered why she was trying so hard to make herself right. She did like Rafael, overt staring aside. And she thought of him often, convict or not, want to or not.

She forced herself up from the sofa and went in search of something to eat. She wanted to take another pain pill, but she couldn't do it on an empty stomach.

In the kitchen she found cold macaroni in a bowl and some summer sausage. She ate what she could, and then she groped for the pills the doctor had given her. The pain in her left hand was terrible.

As she swallowed a pill she thought of the relief it would give her, and then she found herself thinking of another kind of pain, and the relief an unhappy young man might seek.

Then she stiffened.

Don't, she told herself. *Don't make excuses for him. Lots of people know pain, but most of them don't kill anybody. He did.* That meant there was something wrong with him anyway, something the drugs managed to unleash on those poor unsuspecting women.

Lena drank some water and replaced the glass before returning to the sofa. She wasn't going to think about him anymore. He wanted her to keep thinking about him. That's why he said what he did that morning, so she would take each sentence between mental teeth and worry it to death. Well she had news. She didn't care. For one thing, the idea that he could do it with her once and not want her anymore was utterly ridiculous. She knew it and he knew it.

She snorted as she lifted her feet once more to lie down on the sofa. The things men believed.

TWELVE

U PSTAIRS in her room, Eugenia was reading a book she'd
borrowed from the library that morning. The librarian
had looked at her strangely when she filled out the form for a
card, as if she knew her from somewhere. Eugenia shrugged off
the woman's stare and went about her business. She had no idea
why she picked the book she did, about the orphan trains that
operated out of the East during the nineteenth century, taking
orphans and other destitute children to childless homes and
farms throughout the Midwest. Through reading, she learned
most of what she already knew or had guessed. Most of the girls
taken were used as servants rather than treated as daughters. The
boys, though often treated better, became laborers on farms and
in factories.

The associations behind the operation of such activity were obviously the same people Eugenia had encountered as a child in
Fort Grant. The same pious white men and women who appointed
themselves guardians of goodness and masqueraded behind
Christian intentions, all the while hiding their disgust and fear of
the lower classes behind their good deeds.

Eugenia had smiled a grim smile that morning while reading

the tiny article in the paper about the arrest of two local teenagers, both athletes, in connection with the murder of a local prostitute.

Much easier to believe a convicted Hispanic was responsible than to ruin the lives of two high-achieving white boys.

But Eugenia knew in her heart the two boys would be spared. They were, after all, just boys, and no judge in a town as small as this one would send a couple of local jocks away to prison.

Some things never changed, Eugenia told herself, and for the first time in many years she remembered the face of a girl she had known at Vandegrift Hall.

Her name was Martha Box, and she was beautiful. Eugenia was much younger, but she idolized the shy, sweet Martha. Martha had taken special interest in Eugenia as well, helping her with her schooling and looking out for her at the Hall when problems occurred. The day Martha turned up missing was one of the worst in Eugenia's memory. The officials at the orphanage assumed the girl had run away, but Eugenia knew better. Martha was too timid, and she would never leave without telling Eugenia good-bye.

The ten-year-old Eugenia had her own ideas about what happened to Martha, but no one she spoke to would listen to her.

There were boys in town who followed Martha home every day from where she worked at the beauty parlor. These boys hounded her constantly, torturing the shy Martha with their jeers, leers, and insults. Martha often came back to the Hall in tears, but she would tell Eugenia it was nothing, just boys being mean.

Eugenia knew it was more than nothing, and she tried to tell the matron about the boys, how awful they were to Martha and the terrible things they said to her, but the matron wouldn't listen, and eventually she had Eugenia punished because she would not be quiet.

"Martha Box was a tramp," the woman said. "The same as you and every other little guttersnipe girl here will turn out. Now get down to the kitchen."

It was not the first time Eugenia was sent to the hot, sweltering

kitchen, nor would it be the last. All that kept her face from cracking in the heat that day were the tears rolling down her young
face.

The older Eugenia closed the book she was reading and stared
mindlessly at the cover. The loss of Martha was only one of the
many terrible things that had happened to her at Vandegrift Hall.
Funny she should remember Martha now.

She put the book away from her and went downstairs to check
on Lena.

Her daughter was on the sofa still, moaning, but not in pain,
Eugenia saw. The corners of her mouth were curved upward.

An erotic dream, Eugenia guessed, and she chuckled to herself
as she went to the kitchen for something to drink. She poured
herself a glass of orange juice and sat down at the table in the
breakfast nook. There had been no episodes for her that day, and
she was grateful, but perplexed. She was also curious to know why.
The story with the fort officer and his scheming wife had pro-
gressed to the point where the wife discovered the affection between the scout and the laundress, and then the tale abruptly
stopped and became the ghastly vision of the children again, and
the deadly flying bucket.

Was that why she had checked out the book on orphans? Eugenia wondered. Was she still tuned in to them somehow?

A niggling something told Eugenia all was connected, but she
could not for the life of her see how. Nor could she see what part
she was to play in all of this, or even if there was a part to be played.
It was true that a strong sense of purpose was all that was keeping
her sane, but what the purpose was, or why any of it was necessary,
completely befuddled her.

She supposed she wasn't supposed to ask why. She supposed
she was supposed to be doing what she was doing: nothing. At least
she wasn't getting sick anymore.

She looked up with a start when Lena came into the kitchen.
Her face was damp with perspiration, and she took the glass of
orange juice from her mother's hand and downed the contents.

Eugenia watched her and said, "That was some dream you were having."

Lena handed the glass back to her. Then she covered her eyes and began to cry.

Eugenia left her chair in surprise and moved to put her arms around her daughter. "What is it, Lena? What's wrong?"

"Nothing," she said. "It must be the pain pills."

"Nonsense," said Eugenia. "Tell me."

"I can't."

"You can't. Well, all right. I'm not going anywhere. When you want to talk to me, I'll be here."

Lena nodded; then she pulled away and looked at her mother with reddened eyes.

"Mom, let's just go, okay? Let's go home."

Eugenia looked at her daughter's face and wondered what it was that frightened Lena so. Was it the business of the fort and the dreams, or was it something else?

"I can't," she told her in a gentle voice. "Not yet, Lena. Please don't ask me to go now."

"I think I have to," Lena muttered. "I'm going crazy here. I want to go home."

"Suit yourself," Eugenia said, and she patted her daughter on the shoulder. "But you really should wait until after the weekend and the rendezvous thing. Ross will need you, remember?"

"I remember," Lena said. Then she scowled at her mother. "You know damn good and well I won't leave you here by yourself. Why do you act as if I could?"

"Why do *you* act as if you could?" Eugenia asked. Then she smiled. "Lena, you are so precious. I'm so glad you're my daughter."

Lena wiped her face and turned to the refrigerator to refill the glass of orange juice.

"Rah, rah," she said.

Next door, Rafael was just getting home from work. He found some feces in a bag on his front porch and made a face as he walked around to put it in his trash cart. The shit wouldn't stop anytime soon, he guessed, literally, but he hadn't expected anything less.

What he didn't expect was the way Lena's half-conscious questions had made him feel that day.

She was breaking his heart. He was having the damnedest time convincing himself he still deserved to be loved, something his counselor had worked on for years, and here she was telling him she couldn't care for him because a long time ago he went crazy on acid and committed an unforgivable crime.

He knew all that. He knew she shouldn't care. He was a monster who killed innocent women and no one who knew about it would ever love him again. She hadn't told him anything he hadn't already told himself.

But still he hoped.

For the rest of the day Rafael had the terrible urge to break something. Ross kept looking at him, and it was those looks that kept his hands busy with his work.

The minute he got inside the house he called his counselor, and, after the preliminary greetings, Rafael went straight to the problem. After listening, his counselor sighed in his ear.

"Rafael, we talked about this before you left. You were going to give yourself a chance, remember? You were going to try and meet as many young women as possible and not become obsessed with the first single woman you met."

Rafael rubbed hard at his eyes. "I am obsessed with her. She's mean and soft and pretty and a bitch, but I want her. She wants me, too, but because of what I did she won't let herself near me."

"Stay away from her," his counselor advised. "Do your best to avoid her at work, and find someone else to spend your time with."

"I can't even see anyone else. All I see is her."

"Then take off your blinders and start looking. It's a big world,

Rafael. There are women out there willing to give you a chance, believe me. I have to go now, but I'm glad you called. Stay away from this girl, Rafael. She's nothing but trouble for you. All right?''

"Okay," said Rafael. Then he said good-bye and hung up the phone. So much for that. He got up and went to the window that looked out over Lena's house. After a moment he went to the kitchen to eat the sandwich he had brought home with him.

He guessed he was going to have to do as his counselor suggested and forget about her.

There would be other women. He was a good-looking guy, and all he had to do was find a girl who knew about his past and didn't hold it against him.

He found one the next day. Her name was Shanley and she was a Kiowa who had come for the Mountain Man/Indian Rendezvous at the fort. Shanley had long black hair, dimpled cheeks, and a smile that wouldn't stop. She started smiling the minute she saw Rafael, and she didn't stop when he smiled back. He felt Lena look at them, but he ignored her and continued to look at the Native American girl with the smooth brown legs and sweet face. She wore a large jacket over her outfit, but he could see lots of colored beads and buckskin. After he took her order he asked if she had already danced.

"We just finished," she told him. "We dance again later. You should come over."

"What time?"

"Around seven. We're out past the well and the flagpole."

"Good turnout today?"

"Pretty good."

He told her the amount and rang it up at the register. She told him her name and said she hoped he would come. Rafael told her he'd try to get a break at seven, and still smiling, Shanley left.

When Rafael turned, he caught Lena staring at him. She blinked and looked quickly away. He did his best to keep ignoring her, and he skipped lunch later so he could take a long break at seven o'clock. At seven he told the increasingly surly Ross he was leaving, and the man only nodded, not bothering to look up from what he was doing.

Rafael walked across the parking lot to the fort and was asked to pay two dollars before he could enter the grounds. Rafael paid and strolled over the grounds past the flagpole and the well to where a number of people were sitting on benches and listening to a man with glasses and long braids talk about Native American culture. Rafael's gaze moved past the man to the line of dancers behind him. Finally he spotted Shanley. She saw him at the same time and smiled.

One by one the man with glasses introduced the dancers and talked about the tradition behind their style of dance and the meanings of different elements of their outfits. Rafael listened with interest and later watched with awe, captivated by the colors and the level of energy displayed by some of the male dancers. He watched Shanley as she danced, a sort of skip step that still managed to convey grace and elegance and charmed everyone in the audience, including Rafael.

He was still watching her when the man with glasses announced a round dance. Shanley gave him a beckoning nod, and Rafael lifted his brows. *Me?*

Several people from the audience got up to join in, and an old man with steel gray braids looked at Rafael and smiled in invitation as he struggled up from a bench and turned toward the dancers.

"I can't," was all Rafael could think to say.

"Come, brother," said the old man, still with the same smile.

Rafael moved to help him rather than join the dance, but he found himself being led, and then his feet were matching the quick step of the men moving in a circle. The women moved a step or a half step slower, also moving in a circle. The drums and the movement and the voice of the singer began to affect Rafael, stirring him and eventually filling his chest with an odd sense of familiarity and belonging.

Rafael smiled at Shanley in gratitude when he saw her. He wanted to thank her for inviting him and letting him feel the acceptance he was feeling, something he missed so desperately. He never wanted it to end.

He was no different from any of the men dancing in the circle. He was, after all, just a man, and his sin was great, but something told him if he confessed at that moment he would still be accepted by the people around him. Accepted and respected.

His hand tightened on the arm of the old man, and when the dance ended, the old man turned and clapped him once on the back. "Well-done."

"Thank you," said Rafael. He helped the man back to his seat on the bench and turned to find Shanley standing beside him. He took her by the arm and led her to the edge of the crowd, where he looked at her and said, "I need to be getting back. Can I see you later? How late are you here?"

"We're finished for the night. The mountain men take over now. What time do you get off?"

"We're staying open until ten for this thing. I won't get off until then."

"I'll meet you outside the deli at ten," she said, smiling again.

"You don't have to do that," Rafael told her. "I can come to wherever you are."

Shanley shook her dark head. "I'm in a motel room with three other girls. I'll see you at ten." She started away, then she stopped and came back. "What's your name?"

He smiled. "Rafael."

"Do you have a last name?"

"Chavez."

"Okay, Rafael Chavez, I'll see you at ten."

"Shanley, wait." He didn't know why he called her back. He felt he had to.

She paused and looked at him, one dark brow lifted.

"I don't want anyone else to tell you. For the last fifteen years I've been in prison."

She grinned. "What'd you do, kill someone?"

Rafael nodded.

Shanley made a face. Then her dimples appeared again.

"At least you're honest. See you later."

"Okay."

Ross wasn't at the deli when Rafael arrived. Lena said he had gone home with a headache. There wasn't time for any further conversation because much of the crowd at the fort had dispersed and was looking for something to eat. Rafael and Lena were kept jumping for the next three hours, and when it was ten o'clock he saw her go to the door and tell the arriving Shanley they were closed.

"She's with me," Rafael explained, and Lena's face colored in sudden embarrassment.

"Sorry," she mumbled to Shanley, and she hurried to finish closing the shop. Rafael went out before her, but he looked back and noticed Lena having trouble turning the key in the door. Her hand was bothering her, he saw. He told Shanley to wait a second, and he went back to help Lena lock the door.

"I can do it," she said when he reached for the key.

"Give it to me," he said.

"First date?" she asked as she shoved the key at him.

Rafael ignored her and used the key to turn the heavy lock. He handed the keys back to her and took off at a trot to join Shanley. He led her to his car and asked where she wanted to go.

"I don't care," she said with a shrug. "Your place?"

"I guess that means you're not worried or anything," said Rafael.

"Should I be?" she asked.

"No."

"I didn't think so. Let's go."

Rafael nodded and started the engine. He took her to his house, asked her to excuse the mess, and offered her a beer before sitting down beside her on the sofa. She smiled at him again and they began to talk, him asking questions about her life, and her asking questions about his life. Rafael didn't feel uncomfortable because she appeared genuinely interested. At length he confessed the feelings he had felt earlier, during the round dance, and he thanked her for being responsible. She smiled her perfect smile and leaned over to kiss him gently on the lips.

"You're welcome. I need to be getting back now, Rafael. It's after midnight."

"I'll take you." He left the sofa and followed her out of the house to the car. Several lights were on next door, and he wondered who was up. Eugenia, probably.

He took Shanley to her motel, and once more she gave him a tender peck before leaving to go inside. Rafael found himself thinking Shanley was the type of girl he wanted to marry and have children with someday. She was everything he had ever wanted.

He drove around town for a while before going back to his house, and while driving down Main Street he happened to catch a glimpse of two guys, one of them getting the shit kicked out of him, the other doing the kicking. Rafael was tempted to stop, but he knew better than to involve himself. Instead he drove as close as he could and turned the car so his headlights blinded the asshole administering the beating. A tall, blond male threw his arm up over his face and took off running down a side street. The other guy rolled over and started coughing up blood. Rafael went home and called 911.

As he hung up the phone he heard a knock at his door. He went to look outside and he saw Lena standing on his porch wearing nothing but a long white T-shirt. Rafael opened the door.

"What's wrong? Is it your mother?"

"No," she said, and she shook her head. "It's me. Can I come in?"

"No," Rafael said, immediately on his guard. "What are you doing here dressed like that? What do you want?"

She shivered in the cool night air. "I . . . nothing. Just to talk."

"I don't want to talk to you."

"Yes you do."

"Wrong," he said. "It was you who said I could never be anything to you because of what I did. I called my counselor and he said to stay away from you. He said you were trouble. Today I find a girl who doesn't seem to care about my past, and you come running over here with your ass hanging out to make sure I'm still panting after you."

Lena looked at her bare feet. After a moment she said, "You're right. About everything. I don't want you, but I do. I don't like you, but I do. I wish I didn't. I wish I could stop thinking about how good it felt when you were holding me yesterday and taking care of me. I wish I could stop thinking about how it feels when you're near me. I've tried. The more I try to stop thinking about you, the more I think about you."

Rafael closed his eyes and looked away from her.

She touched the screen and said, "Tonight, when I saw you with her, I nearly went crazy. I want you to want me, yes, and I want you to want only me."

He rubbed his face, and in a low voice Rafael said, "Go home and go to bed, Lena. I'm tired."

Lena pulled open the screen door. Rafael reached for it, but too late. She came inside, and, before he could back away, she placed her arms around his neck and pressed herself against him. Rafael attempted to steel himself, but the effort was wasted. She felt too good. She smelled too good.

She took one of his hands and moved it over her thin T-shirt to cup her breast. Rafael groaned and reflexively squeezed its softness; the nipple grew hard and round beneath his palm, causing instant, heated arousal in him and strained breathing for both of them. When she lowered a hand to touch him he jerked and backed away to the wall, taking her with him. He couldn't believe she was doing what she was doing. He kept looking at her eyes, to see if she had overdosed on Percodan.

Her lids were closed, and her hands continued in their pursuit, undoing the snap of his jeans and unzipping his fly. Before she could reach into his briefs and touch him, Rafael grabbed her hand. He wouldn't be able to control himself if she did.

He placed her arm around his neck and lifted her chin with one hand. When she opened her eyes he leaned forward and touched his lips to hers. They shuddered as one and Rafael groaned again, this time into her mouth. He tilted his head and deepened the kiss, loving the taste of her and taking delight in the feel of her tongue against his. It had been so long.

Soon a noise came from her throat, and she tore her mouth from his. She took his hand again and this time placed it between her legs, where he felt the moistness of the fabric of her underwear. Rafael cupped her pubic mound and tried to kiss her again, but she moved her head away and told him she needed him. Right that minute.

He turned her and guided her down the short hall to his bedroom, where she removed her T-shirt and stepped out of her panties without blinking an eye.

Rafael couldn't seem to catch his breath. Slowly he removed his shirt and stepped out of his jeans, and when he was taking too long, Lena came and helped him out of his briefs. He couldn't stop looking at her. She was every bit as beautiful as he had imagined and he couldn't believe this was happening to him. A part of him kept expecting her to start laughing any second and tell him it was all a joke. When she asked if he had any condoms, he went along with it and took one from the drawer and placed it on himself. Any second now, he thought, and he watched her face closely.

But she was already reaching for him again, wrapping her hand around him and causing him to gasp aloud as she slid backwards onto the bed and pulled him on top of her. She didn't hesitate, but guided him directly where she wanted him and then gripped him by the buttocks to pull him inside her.

It was too much for Rafael. Even with the condom he could feel her heat and softness and slippery warmth. He thrust into her once, twice, and then stiffened helplessly in a paroxysm of pleasure. Lena made a noise in his ear and turned her head away when he tried to kiss her. Her breathing was hoarse and uneven and her hips were still moving beneath him, urging him to continue. She didn't have to wait long.

He withdrew from her to remove the condom and explore her breasts with his mouth. By the time he was ready with a new condom, she was writhing on the sheets and touching every part of him with her hands and mouth. Rafael moved over her again and parted her thighs, causing her to moan aloud. Completely taken, he watched her face as he entered her, saw the fire and passion in her, as well as everything she tried to hide, and Rafael knew this was more than just an obsession with the first single girl he had met. She was inside him as much as he was inside her, the only difference being Lena was inside him to stay.

He sank down on her and placed his hands on either side of her head to make her look at him. Her breathing was rapid, her mouth open, and Rafael gently attached his mouth to hers in a deep, loving kiss that surprised both of them by bringing her to violent orgasm. She trembled and shook and finally wrenched her mouth away to gasp for air.

Rafael held her and kissed her face and whispered her name. He told her he never wanted to let her go, she felt so good. She stared wordlessly at him and made a tiny noise in her throat when he gently withdrew from her. He waited for her to speak to him, to say something, but she remained silent. Finally Rafael slept, his arms still holding her close, his face pressed against her warm flesh.

At 3:00 A.M. he awakened to the sound of the front door clicking shut. He sent a hand out to feel the mattress beside him and felt nothing but the sheet. She was gone.

THIRTEEN

D ETECTIVE Morales walked around the hospital bed and looked at the mottled face of the boy under the sheets. His eyes were swollen shut, his mouth split open and taped around the respirator. Both cheekbones were obliterated; his jaw was wired. At four-thirty that morning, the doctors said a blood clot entered his brain stem. The kid who threw the rock that killed Ruanda Beker was now comatose.

And Rafael Chavez just happened to be the one who called 911 about him.

Fate was a funny thing.

The Lake kid came in the door just as Morales was leaving. Lake's face crumpled when he saw his buddy in the bed. Morales snorted and paused in the doorway.

"Feelin' bad?"

Lake ignored him and walked to the bed. "Hey," he said, and picked up his friend's hand.

"Can't testify now, can he?" said Morales. "He can't tell a judge or a jury or anyone else how you told him to throw the rock."

"What the hell are you talking about?" said Lake.

"Oh, I'm pretty sure you know. Now it's become one of those things where you can say you were only joking and you never meant for him to really do it, but he took you serious. Don't expect the DA to drop the charges against you. You're still in for some shit."

"Are you gonna find who did this?" Lake gestured to his friend's purpled face.

"Who do you think did it?"

"Her shithead brothers, that's who. Those assholes were probably waiting for him."

"Ahhh," said Morales, and he put a finger to his head. "Now why didn't I think of that? Guess I never was Dartmouth material, not like some people. I thought I was gonna have to ask my witness what he saw."

Lake looked up. "Witness?"

"Yeah, the guy who called 911. See you later, Lake."

Morales smiled to himself at the frown on the snotty young smart-ass's face and turned to leave the room. He wouldn't tell Lake no one was going to believe the witness no matter what he said, because his name was Rafael Chavez and because Lake's mother had led a lynch mob to his lawn one night. Everyone would say Chavez was trying to get back at her by impugning her son.

And who knew? Morales thought. They might be right.

But he doubted it. Lake was smart. He knew by eliminating the testimony of his partner things would look awfully good for a complete acquittal, with no jail sentence, no probation or black marks to sully his reputation, and only a few dirty looks from people around town.

Still, Morales was going to talk to Chavez, just to confirm what he already suspected. He drove to the deli and parked in front, and when he got out he paused and watched the activity at the fort a few minutes before going inside.

Ross looked perturbed when he saw Morales, but Rafael's face expressed nothing but resignation. Morales saw a woman with dark hair changing the Pepsi canister at the pop machine. He recognized her as Rafael Chavez's neighbor. He inclined his head to Rafael, and after a nod from Ross, Rafael came around the counter.

"Morales," he said. "What can I do for you?"

"Last night you called 911 and reported a fight. I need to know what you saw."

Rafael shrugged. "I saw one guy getting the shit beat out of him. He okay?"

"Nah," said Morales. "Got a blood clot in his brain. They expect him to die soon. What about the guy doing the beating? Did you get a good look at him?"

"He was tall and had blond hair. That's all I saw."

"You don't think you could identify him if you saw him anywhere?"

"No. You know who he is?"

Morales scratched his chin. "You wouldn't get any ideas about messing with anybody, would you? I mean, after they accused you of killing Ruanda Beker?"

Rafael's dark brows met. "Who did you have in mind?"

"Nothing. Never mind. Wait. One more question. You ever see those two guys they nailed for Ruanda's murder?"

"I've never even heard their names, since the paper decided to leave out that information."

Morales laughed. "Yeah, well, it's locally owned, you know. I don't guess much gossip gets passed your way, does it?"

Rafael looked away from him.

"Okay," said Morales, and he peered past Rafael to the counter. "Get me a sandwich? Turkey on wheat, Swiss cheese, mayo, hold the mustard."

He watched as Rafael moved back behind the counter and saw him squeeze past his pretty neighbor. The two of them barely glanced at each other. Morales looked next at Ross, who appeared to have lost a few pounds in the days since Morales had last seen him. He was either in love or had cancer growing in him somewhere.

Morales put it all together as he watched the three of them work. Ross was in love with the girl, who was in love with Rafael, who was a walking piece of shit no female should ever look at. Rafael had probably done it to her once and moved on, which was why she wasn't looking at him, and why he wasn't looking at her. Ross was just mooning over the fact that it wasn't him who had done her.

"Can I get a Diet Pepsi with that?" Morales asked, and he saw Rafael's neighbor look at his distended stomach and smirk.

Morales smiled at her. Maybe he had it wrong. It wouldn't be the first time.

"What did he want?" Lena asked Rafael once Morales was gone.

Rafael didn't look at her. "Nothing."

"He's not still asking you about the prostitute? I read in the paper two boys had been arrested."

"I saw a fight last night and called 911," Rafael said. "He was asking about that."

Lena clasped her hands together. "Was that when you took the girl home?"

"Yes."

She opened her mouth to say something else, but she could see Ross was listening to them so she shut up and went back to finish cleaning up the pop machine. She didn't know what Ross's problem was, but his personality had suddenly done a complete turnaround. She was ready to tell him to shove the job up his ass. She didn't know what stopped her. That morning she almost didn't show up for work. She didn't know how she was going to face Rafael. She supposed she could blame her behavior on the pain pills, but he would see through that excuse the first time he looked into her eyes.

So she went to work and simply acted like nothing had happened.

The trouble was, her body reacted to his nearness even more forcefully than before. Her nipples had been hard all morning and were beginning to chafe. Her underwear was damp and uncomfortable. She couldn't stop thinking about how unusually pleasurable her experience with him had been. There had been only two men in Lena's past, and neither had elicited the response in her that Rafael had. With one long, sensual, heartfelt kiss he had shattered her into a thousand little pieces right there in his bed.

Again, she had to question if it was him or his dark background that turned her on so much. She hoped it was him, because the alternative would make her one sick weirdo.

She glanced at him again. He was obviously upset with her for leaving him the night before. He wouldn't even look at her. She eyed the definition in his arms and the curve of his chest and remembered how it felt when he held her close, the hardness and strength of him. She thought of the feel of his buttocks under her palms and shuddered. She took a deep breath and jerked her gaze away when he looked up.

At that moment Ross took off his apron and muttered something about a doctor's appointment. He told Rafael he'd be back as soon as he could and went out the door without saying a word to Lena. She looked at Rafael, but he turned his back on her. Lena didn't move behind the counter until a customer came in, and for the next half hour she and Rafael worked side by side without saying a word to each other. When the place cleared out again he went to wipe off the tables, and, unthinking, Lena followed him. She moved behind him and slid her arms around his waist; she pressed herself against his backside and rested her face between his shoulder blades.

Rafael stiffened. His voice came out hoarse.

"Lena, what are you trying to do to me?"

She tightened her arms around him and then dropped one

hand to the front of his jeans and squeezed. He drew a sharp breath and pulled her hand away. "What are you doing?"

"I want you to make love to me," she said, and it was all she could do to look him in the face.

"No."

"Yes. You're all I can think about. I'm driving myself crazy."

"You're driving me crazy. Why did you leave?"

She looked at the floor. "I don't know."

He pulled away from her and started behind the counter. Lena reached for his hand and tugged until she could kiss his palm with her lips.

His gaze lowered, and she could see a tremor run through him. She went on tugging until he was following her into the bathroom. She shut the door behind them and locked it, and then she removed his apron and lifted his T-shirt to touch the warm flesh of his chest with her mouth. She kissed one hard brown nipple and glided her hands over his smooth skin before reaching for the snap on his jeans.

"I don't have a condom," he said, his breathing unsteady.

"Sssh," she said, and she quickly unfastened her own jeans and slid them down to step out of them. She pushed her underwear down, and then she turned around and placed her hands on either side of the sink, with her back to Rafael. He saw what she wanted, and she noticed him swallow as he stepped up behind her.

When he entered her she sucked in her breath and closed her eyes. A moan escaped her. He placed one hand under her rib cage and used the other to cup her pubic mound, his fingers reaching down and probing the moistness he encountered. Lena moaned again and spread her thighs wider, taking him deeper inside her. Rafael buried his face in her hair and she felt the warmth of his breath on the back of her neck. When his lips touched flesh her knees began to buckle. She felt as if she were melting from the inside out. He was in every part of her. His fingers and his mouth and his gently grinding hips.

He whispered her name against her neck, and Lena began to jerk. It was happening again. Her fingers gripped the side of the sink so hard her knuckles turned white. She squeezed her eyes shut to savor every second of what was happening to her body. He said her name again and a small cry escaped her throat. He held her tighter and began to stiffen. His breathing stopped. Soon he was withdrawing from her and turning her around.

"Let me kiss you," he begged as she averted her face. "Please."

Slowly she turned toward him, and she lifted her lids to look at him. His dark eyes held naked emotion and a blatant hunger that frightened Lena. He took her face between his hands and lightly touched his mouth to hers, then he gently increased pressure, and soon he was drawing her into the kiss, until her arms were twined about his neck and she was kissing him with nearly as much passion as he kissed her. Lena had never enjoyed kissing anyone so much, or felt so deeply stirred by the act. Twice he stopped kissing her to tell her how beautiful she was, and how she made him feel, and he made her look into his eyes as he said it. Instead of squirming away, Lena buried her face against his neck until he lifted her chin to kiss her again.

"Why are you so uncomfortable?" he whispered finally.

"I'm not."

"You are. I can see you are."

She lifted one shoulder a fraction. "You're embarrassing me."

He smiled. "My baby blushes."

She said, "If you really knew me, you'd know I don't like to be called baby."

"You're not used to being my baby yet."

Lena thought about that. Then she said, "I am the first single woman you've been exposed to since leaving prison."

"I don't want anyone else," he said. "You're all I've been able to think about since the first time I saw you." He touched her cheek then. "Do I make you feel good?"

Lena's lashes lowered. "You know you do. I want to do it again."

"We can't," he said. "We've been in here too long already. Ross'll be back any minute." He paused then. "Will you come over tonight? After work?"

"You come to my house first," Lena suggested. "That would make Mom happy."

Rafael smiled widely, and Lena was struck, painfully so, at how handsome he appeared when he smiled. She massaged away the sudden ache in her middle and reached for her jeans and underwear. Later, after Rafael had left her alone in the bathroom, she looked at her reflection in the mirror and blinked. She didn't look like herself.

Lena frowned and said, "Just what the hell do you think you're doing?"

Besides having the best sex of her life with a man who'd had nothing but his hand for fifteen years.

She hoped.

She left the bathroom and saw Rafael look searchingly at her, as if she might have used the time alone to change her mind. She walked behind the counter and pinched him on the bottom. "Hey, baby."

He smiled at her again, and once more she experienced a sweetly painful twinge in her middle.

Ross came back and headed straight for the bathroom. He came out with a funny expression on his face, and he looked hard at Lena and Rafael, but both ignored him.

Shanley came over from the fort and invited Rafael to come back for more dancing, but he explained he already had other plans for the evening. Shanley looked momentarily disappointed, but she went away still smiling. Lena had to respect her for that.

She felt like smiling herself, the kind of goofy smile people smiled when they felt good about everything.

Her old self was still having fits, still asking all the old questions and still searching for a mental crook to drag her back from the abyss, but the happy Lena wasn't listening. Each time she looked at Rafael she felt like sighing. The things he did to her. The way he made her feel.

She didn't know how she was going to explain all this to her mother.

Then she wondered if she even had to explain. Her mother had worn a knowing look the night Lena burst out crying, but she had remained wisely silent.

She hoped her mother didn't think she was in love with Rafael. She wasn't, not really. She was simply incredibly physically infatuated with him. His body was so beautiful. His hands. His mouth.

Lena shuddered once more and looked up to find him watching her. Her eyes closed as he smiled at her again.

FOURTEEN

ROSS was certain he smelled sex in the bathroom, but he was already convinced he was going crazy, so he refused to dwell on what his nose was telling him. And he couldn't see any visible change in the way Lena and Rafael treated each other, so he supposed it was all his imagination.

The traitorous part of his own mind that was turning on itself and driving him mad.

Imagination.

That's what it was when he saw Martha Box sitting in a chair in his living room. And when she turned to him and smiled her beautiful smile, that was imagination, too. Or a hallucination.

The doctor didn't know what to call it, other than a "delusional" something or other. He wanted Ross to visit a psychiatrist friend, and Ross told him to go to hell. All he wanted was some pills so he could sleep at night instead of wandering his house and seeing dead women.

His physician refused to prescribe any sleeping pills, so Ross was right back where he started. He thought of going to another doctor, but there weren't that many in town, and all of them knew one another so he was sure to be found out eventually. Not that it bothered him a great deal what any of them thought. Still, he was a businessman and generally respected around town. He didn't want his reputation to suffer needlessly.

Lorraine had been working on that already. When Ross walked into his doctor's office, the nurse behind the desk smiled in understanding at his complaint.

"Lorraine said you were going through something of a mid-life crisis. It affects everyone differently."

Ross nearly snarled at the woman.

Later, on the way back to the deli, he stopped and bought a twelve-pack of beer. He was going to get some sleep that night, one way or another.

So determined was he that he opened one can in the car and downed it before he got out of the truck. An early start couldn't hurt, he decided.

Once inside the deli he headed straight for the bathroom to check his breath and rinse out his mouth. It wouldn't do for any of the customers to smell alcohol on his breath.

He would have eaten something, but lately food had no appeal for him. He ate when he absolutely had to have something in his stomach, and then only a small amount. If he ate more, everything threatened to come up and out.

Amazing what the mind could do to the body.

The last of the afternoon went quickly and passed into early evening, with a blur of customers from the fort. Ross made a couple of trips to the truck to drink a beer, and in so doing managed to keep his thoughts away from the direction they seemed determined to stray. At ten o'clock he felt just a bit of a buzz, nothing he couldn't handle. He told Rafael good night, grunted at Lena, and went about locking up the place. At home he proceeded to drink one beer after another until he passed out on his couch.

At a quarter past one he awakened with a start. Something had touched him. Something with cold hands had touched his arm. She was back again.

"Oh, shit," he mumbled as he slammed his lids shut and rubbed at his face. His head was thick. He felt sick.

Not real, he told himself. She was not real. She was a creation of his mind, brought on by memories of and thinking about Vandegrift Hall.

Ross held his head in his hands and wondered why he was doing this to himself. He had done nothing to Martha. He never laid a finger on her. Why was she picking on him?

Then he had a sudden thought. Opening his eyes to mere slits, he rose unsteadily off the couch and made his way to the kitchen to find his phone book.

He was going to call those other three guys, the ones who had been there with him on that day. The guys who had done it to Martha Box.

It took him a minute to think of their names. He could see their faces in his head, but his alcohol-numbed mind was having trouble with their names. Two of them didn't live in town anymore, he knew, but one of them still did. Which one was it? Jesus in Heaven, he couldn't think.

Rad Lanyard. That was the one. Rad, with his long thinning hair, bushy sideburns, and an act as a folksinger out at the hotel on the highway. Ross had seen him a couple years ago and thought he looked like an old Neil Young, only uglier.

Ross looked under the L's in the phonebook and found three Lanyards with the first initial R. He dialed the first one and asked for Radburn Lanyard.

"Rad?" responded the person on the other end.

"Yeah," said Ross. "He there?"

"No, no, this is his cousin, Ron. Rad lives in a trailer in the court on the south edge of town. He don't have a phone."

"Okay, thanks. Does his trailer have a number?"

"You can't miss it. It's the one with the refrigerator in front."

"A refrigerator?"

"Padlocked and everything. He keeps his beer in there."

Ross glanced toward his own kitchen and the empty beer cans on the counter.

"I appreciate it," he said, and started to hang up.

"Wait," said the cousin. "Who is this?"

"An old friend," said Ross. "Rad and I went to school together."

"Huh," came the reply. "I thought all Rad's friends were dead now."

Ross blinked. Then he said, "Thanks again," and he hung up the phone.

He looked cautiously around himself, to see if Martha was still there. Out of the corner of his eye he caught a flash of auburn, and he quickly looked in the other direction.

A peek at his watch told him it was 1:35. Most lounge acts in the area finished up around one-thirty.

After scooping up his keys and his wallet, Ross headed out the door and went to get inside his truck. His head felt clearer, and he drove with purpose to the south edge of town and the poorly lit mobile home court located just off the highway. Dogs barked and one or two security lights popped on as Ross drove through the court looking for a refrigerator. A ripped screen door on a trailer with what appeared to be fire damage opened and the light that came on illuminated a man with a shotgun in his hands. He looked with suspicion at Ross, and, heart beating triple time, Ross slowed to a stop and rolled down his window.

"I'm looking for Rad Lanyard."

The man said nothing, only gestured with the end of his shotgun to keep going.

"Thanks," Ross muttered, and he rolled up his window again.

Cousin Ron had been right about not being able to miss Rad's trailer. It did have a refrigerator in front, and Ross's headlights picked out the wild colors of the nude bodies painted on the door.

Rad hadn't changed much, Ross found himself thinking.

Parked beside the trailer was a dinged and damaged twenty-

year-old Datsun. Ross parked next to the Datsun and left his truck
to go and knock on the trailer door.

"Get outta here, you little bitch!" someone yelled from inside
the trailer. "I told you never to come here again."

"It's Ross Schweig, Rad."

The door was abruptly yanked open. "Ross Schweig?"

"Yeah."

"Oh. Shit. Come on in. I thought you was someone else."

Rad looked worse, if possible, than the last time Ross had seen
him. His hair was even thinner, his sideburns bushier, and he was
missing several teeth. Ross knew this because Rad was smiling at
him.

"How you been?" Rad asked as he led the way inside his living
room.

Ross shrugged. "Same as last time I saw you. You?"

"Great. Hell, I'm still swingin'. You want a beer?"

"No." Ross was looking around himself for a place to sit. He
chose a brown chair with a quilt thrown over the cushion. His nostrils wanted to shut at the smell of the place. Rad lifted his beer
and took a long swallow before moving over to sit down on the
piles of clothes and papers on the couch. "So, Ross, what brings
you out here at this time of the morning? We ain't exactly been
pals these last twenty or thirty fucking years, now have we?"

Ross glanced up at Rad's acerbic tone. "No, we haven't. Which
reminds me to ask about Sharp and Lewin."

He had remembered their names on the way over.

And wondered how he could ever forget.

"Damn," said Rad. "I ain't thought about them in a while."

"You know where they are?"

"Both been dead for years. Sharp had his face blown off by a
buddy in a hunting accident. Lewin drowned in a damned flood."

"You didn't go to their funerals?"

"Nah. Both of 'em out of state. I heard about Sharp from his
sister, and Lewin's cousin Roy told me about him." Rad took an-

other drink and laughed. "They're dead, I'm drunk, and you're
. . . what the hell are you, Ross? A sandwich maker?"

"That's right," said Ross.

"Much money in that?"

"Enough."

Rad's red-rimmed eyes peered closely at Ross. "You appear a
little tired, son. But you look good. Better'n me, anyhow." He
belched. "Go on and say what you got to say, so I can stretch out
and get some down time."

"Martha Box," Ross said, his tone blunt.

Rad didn't even blink. "Who?"

Ross repeated the name.

"Never heard of her," said Rad. "She sayin' I heard of her?"

Ross's nostrils flared. He couldn't believe the bastard's brain
cells had all been fried by booze. He had to remember.

"She was from Vandegrift Hall," said Ross.

"Vandegrift Hall?"

"The old orphanage," Ross said in a tight voice. "I'm sure you
remember the old orphanage at the fort?"

Rad looked momentarily uncomfortable. "Yeah, yeah, sure I
remember the fort."

"Not just the fort, Rad. Vandegrift Hall. Where all the 'white
trash' used to live."

"Oh. Oh, yeah. Okay, I gotcha now."

Ross wanted to get up and smack him at the light of compre-
hension that entered his eyes. Here he was, one step below white
trash himself, and he still thought he was somehow better than
those other poor kids.

"So what about . . . what did you say her name was?"

"Martha. Martha Box." Ross snorted. "You're a lying son of a
bitch, Rad. I can see right through you. You know exactly who I'm
talking about, but you're pretending you've blocked it out. Well I
thought I'd blocked it out, too, but it was all still right there, just
waiting for me to slip up once."

Rad was staring at him. "Man, I swear I don't know what the hell you're talking about."

Ross nearly leaped out of his chair. He stood over Rad and heard his voice become a hoarse growl.

"You're telling me you don't remember Sharp and Lewin pushing her into your car and you driving out to the old Hickok place behind the fort? You're telling me you don't remember catching her when she ran, and holding down her legs while Lewin sliced through the tendons in one ankle? You don't remember punching her in the stomach when the blood pouring from her foot made a mess of your brand-new Levi's?" Ross hunkered down and got right in his face. *"I* remember, Rad. *I* remember."

Rad's eyes had taken on a glazed look. He stared without blinking right through Ross, his mouth hanging slightly open, his hands quivering. The beer in his hand slipped to the floor and spewed foam everywhere.

"You ran then," Rad whispered finally. "That's when you ran."

"I did," said Ross. "And I've never forgiven myself. I have to ask you something now, Rad. I have to ask you what you did with Martha. I don't want to know what you did *to* her after I left; I just want to know what you did *with* her."

"I . . . we . . . I . . . can't remember."

Ross got in his face again. "Don't tell me that, you sorry son of a bitch."

Rad gave him a shove and pushed him away. "I can't *remember.* Jesus, I swear I can't. All I remember is . . . is watching Sharp. . . ." At Ross's warning look he allowed his voice to trail off. He tore at his thinning hair with his long-fingernailed hands and said, "Why did you come over here? Why're you doin' this?"

"I don't know," Ross said, his voice still angry. "Because things are happening and things are changing and there's nothing I can do to stop it. These women are making it happen. I think that's what's causing all this to happen now. Eugenia. Eugenia started something when she came to my store that day. I can't find any other explanation."

Rad was staring at him again. "Who?"

His mouth opened in automatic explanation, but Ross soon shut it again. Rad wasn't worth the effort. Ross shook his head and turned to leave.

"Hey, wait," said Rad. "What're you gonna do?"

"About what?"

"About . . . you know. About Martha."

Ross had no answer for him. He simply turned and walked out the door.

FIFTEEN

E UGENIA was back with Audrey and her lover in the dimness of Audrey's tiny room behind the fort's laundry. The handsome, dark-eyed scout was so tender and gentle and loving it made Eugenia's heart swell to see them together. Audrey clung to him, unwilling to let him go for even a moment. She needed him, as much as he needed her. As Eugenia watched them settle together in sweet repose, she noticed how Audrey's features seemed to shift, blending somehow with those of another young woman very familiar to Eugenia. The scout, too, appeared different in the dim light.

Before the sleeping Eugenia's mind could wonder at the changes, the scene shifted and she was in the bedroom of Annabeth and John Dixon. Annabeth was hovering over her husband in his bed, seemingly attempting to wake him. Eugenia could see that he was in fact awake, but he was ignoring his wife. Annabeth grew angry and reached to light a lantern, determined to see if he was avoiding her. When she raised the wick, the glow illuminated her face.

Again, Eugenia became confused. The blonde was not Annabeth's face at all now, but another face. A familiar face with an angry, strident voice.

The man in the bed was no longer John Dixon, but now resembled someone Eugenia knew as . . .

Awareness began to fade before the name could register, and Eugenia awakened utterly perplexed. What was happening now? Why were the faces changing?

Suddenly, without warning, she experienced the memory of the matron called Mother Wimley grabbing her by the upper arm and shaking her so hard she actually dislocated the young Eugenia's shoulder. The pain was excruciating, and Eugenia lost consciousness. When she awakened, she heard Mother Wimley explaining to the doctor how she had caught the idiot girl in a tree, and how a branch had given way.

"Liar," Eugenia had whispered, and though the doctor heard her, he averted his head and pretended he hadn't. When he was gone, Eugenia had her hair pushed aside and her ear pinched until it bled. Mother Wimley was in a fury.

"You will speak to no one for a week," she seethed. "If I hear you open your mouth, it's into the closet with you. It's *you* who are the liar, always telling people about these visions and voices you hear. You only want to make yourself appear special, and I'm here to tell you that you most certainly are not. You're a wicked little child, and you're lucky anyone will have anything to do with you."

"Monster," the adult Eugenia whispered to the memory. The woman was a monster. But no more monstrous than the white-haired matron who threw the bucket at the little boy.

Unable to continue in her thinking, she left her bed and wandered down the hall to look in Lena's room. Her daughter's bed was empty.

Eugenia sighed to herself, thinking of the way Rafael had looked at Lena, and the way Lena looked at Rafael.

For a fraction of a second, she glimpsed a piece of a dream. A dream of peacefully slumbering lovers with limbs entwined. . . .

The image vanished as quickly as it came, leaving Eugenia

once more confused. She pinched the bridge of her nose and went downstairs to make a cup of tea for herself.

There were no lights on next door, the house was dark, and Eugenia imagined Lena would be staying with Rafael for the rest of the night.

She was surprised at her daughter, but only at the fact that it had taken her so long to give in to attraction.

There was no mistaking Rafael's feelings; one look at his expressive face said he was in deep, and Eugenia was a little worried for him. Lena was unpredictable, to say the least, and Eugenia didn't know how she would react to being in love. If she knew Lena, then her daughter would deny every emotion, telling herself anything but the truth. Rafael's emotions, on the other hand, were right there for anyone to see. He hid nothing of what he felt, and Eugenia wondered if this would frighten the reserved Lena.

It was exciting in a way, seeing her daughter smitten for the first time. It reminded Eugenia of her own first love, and the time she had convincing herself that he truly did love her. Such things were simple for most people, but after Mother Wimley's teachings it was a struggle for Eugenia to believe in her own self-worth.

Still, she had survived and even prospered. And now she worked with children the rest of society found "difficult."

Thinking of the kids she worked with made her smile. She missed working and being useful. Lena had the right idea, going to work for someone and making use of herself.

Tomorrow, Eugenia decided, she would go to work with Lena and sit down for a talk with Ross Schweig. It was time she found out how much of the town had changed and how much remained the same since she had been gone. Eugenia was certain the latter would be greater than the former, if they were talking about people, anyway.

Next door, Lena stirred and moved to the edge of the bed. Rafael's hand caught her arm. "Lena?"

"Going to the bathroom," she mumbled. "Be right back."

He released her, and she stumbled across the darkened room to the hall. The bones in her legs felt as if they had been unused for weeks. Her mouth, when she turned on the light in the bathroom, looked twice its normal size, swollen by endless kisses. Parts of her skin were abraded by the hint of stubble on his face; her breasts still felt heavy and swollen. She hugged herself and sat down on the toilet to pee. The toilet paper felt rough against her sensitive flesh.

When she got back in bed he immediately reached for her to draw her close. She nestled against his chest and inhaled the scent of his warm skin. She pressed her lips against him and felt his hand squeeze her waist in response.

She had never stayed over with anyone before, much less actually fallen asleep.

Neither had she made love for half the night and been so utterly exhausted before.

Everything with Rafael was new. Everything was warm and sweet and passionate and exciting and completely novel to Lena.

She pressed her naked body against his and closed her eyes at the tiny spark of desire she felt. She couldn't believe it, but it was there. Sleepy and sore as she was, she wanted him again. She sent her fingers down to run through the dark, curling hairs below his navel, and soon she heard him groan. She allowed her circling fingers to travel lower, and a smile curved her lips. He was going to give her what she wanted.

Four hours later he awakened her with a kiss and a swat on the buttocks. "Come on, let's run."

"Coffee," she protested. "I need caffeine."

"Wuss," he said, but he went to make her some coffee.

Lena rose groggily from the bed and lifted her arms high above her head in a stretch. She had been dreaming of something strange having to do with horses and men in grimy, sweat-stained uniforms, but the dream escaped her the moment she awakened. She shook her head and pulled on the T-shirt and drawstring shorts Rafael had laid out for her. They were big, but they would work. She had worn her running shoes to work the day before, so she needed nothing else.

She walked into the kitchen and mumbled a thank-you as Rafael handed her a cup of coffee. She looked around for some sweetener, and he offered her a sugar bowl.

"No, I'll take it black," she said. "You don't drink coffee?"

"Occasionally." His dark eyes were studying her intently, and finally she put a hand on her hip and said,

"What?"

"Nothing. I was just looking at you."

"Do I look that much different to you in the morning?"

"A little sleepy-eyed. It makes me want to take you back to bed."

The warmth of his voice put color in her face. She turned from him and tilted her coffee cup to her lips. When she lowered the cup again she said, "Yesterday I heard you telling Ross about your degree in communications. What are you going to do with it?"

"Whatever I can," Rafael answered, only mildly nonplussed at her abrupt change of subject.

"Not many options around here, I suppose?"

"Not for me."

"What about when you're off parole? Will you go somewhere else?"

"Count on it."

Lena lifted the cup in front of her mouth again.

"Where?"

He shrugged. "I've thought about it, but haven't made any decision. When the time comes, I thought I'd send out some résumés, see what comes back."

"It made me look at you differently," Lena confessed. "I mean, I was already looking at you differently, but—"

"I was hoping for that effect," said Rafael with a grin.

Lena put the cup on the counter. "You mean you told Ross so I would hear?"

"Yep."

"You dog."

Rafael lifted a hand. "A dog I may be, but I'm a dog with a degree."

Lena picked up a dish towel and threw it at him. He laughed and went after her, chasing her out of the house and down the sidewalk. They ran hard for a quarter of a mile, then settled down to a pace comfortable for both of them. Lena enjoyed seeing him run. She liked to watch the muscles pumping in his legs and back and shoulders, and the sight of the perspiration dampening his skin and hair made her heart beat even faster. When a stoplight halted them at a busy corner, they jogged in place for several moments, looking at each other's faces and saying nothing. The intensity of Rafael's gaze was too much for Lena; she had to look away.

At the next stoplight she felt him looking at her again, and she looked at everything but his face. He stopped moving and reached over to touch her cheek. She glanced at him, and in a voice barely above a whisper he said, "I'm happy."

"Me too," she said, her own voice breathless.

Then the light changed.

By the time they reached home they were walking hand in hand, talking about Lena's job back in Eugene and laughing about the wages they were receiving from Ross. As they rounded the corner, Lena saw a tall, blond male bound away from Rafael's porch and hop into a blue Camaro.

"Who the hell is that?" muttered Rafael under his breath, and Lena watched with him as the Camaro sped past them up the street.

Lena blinked as they approached the house. Dozens of black and white glossy photographs, 8×10's, had been stuck to the outside of Rafael's house and porch. She dropped Rafael's hand and moved to pull down a photograph.

The horrible image immediately caused her to recoil and drop the picture. Rafael stooped to pick it up. His skin went gray.

"What is that?" Lena asked, the horror she felt making her voice rough. "Rafael, what is that?"

Then she knew. She saw the emotions take shape in his face. Remorse. Guilt. Anger.

She began to back away from him. He couldn't have done such a terrible thing. He couldn't have created the image on those police file photographs, that of two women, horribly battered and mutilated, their faces lost somewhere in blood, bone, and tissue.

Everywhere. The horrible images were everywhere she turned, and Lena's stomach began to churn. She backed even farther away, and Rafael reached for her.

"Lena, don't."

"Don't?" she echoed. "You did this, didn't you?" she said and pointed to the photographs. "You did this. These are the women you killed."

Rafael swallowed.

"Deny it."

"I can't," he said in a low voice. "But I am not that person, Lena. I am not him. Please, please don't back away from me."

Lena kept moving. "Why didn't you tell me? Why did you keep this from me?"

"I didn't keep anything from you," he said, and he made a step toward her. "I told you what happened. I told you about my addiction."

"You didn't tell me about *this,"* Lena nearly shrieked, and she pointed again.

"I'm sorry," he said. "I'm sorry. How could I?"

Lena hugged herself. She felt sick. "I can't believe what I did with you. I can't believe I let you touch me."

Rafael's jaw began to tremble. "Lena, don't do this. Please don't do this."

"Tell Ross I quit," Lena responded, and she turned her back on him.

"I'm *sorry,"* Rafael shouted at her. "I'm sorry for what I did. I've been sorry half my life. What else do you want me to do? I can't change it. I can't bring them back and apologize for being temporarily insane. Lena, please, don't run away. God, if you knew what you mean to me. If you knew how much I . . .''

His voice died with a bitter curse as her steps quickened. Lena glanced over her shoulder to see him hitting and kicking the wooden porch beam in a fury, his face nearly scarlet. Angry tears streamed down his cheeks, and his teeth bit into his lower lip hard enough to make blood well up and stain his chin.

Everything inside her said to go to him and make him stop, throw her arms around his waist and keep him from hurting himself. But the photographs were all around him, and she knew she couldn't look at those again. She went on.

Eugenia looked up as Lena came in. ''What?'' she said immediately. ''What's wrong?''

Lena only shook her head and continued toward her room. Eugenia followed and had the door slammed in her face. Then she heard her daughter sob, long and despondently loudly.

''Lena, open the door,'' she said, and when she received no response, only heard more crying, Eugenia went down the stairs and out the front door. She found Rafael, face and hands bleeding, tearing photographs from the front of his house.

He turned when he saw her, and the reddened condition of his eyes made her reach instinctively out to touch him. He veered away from her and shoved one of the photographs into her hands instead.

''This is what I did all those years ago. This is why I went to prison for half my life. I deserved to be there. I've never said I didn't.''

Eugenia studied his tortured face; then she glanced at the photo. Her gorge rose, and she calmly handed it back to him.

''If you did that, then yes, you deserved to be there,'' she said.

Rafael met her unwavering gaze. ''The only reason I didn't get the death sentence is because I was under the influence of illegal substances at the time of the killing. I served the time they gave me and paid every penny of my restitution. I wrote letters and apologized to the family face-to-face. I got down on my knees and begged their forgiveness for what I did."

"Did they forgive you?"

"No. But I had to ask."

Eugenia kept her eyes on his face to avoid looking at the pictures. His dark gaze was fixed on the grisly images. Fresh blood ran down his chin and splattered one of the photos in his hand. He held it out and said, "I'm not that person anymore. I've done everything I can to *not* be that person anymore."

"I believe you," she said. "I don't think you were ever that person, Rafael. What's more, and if you don't mind my saying so, I don't think you've ever had the chance to mature like a normal man, particularly where emotions are concerned. You've never learned how to hide what you're feeling, and that puts you at a disadvantage with someone like Lena, who's used to hiding everything from everyone."

He turned abruptly away. "Thank you for the analysis, Eugenia. I'm sure you're right."

"Rafael?"

He didn't look at her; he went about taking down more photographs. "What?"

"She's upstairs right now, crying like I've never heard her cry."

Rafael kept his face averted. "She's not crying for the reasons you think."

Eugenia weighed the impulse before she said it, but in the end she couldn't help herself.

"Lena's never cared for a man before. You frighten her in more ways than one."

He stopped what he was doing, and when he turned to look at her his eyes were black.

"Lena was just playing with me, treating me like the slobbering idiot I am and looking to make a fool out of me because she thinks I deserve it. You know something? I do deserve it."

"You'll feel differently tomorrow," Eugenia told him. "So will Lena."

"Lena told me to tell Ross she quits."

Eugenia looked at Rafael's still bleeding hands and face. "That's nice," she said. "Lena quits, and you're likely to bleed all over the menu. Mr. Schweig is going to be fed up with the both of you."

"He already is," Rafael muttered. "Or at least he acts like it. I don't know what his problem has been lately."

"Come on," Eugenia said, and took him by the arm. "Let's go in and get those hands taken care of. Do you have bandages?"

"Just Band-Aids. I don't have any gauze."

"I'll go home and get some. You go in and start getting cleaned up. I'll be over shortly."

"You don't have to do this, Eugenia. I can handle it."

"I know you can, but allow me to feel needed for ten minutes, all right? I've been feeling incredibly useless."

He opened his mouth again, but wound up merely nodding. After a quick sweep that took care of the rest of the photographs, he went inside his house and Eugenia went inside hers.

A splotchy-faced, red-eyed Lena met her at the door. "What did he say?"

"About what?"

"About those pictures."

"What could he say, Lena? Someone wanted to hurt him badly, and they did."

Lena shook her head. "They were trying to warn us. Only a monster could have done what he did."

Eugenia sighed. "I'll wager he was seeing monsters when he did it, Lena. You're perfectly aware of how drugs can alter the mind's perception."

"Why are you making excuses for him?"

"I'm not. I'm only telling you what you already know and for some reason want to reject."

Lena's lower lip threatened to quiver. "I'll never be able to look at him again without seeing those pictures."

Eugenia went past her to the bathroom and Lena followed, eyeing her mother's activity with unease.

"What are you doing?"

"I'm going to help him."

"Why?"

"I don't know why. Maybe because my daughter cares about him more than she's willing to admit."

Lena blinked and looked at her mother.

"God only knows why he's chosen you to fall for, Lena, but he has, and the one thing he needs more than anything is to know someone somewhere has forgiven him."

"God only knows?" Lena repeated. "Thanks so much, Mom."

"You don't make it easy for a man to care, Lena."

"I don't have to," Lena said, her voice defiant. "Why should I?"

"No reason," Eugenia said and exhaled. "No reason at all. I'll be back later."

Lena blinked again. "Did he break anything?"

"I don't think so." Eugenia started out, then paused. "Were you serious about quitting the deli?"

Her daughter looked at her hands. "I don't know."

"Well, you don't have long to think about it. You're due at work in an hour."

Eugenia left her daughter still gazing downward, and for a moment, just a moment, she would swear she was looking at Audrey, the girl from her visions, and not Lena. The idea sent a terrifying spasm of fear through Eugenia.

SIXTEEN

RAFAEL winced as Ross took his bandaged hands and held them up.

"You get in a fight?"

"No." Rafael told him what happened at his house that morning, leaving out the parts having to do with Lena.

"You got mad and hit a piece of wood? You screw up your hands like this over some pictures?"

"Yeah."

"Can you move 'em? Can you make sandwiches today?"

"Yeah, sure."

Ross dropped his hands and looked past Rafael out the window. "Where the hell is Lena? I have some errands to run today."

Rafael was silent. Eugenia had asked him not to say anything about Lena's decision to quit. He asked her why, but she wouldn't say, just to wait and see what happened. Lena was unpredictable, she said.

That much he knew.

"I can handle things, Ross," Rafael offered.

Ross snorted. "With those hands?"

"I can handle it. Go and do what you need to do."

"Forget it. When that snotty little bitch gets here, let me know."

"Hey," Rafael said before he could stop himself.

"What?" Ross had been heading for his office, but he stopped to glare over his shoulder.

Rafael compressed his lips and said nothing. He needed the job more than he needed to defend Lena.

Ross's eyes narrowed. "Just general principles, or are we suddenly hot after our sister superior?"

When there was no answer from Rafael, Ross went into his office and slammed the door behind him. Rafael exhaled and hurried to get the bread made and into the ovens. He couldn't wait for the day he was off parole. He couldn't wait to tell the people in town, including Ross Schweig, to kiss his ass.

He cleaned everything behind the counter, put the risen bread dough in the ovens, and was changing two of the canisters on the pop machine when Ross came out of the office and walked through the deli to the door. He said not a word to Rafael, just went out and got in his truck. Rafael flexed his aching hands and muttered under his breath about Dr. Jekyll and Mr. Schweig. Then he went back to work.

Lena came in during the lunch rush, and while Rafael was surprised to see her, he said not a word. She moved behind the counter and put an apron on, and when the rush was over, she went about wiping down the tables and sweeping the floor. Rafael was tempted to speak, ask her how she could bear to be in the same room with such a disgusting animal, but he kept his mouth shut.

Ross came back around one, and he told Lena if she was ever late again not to bother showing up at all. Lena surprised Rafael by apologizing to Ross. Rafael moved to where he could look at her face and see if she was serious.

She was.

He blew air out his nose and walked away. He couldn't figure her out. Nice to the guy who treated her like shit, and shitty to the guy who was nice to her.

As the afternoon wore on he became more and more restless, wanting her to say something and at the same time not wanting her to say anything, because he knew it would be something he didn't want to hear. He couldn't look at her for very long. When he did he saw her face as it looked resting against the pillow next to his, relaxed and affectionate and happily satisfied. Rafael refused to believe she could turn it off just like that. Unless she had in fact been playing with him.

Which was entirely possible, he guessed, as he caught a glimpse of a smirk while she watched Ross hack away in irritation at a slab of meat.

Why did she come back? Rafael wondered. *To laugh at us stupid jerks? Make fun of us?*

Eugenia came in around three, and she asked Ross if he could spare some time to talk with her.

Ross barely looked up. "What about?"

"About town," she said. "Lena may have told you I used to live here many years ago. I was curious—"

"Nothing has changed," snapped Ross. "It's still the same shithole it ever was. And we're all still the same dumbshits living here."

Eugenia blinked. "I see I've come at a bad time. Forgive me."

Ross did look up then. He took several deep breaths and visibly attempted to relax himself.

"I'm sorry," he said. "It is a bad time."

"I'll just . . . be going," said Eugenia, and she waved to Lena and then to Rafael before walking out the door. Rafael glanced at Lena and saw that her nostrils were flaring in anger. Her mouth opened, but at that moment Ross went rushing around the counter to go out after Eugenia. Rafael and Lena stared as he jerked open the door and called out. Eugenia stopped, and Ross approached, his hands held out in front of him. Words were exchanged, and Rafael saw Eugenia begin to back away, an uncomfortable smile frozen on her face. Rafael gaped in the next moment as Ross fell to his knees and appeared to begin begging for something.

It was Lena's turn to rush around the counter, but she stopped as she reached the door. Eugenia had bent down and helped Ross to his feet. Her face was full of concern as she led him away from prying eyes, over to her car. The two of them got inside, and Lena saw Ross cover his eyes and begin to cry.

"What the hell is going on?" she said to no one in particular.

Then a customer approached the door and wanted to be let in.

Business picked up again, and when Rafael next had a chance to look out the window, Ross and Eugenia were gone. Lena looked out the window frequently, but she said nothing. When it was finally time to close, Rafael took the spare keys from Ross's drawer and locked up the place. He asked Lena if she wanted a ride home, but she ignored him. He opened his palms and walked to his car.

At home he looked for the blue Taurus in the drive next door, but it was nowhere to be seen. He pulled his Escort into the garage and turned off the engine. He was thinking about Ross and wondering where Eugenia had taken him when he saw something out of the corner of his eye. He shut the garage door and had just turned around when he was viciously bludgeoned over the head. Rafael heard the sound of metal ring after it connected with his skull. The ringing sound seemed to go on forever as another blow came, and then another. He wasn't aware of falling to the ground, but suddenly his hands were full of dried brown grass and his ribs were being assaulted by what felt like a steel-toed boot.

From far away he heard a screech, and then shouting, and suddenly his attacker was gone. Rafael moved his hands beneath him and attempted to use his arms to lift himself off the ground. Blood poured down his forehead into his eyes and he squeezed his lids shut. His head spun. He was going to lose it soon. He felt hands on his arms and he opened one eye to see who it was. Lena's jaw was quivering with fury. Rafael wanted to fall back to the ground; instead he said, "Someone thinks like you do, Lena."

He never heard her reply; the effort of speaking took him into unconsciousness.

When awareness returned to him he opened his eyes to see Detective Morales leaning over him and speaking loudly into his face.

"Wake up, Chavez. I don't have all day for this."

Rafael moaned.

"Come on now, you been beat up before, I know. Who did it this time?"

"Drink," Rafael croaked. His throat was parched.

Morales picked up one of his hands in the same way Ross had done earlier. "I guess you got one or two shots in at him, huh?"

Rafael's eyes rolled away from the detective's face. From the looks of the room, he was in the hospital. He could feel a binding sensation around his middle and he assumed his ribs were taped. The throbbing in his head was so painful it made his eyes and nose hurt.

"I need something to drink," he said.

"Here." Morales reached impatiently for a glass on the tray beside him and filled it with water from a Styrofoam pitcher. He shoved the glass at Rafael and watched even more impatiently while he gulped water from the straw. When he was finished, Morales nearly snatched the glass away.

"Now," he said, "what did you see?"

"Nothing," Rafael whispered.

"Nothing. Uh-huh. Well, your neighbor said the guy was big and tall, and he had a black stocking cap on his head. In late September. It's still a little warm for that. Who was it, Rafael? Anyone you know?"

"Probably the same guy who plastered my house with police file photographs," Rafael ventured, and he had the pleasure of seeing surprise lift Morales's eyebrows.

"Come again?"

Rafael told him about the photographs, the blond man, and the blue Camaro. When he finished, Morales was shaking his head.

"You know who it is?" Rafael asked.

"Yeah, but I ain't telling you."

"The same guy who beat up the kid?"

"Yeah."

"Because I saw him do it? Because he thinks I can identify him? That's why he's doing this?"

"Beats the shit out of me," said Morales. Then he smiled. "Or you, rather."

Rafael inhaled away the urge to call him a prick and said, "How did I get here?"

"Your neighbor brought you here."

"By herself?"

"Don't ask me." Morales moved away from the bed and toward the door. "You sure those were police file photographs?"

Rafael nodded; then he winced at the pain nodding caused. He wanted to ask for a pain pill, but he didn't know how he was going to pay the bill as it was; he certainly didn't want to add to it. He wished Lena had left him the hell alone. She was good enough at it.

She appeared as if on cue, and Rafael gritted his teeth and attempted to sit up as she entered the room.

"Why the hell did you bring me here?" he asked her. "You think I've got the money to pay for hospital rooms and emergency care?"

She blinked in surprise at the attack, and then came back just as vehemently. "You were bleeding all over the place. I thought you might have a skull fracture. What was I supposed to do?"

"You brought me yourself?"

"The hospice man who takes care of your other neighbor gave me a lift home and helped me."

Rafael stared at her. She wouldn't ride home with him, but she hauled his ass to the hospital he couldn't afford. "Why are you still here?" he asked.

"I drove your car."

"Get out," he told her.

"No, I have something to say."

The pain in Rafael's head made his eyes begin to water. "Goddammit, will you please just go? Haven't you fucked me over enough?"

She came to the edge of the bed. "Don't you dare speak to me that way. You're the one who's been hiding things, pretending to be something you're not."

Rafael nearly shouted at her. "I haven't pretended *anything*, Lena. I've been honest with you from the start. I told you what I did, and forgive me for wanting to spare you the details, but I've been witless from the first moment I saw you. You know that, and you've done nothing but play with me ever since, you heartless, fucking ballbreaker. Now get out of here."

Lena leaned over and slapped him across the face, causing the pain in his head to shoot sparks across his vision. Instinctively his fist came up, but there was no will to follow through. He dropped his arm and abruptly turned his face away. Lena's voice, when it came, was shaky, but he couldn't look at her.

"I've never experienced anything in my life like the rage I felt when I came around the house today and saw what that man was doing to you. I wanted to kill him. I wanted to pick up something and beat his face in . . . the way I saw in those pictures this morning. I don't know what that means, Rafael, but if it means I care, then I'm not so sure I want to. I'm not sure it's *right*."

"Lena, just go," Rafael said, still not looking at her.

"I can't," she said. "That's what I'm trying to tell you. Right or wrong, I can't seem to leave you alone. I can't help wondering if there's something wrong with me."

"Because you care about me? Jesus, Lena. Get out. Go home. Go back to Oregon and pretend you know what the hell you want.

I know what I want. My head's on straight, no matter what you or anybody else thinks."

"I'm sorry I hurt you," she said, and he felt her hand cover his. He tried to tug it away, but she held on. He turned to look at her finally, and the dark confusion in her eyes made him swallow.

"Go home," he said to her again.

"No. I'm staying." She lay down on the bed with him and eased herself over to hold him across his middle. She pressed her lips to his temple and began to kiss his bruised and bandaged forehead. Rafael closed his eyes and held himself as still as possible, and when her mouth sought his, he refused to allow himself to respond. She wasn't going to hurt him again. She wasn't going to make him crazy.

"I used to know what I wanted," she said when she pulled away. "You changed everything."

"I'm not listening to you," he said, and he turned his face away again.

Lena took his chin and brought him around to look long into his eyes. "I need to be with you. I need to find out who I was meant to be, who I've been running away from all this time. You don't realize how different everything is with you."

Rafael twisted out of her grasp. "You're not jerking me around again, Lena. I'm not falling for this sweet bullshit so you can knock my dick in the dirt again tomorrow or the next day."

Lena's mouth snapped shut and her nostrils quivered with anger. A nurse entered the room then and cleared her throat. The nurse informed Rafael it was the doctor's suggestion that he stay overnight, in case of concussion. Rafael bluntly told her there was no way in hell he could afford to stay in the hospital another minute, and he was leaving as soon as he found his clothes. Lena left the bed and opened a closet near the door, while the nurse stood and tried to argue. Rafael refused to listen.

"Here," said Lena, and she tossed his briefs to him.

Rafael caught them and swung his legs over the side of the bed.

The pain came back to him in a dizzying rush, but he was determined to leave the bed and the room and go to his own house.

The nurse gave up and left the room. A doctor came in next, but Rafael had his jeans on and was standing on his own two feet. His answer to the doctor was the same, "You can't make me stay here. I'm going."

The doctor turned impatiently and spied Lena. "Make sure he stays in bed, or at least immobile, would you?"

She said nothing, only nodded.

Rafael left the hospital and tried not to lean too heavily on Lena, who walked him out to his car and put him in the passenger seat before climbing in behind the wheel.

The ride home was silent, and as she pulled into his drive Rafael happened to spy a car in the side mirror, a Camaro, sitting just off the street around the corner.

"Son of a bitch," he muttered.

Lena looked at him. "What?"

"The Camaro. It's around the corner."

"I'm calling the police," said Lena.

"Don't bother. He's already leaving." Rafael closed his eyes. It hurt even to talk.

"Okay." Lena turned off the car in the drive beside the porch. "Let's get you inside. I'll come back and put the car in the garage."

"You're not staying here," Rafael told her.

She looked at him. "I am."

"No. He knows I'm home again. He might come back."

"Which is exactly why you need me here to protect you," said Lena.

Rafael managed to look at her. "Protect me?"

"You're a con and can't have a gun. I have one, and I'm going next door to get it as soon as I get you in bed."

"You carry a gun?"

"Two single women traveling across country?"

"Is it licensed?"

"Of course."

"You're licensed to *carry* it?"

"I didn't say that."

She ignored his frown and left the car to come around and open his door. She helped him out and up to the front door of the house, fumbling for the right key until he picked it out for her. Once inside, she walked with him to the bedroom and settled him on the bed, reaching for the snap of his jeans and untying the laces on his shoes to slip off both items of clothing. He struggled with his shirt and she knocked his hands away and pulled it over his head for him.

His bare chest goose-pimpled and his nipples hardened as Lena ran her hands over his skin. She bent down to kiss his mouth before leaving him to rest. Rafael gazed at her concerned features and wondered how he was ever going to get over her.

SEVENTEEN

I knew it," said Ross as he stared with glazed eyes at Eugenia Fairfax. "You knew her. You're causing this to happen to me."

Eugenia blinked. "I swear to you, Mr. Schweig, I have nothing to do with anything that's happening to you. Yes, I knew Martha Box, and yes, I adored her, but I haven't thought of her in years. Well, I did think of her just the other day, but it was while thinking of the orphanage and my experiences there." She paused a moment and studied Ross. Then she said, "I have to ask you, Mr. Schweig, why *you* think you're having these so-called visions of a girl you barely knew. You didn't know her, did you?"

"No," he said quickly. "I didn't know her at all."

Eugenia went on looking at him, and Ross grew increasingly uncomfortable. They were sitting in his home, on his sofa, drinking his coffee. He couldn't believe he had fallen apart in front of her—in front of everyone—but he had, and his knees still ached from kneeling on the concrete walk in front of the deli. He was hoping some of the people who had seen him thought it was all a joke, maybe a proposal of marriage or something.

He was also hoping no one had seen him crying in her car afterward.

God, he felt like such a fool. And now to have her looking at him like this, as if she knew everything already and was only waiting for him to spill his guts.

"I would never have believed it of you," she said in a soft, quiet voice.

Ross nearly dropped his cup. "What?" he demanded.

Eugenia shook her head and opened her purse. She reached for her keys. "We've spent the entire afternoon talking about everything but the thing you want to talk about. Now that we're close to the subject, you're backing away."

"I'm not. You're accusing me of something."

"I suppose I am."

"Why? What do you think you know?"

"Nothing. All I remember is some boys who were very cruel to her. Cruel because she ignored them and wanted nothing to do with them."

"I don't know what they did with her," Ross said, his voice desperate. "I've asked and tried to find out, but I don't know what they did with her. I left. I couldn't stay and watch. I ran away."

"Watched who?" Eugenia asked, her voice cautious.

"The guys I was with. Just guys."

"Where did they take her?"

"The old Hickok place, behind the fort," Ross answered without thinking.

"To do what?"

"I don't know. I don't know. I didn't stay. I told you, I ran away."

"And did nothing to stop them," said Eugenia.

Ross looked at her and opened his mouth, but nothing came out. His eyes felt as if they were bugging out of his head, because suddenly it was Martha sitting on the sofa next to him, holding keys in her hand and gently shaking her head as she looked at him.

And did nothing to stop them.

"Sorry," Ross managed in a whisper. "I'm so sorry, Martha. I was scared."

Eugenia was blinking again, and the red hair slowly darkened and the eyes turned a chocolate brown. Ross cleared his throat.

"Dammit, will you listen to me? I tell you, Mrs. Fairfax—Eugenia—I'm fighting hard as hell to stay with it, but I think I'm losing."

"We should go to the old Hickok place," she said, and his lids came up as he stared at her.

"What for?"

"To look around."

"For a grave, you mean? For bones sticking up out of the ground? What the hell are you talking about?"

Eugenia spoke calmly. "We're both experiencing psychic episodes, Mr. Schweig. We may get some impression while we're there; something may speak to us now that would normally remain silent. Are you willing to accompany me, or shall I go by myself?"

"Forgive me, Eugenia, but I'm wondering, as I have been all along, if there's not something wrong with you. Something that causes things to happen to other people. You come to town and all kinds of—"

Eugenia stood. "I think this is the point where my daughter would call you a pig. Good-night, Mr. Schweig."

"*Night,*" he said. "You said it right there. What are you going to find at night?"

"Nothing, I suspect. That's why I'm going in the morning."

"I've got to work," said Ross.

Eugenia kept moving toward the door. He got off the sofa and followed her. "What are you going to do if you find anything? Have you thought about that?"

"Yes," she said. "Just now."

She said nothing more, only walked outside and left him standing and holding the door. Ross began to panic.

"Eugenia," he called. "Don't do anything on your own. I'll come with you in the morning. Call me before you go."

She didn't respond, just went on and got inside her car. Ross knew he couldn't let her go by herself. What if she really did find something? What if she intended to bring in the authorities?

A crackpot, he told himself. She was a bigger crackpot than him, good-looking or not.

As he watched her drive away, a thought occurred to him. He immediately shied away from it; it wasn't the sort of thing a man like him would do. But these were unusual circumstances.

He shut the door and went inside the house to pick up the phone and call Lorraine Lake.

Eugenia was more confused than ever as she left the tortured Ross Schweig. She had no idea why he was experiencing what he was experiencing. It had nothing to do with her, she was certain of that. It was his own guilt over Martha, and what he assumed had happened to her.

His assumption was probably right. And if they had in fact killed Martha after doing whatever they had done to her, her body was likely to be in the vicinity of the old Hickok place. They wouldn't have risked moving the body anywhere or doing anything too involved with it. People had been using the old Hickok place for dumping bodies long before it was the old Hickok place.

Eugenia nearly slammed on the brakes at the last thought recognized by her conscious mind.

Dumping bodies.

She breathed in deeply and felt a pain tear at her chest as she remembered the way things ended for Audrey and her beloved scout. She hadn't come to that part yet. She wasn't even close to reexperiencing their untimely end. How could she have forgotten for even one moment the fate that befell the two?

Eugenia spoke to the car's ceiling as she went on driving. "I'm ready for this to come to an end now. I want to go home. I want *my* home."

The Victorian house was dark and empty when she arrived, and Eugenia went inside, put her purse down, then walked next door to see if Lena was there. She was. Her expression was wary as she opened the door, and Eugenia looked at her in surprise.

"What's going on?"

"Hi, Mom." Lena sounded relieved. "Come in."

Eugenia went inside. "Where's Rafael?"

"Asleep. After work he was attacked. I saw the man who did it, but not well enough to identify him. Rafael didn't see him at all. I took him to the hospital, but he wouldn't stay."

"Is he all right? Was he badly injured?"

Lena looked at the floor. "I've been watching him. He seems okay. He's still upset with me."

Eugenia left the foyer and went to sit down on a chair in the living room. She looked around herself and decided Rafael's mother had very good taste. Everything was old, but still stylish. And the house was relatively clean, for housing a bachelor.

Lena sat down on the sofa. "Where did you go with Ross?"

"His house. He was very disturbed."

"No kidding. What about?"

"Martha Box."

"Who?"

"A girl who befriended me at the orphanage many years ago. Martha disappeared one day and was never seen or heard from again. Ross thinks he knows what happened to her. He was there with the other boys on that long-ago day, but he says he ran away and didn't see what became of her."

Lena's mouth was hanging open. "Are you talking about a murder?"

"I think so, yes," said Eugenia.

"Is that why we're here?" Lena asked. "Is that why you're having the dreams, because of Martha?"

"I don't know," Eugenia told her. "Ross thinks I've come here to torment him. He thinks I'm the devil in disguise, or some other foolishness. He's convinced that because I knew and loved Martha, I've brought all his memories of her and the events surrounding her back to him."

"What a crock," said Lena. "Is he crazy?"

"He thinks he's headed in that direction. Tomorrow morning I'm going to the old Hickok place and have a look around. Ross said he wanted to come with me, but he may change his mind before morning."

"What do you think you'll find?" Lena asked. She was staring worriedly at her mother.

Eugenia lifted a shoulder. "Martha."

"You can't be serious."

"I don't know what I am anymore. I'm sick of it all."

Lena blinked. "Are you saying you're ready to go? You want to leave now?"

"I'd like to, yes, but I can't. It would be like walking out of the theater after watching three-quarters of a movie." She paused then and looked at her daughter. "Are you still eager to leave?"

Lena said nothing, only shook her head.

"Because of Rafael?"

A nod.

"Do you think you'll ever be able to leave him?"

"Of course," said Lena. "Just not now."

Eugenia smiled. "You're fooling yourself. The longer you stay, the deeper you—"

"I'm not in love with him, Mother. It's not like that."

"Well tell me then, Lena, what is it like? I'm curious."

Lena stared at her mother. "You're making fun of me."

"I'm not. As I said, if it's not love, then I'm curious to know exactly what it is."

"I care about him, all right? I do. Just not that way. Not the way you care about someone you're in love with."

"Meaning what? You wouldn't die for him, or some such nonsense?"

Lena turned cold. "You have no idea where I'm at, so I don't know why we're even discussing this."

"I do know where you're at, Lena," insisted Eugenia. "You're in the home and at the bedside of a man who makes you think and do things you never dreamed possible. He makes you see differently, breathe differently, and you lose a part of yourself and become a little less Lena every time he touches you, because you're giving him something you'll never give anyone else. And you love it. You love the feeling that your identity is merging with his to create something separate from either of you. It's a bond that will last the rest of your life, if you're lucky."

Lena looked at her mother and said, "You're talking about you and Dad, not me. I'm not giving away anything, and I don't need some man to come along and make me whole, Mother. I am whole."

Before Eugenia could reply, a voice from down the hall hailed Lena.

She hurried to go to him, and a bitter smile twisted Eugenia's mouth. She thought of saying something about how quickly her "whole" daughter had jumped; instead she followed Lena to the bedroom and pulled a face when she saw Rafael's injuries. Lena was already sitting on the bed and touching his arm.

"Nothing," she said. "Nothing's wrong."

"Hello, Rafael," said Eugenia, and she stepped to the bed. He looked relieved to see her.

"I heard you arguing."

"I'm sorry. Did we wake you?"

"No." He gritted his teeth and attempted to sit up.

Lena pushed him down. "What are you doing?"

Rafael scowled at her. "Trying to get up and take a piss."

"You're not supposed to get up."

"You want me to pee in bed?"

"I'll get you something to go in."

"You'll get the hell out of my way and let me go to the bathroom. Eugenia . . ."

He extended a hand to her and Eugenia moved forward to help pull him up. Lena's mouth worked and she determinedly placed herself on the other side of him, placing his weight against her as he left the bed.

"You don't have to snarl at me," she said to him. "I'm only trying to do what the doctor said."

The three of them were in the hall when the sound of glass shattering stopped them in their tracks. They looked at each other, and Eugenia started forward, but Rafael held her back. "Wait," he said. He turned to Lena then. "Go see if anything's on fire."

Lena released him so that she could walk to the end of the hall and look into the foyer and living room. When she returned, her face was pale.

"What was it?" asked Eugenia.

"A baseball bat," Lena said in a low voice. "It's covered with blood. Somebody threw it through the living room window."

Rafael looked at Lena and seemed to be holding his breath. Eugenia saw her daughter's throat hitch as she turned her face away. Then she turned abruptly back and reached for Rafael. She put her arms around his neck and pressed herself hard against him, pushing him to the wall. Eugenia released his arm so he could place it around her daughter.

She looked at them holding each other, Rafael's jaw twitching, and Lena close to tears, and Eugenia walked quietly through the house to go and call the police.

EIGHTEEN

JOHN Dixon glanced at the laundress with a pained expression. Her white hair made her look older than her years; she was still a healthy, vital woman, with arms as thick and strong as any soldier's. Most single women were married within weeks of coming to a fort. Not this woman. Her voice was too harsh, her bearing too masculine. Her face was hard, made ruddy by the steamy water used in the laundering of fort uniforms and bedclothes.

The way she was looking at him made Dixon wonder if she expected payment for what she had just told him.

"Yer lady wife said I should come and tell ye what I seen," she repeated for the third time. "She said ye be wantin' to know about these goin's on."

"Thank you," Dixon said for the third time. "You're free to go now."

Her dark brows rose nearly to the crown of her white hair. "What're ye goin' to do? Why, back home we'd have had her—"

"You're not back home, my good woman, you're here in Kansas, and we are bound by civility and courtesy to our fellow human beings."

"But she's sleepin' with a filthy brown heathen. She's matin' with him like he's a regular man, fit to marry an' all."

"Madam, you may go now," Dixon said loudly, and the steel in his voice caused the white-haired laundress to turn and stomp out of his quarters, muttering under her breath about how things would have been for Miss Audrey back home.

When the door slammed behind the woman, John Dixon's head sank into his hands.

He had known, of course; had guessed, simply by witnessing the light in Audrey's eyes and the warmth in the scout's dark orbs when they chanced to pass on the grounds. Dixon had chosen to ignore the implications, telling himself she would not lower herself in such a manner, would not leave herself open to the condemnation she was sure to face should they be found out. And, too, he had falsely believed and eagerly told himself she was only flirting with the scout to make him, Dixon, angry and jealous. She knew how Dixon felt about her. She knew how deeply ran his emotions where she was concerned. She would not betray those emotions.

"Yer lady wife said ye be wantin' to know."

Annabeth, the omniscient one.

The golden viper.

She knew what was in Dixon's heart and had not wasted a single moment in sending the washerwoman to his quarters.

Dixon's fingers played with the butt of the revolver on the desk before him.

He turned the barrel toward himself, and sat for long minutes with one finger on the trigger, thinking.

Finally, his heart diseased with despair, he called to his aide. The door opened and the tall, gangly blond strode to the desk and stood at attention.

Dixon kept his voice low and told his aide what needed to be done. He knew he could trust the young man; he had performed a similar service for Dixon on a previous occasion.

The aide fought to keep the smile from his face, but it was too much for him. He was happy to be of use. Eager to make himself indispensable to the commander and be in a position to blackmail the man, should he ever find the need.

It was a shame the commander kept falling in love with these young girls, when he had such a fine-looking woman at home. He couldn't expect the aide to kill every girl who spurned him. Not without some recompense.

Dixon's nostrils flared, as if reading the aide's mind and hearing the thoughts aloud.

"Of course you'll be granted extended leave and whatever else you feel you require."

"Same as last time'll be fine," said the aide.

Dixon's blue gaze rose to meet that of the smirking younger man. "This is not the same."

"It ain't?"

"No," breathed Dixon. He was genuinely in love this time. Audrey was everything to him.

"You want me to do him first, so she can watch?"

Dixon went still; then he nodded, and said, "As soon as possible. And this time make it look like a double suicide."

"Suicide?"

"Yes. Their relationship was doomed from the very beginning. Everyone will understand."

The aide shrugged. "If you say so. Will that be all, Commander?"

"For now," said Dixon, and he allowed his head to fall into his hands again once the younger man was gone. Some day soon he was going to have to arrange for an accident to befall his young aide. Perhaps an ambush by Indians, or a fall from his horse. The accident would, of course, be fatal.

Dixon lifted his head and picked up the top piece of paper from a stack on his desk. The words blurred when he tried to read, and he found himself thinking of Annabeth again. Annabeth delighted in finding him out, in revealing his heart's desires and smashing them with the heel of her tiny boot. It galled her to know she was never the object of her husband's attentions, never the one he lusted, pined, and yearned after with such forceful intensity. She was nothing he wanted. Nothing but cold flesh and a frigid smile.

She followed him to various camps and forts to make certain he stayed out of "romantic mischief," as she once called it. She despised his romantic soul and called him a vain, ridiculous old fool.

Dixon fingered the butt of his revolver once more and, thinking of Audrey, began to wonder if Annabeth was right.

He thought of calling his aide back and telling him he had changed his mind, but the image of soft white skin melded with brown in a passionate embrace stopped him.

Dixon picked up the paper once more and stared at the words until his concentration began to focus. Running a fort required a clear mind and a firm hand. John Dixon had both.

Eugenia's lip curled as she watched the commander turn the barrel of the revolver away from himself and attend to the business on his desk.

She awakened in the chair she had fallen asleep in and stared into the dimness of the room.

The bitter, tattling white-haired laundress was the same woman, who, years later, threw the bucket at the little boy.

How could that be? Eugenia asked herself. The fort dreams took place in the mid 1850s, and the orphanage dream took place at the turn of the century, nearly fifty years later. How could it be the same woman?

And why did John Dixon suddenly resemble Ross Schweig? Why did she now think of Lena and Rafael, when Dixon's thoughts fixed upon Audrey and her scout?

Was there some sort of parallel existence at work here? she wondered. Or was she simply linking present day facts with her knowledge of the past.

That was it, she told herself. Her subconscious mind was creating the similarities and drawing the parallels.

Unless the white-haired laundress had been reincarnated as the orphanage matron.

Eugenia blinked. Perhaps Dixon had had the complaining washerwoman killed along with his aide, erasing all possible evidence of his misdeeds. That would explain her appearance fifty years later, as the wicked, ruddy-faced matron.

"You're reaching," Eugenia whispered to herself in the darkness, and for a moment she wished she was not in the house alone. Another presence would have been a comfort to her, diversion from the thoughts circling her brain.

She knew she didn't want Lena and Rafael to be Audrey and the scout. She didn't want to walk next door and find them both hanging from the rafters of the ceiling, the way the smirking aide had left Audrey and her lover.

She blinked again as she thought of the police file photographs and the bloody bat thrown through Rafael's window earlier. The man who attacked him was the aide. Eugenia was suddenly sure of it.

Then she shook her head.

"Listen to you," she said aloud. "You sound as crazy as Ross Schweig said you were."

Maybe even crazier.

NINETEEN

ROSS sat on the hassock in front of Lorraine's sofa and looked earnestly into her face. "I'm sorry. The same thing happens every time I get close to someone. I get scared and run."

"You're sitting here telling me it's not because of those two Fairfax women that you dumped me?" Lorraine's eyes were slitted with distrust.

Ross tried to smile. "Lorraine, I got caught up in their problems, is all, and I used my involvement as an excuse to get away from you. I never cared for either one of them, and to tell you the God's honest truth, I think they're both bad news."

Lorraine lifted her chin. "How do you mean?" she asked. "Are you talking about their defense of Rafael Chavez?"

"No, no, not just that. They're strange, Lorraine. Weird. The mother has these dreams and visions, and the daughter I'd swear is a man-hating lesbian."

Lorraine leaned forward and Ross could see he had her full attention.

"What sort of visions?"

"About the fort, I think. And Martha Box. Do you remember her?"

"No. Who was she?"

"She lived at the Hall the same time as Mrs. Fairfax. Martha was always coming on to the guys around town—you know how those girls from the Hall were—and a few of the guys took her up on it one day, only things got out of hand and Martha got hurt."

"You were there?" Lorraine interrupted. "You were one of the boys involved?"

"Yeah, but I didn't stick around to see what happened. I left before things got hairy. All I knew is that Martha was never heard from or seen again. I didn't ask any questions. I didn't want to know. But here comes this Fairfax woman years later with her visions and dreams and things, and suddenly *I* start getting visions of Martha. It's been driving me crazy, Lorraine, and if I didn't know better, I'd swear Eugenia Fairfax did something to me."

Lorraine was frowning. "Like what?"

Ross threw open his hands. "I don't know. How the hell should I know? I'm just telling you it's really weird all the goings-on since she's been here."

"What? What else has been going on?"

"Things," Ross said, irritated. "It's like she came here to dig up some dirt in our past, maybe to pay us back for the way we treated her or something, I don't know."

Lorraine sniffed. "Their attachment to Rafael Chavez should have said something to you. I don't know how you could have hired that scum—"

"Rafael is a good worker," Ross said. "I was giving the guy a break."

"Do you have anyone to replace him?" Lorraine asked.

Ross looked at her. "Replace him?"

"It came over the police scanner that he was attacked and beaten quite severely earlier this evening. I doubt he'll be in to work for you tomorrow."

"Where did it happen? At work?"

"No, at his home. The younger Fairfax woman took him to the hospital."

"I'll be damned," Ross said under his breath, and he looked at Lorraine. "Who did it?"

"The police have no idea."

"Do you?"

"Of course not. What makes you think I would?"

Ross looked at his hands. "You know just about everything that goes on in this town, Lorraine. Not much gets by you."

Her eyes narrowed again. "I didn't know about Martha Box, now did I?"

"It wasn't something we went around broadcasting. Two of the guys who did it are dead now, and the third jerk is a drunken musician who can't remember his own name, let alone what happened with a girl over thirty-five years ago."

Lorraine studied him for several moments, causing him to look away from her and about the room. Finally, she said, "What do you want from me, Ross? Why are you here?"

He looked at her and opened his hands. "I'm here because I need you. I never realized how much. I need you to make her stop and go away. I need you to help me forget about Martha again and be who I was before those two women came to town. I'm asking for your help, Lorraine. For God's sake don't turn me away."

She made no move toward him, only went on eyeing him.

"What do you suppose happened to Martha Box, Ross?"

"God only knows. I was ashamed of my involvement then, and I'm ashamed of it now. I can't have Eugenia Fairfax digging up the ground around the old Hickok place thinking she's going to find something."

"Is that what she's planning to do?" asked Lorraine.

Ross nodded. "Tomorrow morning."

"Who told her to go there?"

"I did."

"What were you thinking?"

"Me? I was thinking about Martha, and the way she's been driving me crazy. I thought Eugenia was going to help, but something tells me she's only going to make it worse, because what if she does find something? I'll be in trouble.''

"You said you didn't do anything," reminded Lorraine. "You said you ran."

"I did," said Ross. "I couldn't watch."

"Then you should have nothing to fear."

"Nothing but Martha." Ross left the hassock and walked with angry, jerky steps to the door. "I'm sorry I came and bothered you. I don't know what I thought you could do. You have no reason to do anything for me."

"That's right," said Lorraine, maintaining her position on the sofa. Her son came to the door and twisted the knob just as Ross was ready to grasp it. He stepped away and snubbed the tall blond on his way out. Lorraine's son sneered at him.

"What the hell did he want?" he asked his mother when Ross was on the porch and walking to his truck.

"I'm not sure," said Lorraine. "He was acting very strangely."

"Was he drunk?"

"I didn't smell anything."

"Could've been vodka."

"No, I know the signs. He wasn't drinking." She looked up then. "Where have you been? It's nearly one o'clock."

"Out with some friends," her son answered.

"Who?"

"No one you'd know."

"Where did you meet them?"

"At school. Jesus, what's with you? Why are you grilling me all of a sudden?"

"Rafael Chavez was severely beaten earlier. Do you know anything about that?"

"Somebody does, I'm sure."

"What kind of an answer is that? I asked you a direct question."

"No, I don't know who beat him up."

"It was one person, acting alone. Someone tall, with a stocking

cap on his head.'' Lorraine looked at the stocking cap sticking out
of her son's jacket pocket.

"You'd better be careful," she said. "You're not invincible,
you know."

Her son only smiled at her.

TWENTY

L ENA awakened in the same moment as Rafael and they lay looking at one another until Rafael shifted away from her. The coolness emanating from him disappointed Lena. He was still holding back from her, still being cold instead of warm and reaching for everything but her to hold on to in the middle of the night. She couldn't blame him. She had been thoughtlessly cruel the day before about the pictures. Anyone would have done the same, she told herself. Her reaction had been normal. She believed she had made up for it last night, by not running away at discovering the bloody bat. She wanted to run; the sight of the thing sickened her. But the idea of the pain it caused Rafael meant more to her than her own repugnance. The expression on his face did more to convince her than any words he could speak; he would never have done what he did if not under the influence of illegal substances. Rafael was the person he claimed to be, sincere and remorseful, willing to face the scorn of an entire community for a chance to start over again.

In her heart Lena knew he was good, without having her mother tell her. But she had waited and hoped against hope to find someone meant just for her, and there was difficulty in accepting the fact that her someone happened to be a convicted murderer just out of prison. He couldn't know how difficult it was for Lena to trust or rely on not only him, but anyone. He didn't know the problems she had giving of herself.

All her life she had stood by and watched her father attend her mother. Her mother was so *needy,* there was little room left for attention to Lena. Not that Lena minded. She loved her mother and gave the same as her father, without thinking, without questioning; it was just what they did.

Lena considered herself strong and resilient as a result, but as she grew older her resiliency translated itself into a wariness of other people that prevented her from fully enjoying intimate or even casual relationships. In Lena there was a constant subconscious struggle against identifying with her mother and being considered needy at any time by anyone. Consciously, she told herself she was just being careful.

For years Lena had known someone somewhere had treated her mother badly; had guessed that the results of such treatment created the vulnerability that made Eugenia cleave to her husband and seemingly ignore the needs of her daughter. Lena believed Eugenia purposely tried to make her daughter stronger than herself, and Lena had responded, cloaking herself in strength, calling it superiority, never counting on someone like the overtly male Rafael coming along, someone who made her forget her cautious ways and ignore the clamoring, fearful voice inside and care about nothing but being female.

She reached over and stroked the black hair on the back of his head, loving its silky texture. Then she ran her fingers down his neck until she saw his flesh goose-pimple.

"Does your head hurt this morning?" she asked.

"Aches," he mumbled.

"I dreamed about you last night," Lena told him. "You were a young boy, ten or eleven, and you rode a bike down this street."

"My mother didn't buy this house until I was gone," he said.

"You never rode down this street?"

"Maybe once or twice, I don't remember."

Lena propped her head on one elbow. "What were you like then, Rafael? Was it just you and your mother?"

"I never met my father," he answered.

"He died before you were born?"

"No."

"Oh. Were you . . . did you and your mother have a good relationship?"

"My problems had nothing to do with her. She was a good, hard worker. Everything she did, she did for us."

"Then where did your problems come from?"

"I don't feel like talking about this right now, Lena."

"I do," she said. "Tell me."

Rafael turned his back on her. "Ask me about the pederasts in prison. I'll tell you about them."

She made a face. "You never . . . you weren't . . . were you?"

"What difference would it make to you now?"

"None, I guess. Were you still taking drugs in prison?"

There was a pause before he answered: "Yeah, for a long time."

"What made you stop?"

He was silent again for some moments. Then she heard him say, "Probably the same reasons I started. I was a fatherless speck of brown with a shitty attitude. It was time to take responsibility for myself and be a man instead of a worthless cell house fixture with a habit."

"It must have been hard," Lena said in a quiet voice.

Rafael said nothing.

She rolled toward him and lifted herself to place her arms around him from behind. She began to kiss the back of his neck and the lobes of his ears, tickling him with the warmth of her breath.

Abruptly he turned to her. "Aren't you worried, Lena?"

She lifted her brows. "About what?"

"Sexually transmitted disease? We haven't used condoms since the first time."

"Aren't *you* worried?" she countered. "What do you know about me?"

He breathed out impatiently. "I know you're not promiscuous."

"How do you know?"

"You're too mean to be promiscuous. You never let anyone near you."

Lena bristled. Then she relaxed and even smiled a little. "The first night I was here I snooped through the bundle of papers on top of the secretary in the foyer. In the year before your release you were tested twice for STDs. You came up clean both times."

Rafael regarded her with an impassive expression. Then he asked, "What are you doing to protect yourself?"

"Norplant."

"What?"

Lena explained it to him and showed him the barely visible capsules beneath the skin of her underarm. She thought to herself he looked relieved, but in the next moment she would have sworn he appeared disappointed.

"Isn't it a little late to be asking all these questions?" she said.

His mouth twisted. "My passion for you prevented my asking before."

"And now that your passion has dimmed, you're covering your tracks?"

He looked at the ceiling and refused comment.

Lena moved to hover over him, and when he turned away from her she sat down hard on him, straddling his middle.

"I can change your bandages," she said, "or we can make love. The choice is yours."

"I don't want to make love to you again," said Rafael, and Lena felt herself go still with shock and a hurt she would never have believed possible.

"Why not?" she asked, her voice barely a whisper.

"Let me see if I can remember exactly how you put it to your mother last night. 'I care about him, but not the way you care about someone you're in love with.' Wasn't that what you said?"

Lena stared at him. She could not deny the words had come from her. Could not take them back.

"I was only trying to protect myself. If my mother believed I was in love with you, we'd be picking out napkins and a wedding dress right now."

Rafael looked at her for what seemed a long time. Then he said, "I'm not interested in just fucking you, Lena. I can find that if I need it."

"I'm aware of that," Lena snapped. She crossed her arms over her chest. "What do you want from me, Rafael?"

"I want you to love me."

Her lashes lowered as she blinked. When she made no response, he made a slight bucking motion with his hips.

"Get off."

She stayed put. "You've never said you love me."

He stared at her, his eyes round. "You don't know? You can't see it when I look at you, or feel it when I touch you?" He struggled to sit up. "I don't want anyone else. I've told you that."

"What kind of future can you possibly see for us?" Lena wanted to know.

"I can't see any future for us," he answered. "Not when you think there's something wrong with you for caring about me."

"You're not being fair," she said. "You have to admit a woman would think twice before—"

"I admit anyone would think twice," he interrupted. "And I'm doing all I can to prove myself, but I don't know why, because no matter what happens between us, you're still ready to go home to Oregon without me."

Lena's mouth tightened. "I have to go home. I work with my mother. It's my job."

"See? You're not prepared to compromise any part of your life."

"Why should I be?" she asked, suddenly angry. "What the hell do you want from me?"

Rafael's dark eyes went black. "I want to get out of bed today and go look for that wedding dress. I want to take those things out of your arm and start having babies with you. That's what I want."

The anger drained from Lena in a second and her entire body flushed at the way he was looking at her. She couldn't believe she was responding to him this way, not at the suggestion of having babies, but her middle was contracting and her breathing had gone shallow.

"This is crazy," she said. "You haven't thought anything through, you're just talking. You have no job, Rafael. Not a decent one, anyway. And you're still on parole. What are you planning to tell your children when they ask about you?"

"The truth," he said, and he pushed her off him to the other side of the bed. She sat on her knees and watched him swing his legs slowly out of bed. He sat on the edge of the mattress, his fingers gripping the sides, and she could see he was experiencing dizziness. Instinctively she reached for him, moving to wrap her arms around him again. She felt him exhale in a long sigh. "Lena," he said, "if you're not going to be a part of my life, I want you to get out of it."

"I don't want to get out of it," she told him. "Can't we just be together and not talk about any of this?"

A noise of frustration came from him. He took one of her hands and placed it on his taped chest over his heart.

"While I was locked up I used to dream about the woman I'd find when I got out. She would take her time getting to know me, and I would be patient, letting her see who and what I have become, so she might possibly grow to love me. When I get out I find a woman who acts like I'm dogshit, can't bear the sight of my crime, and tells me she could never love me because of what I once was. The hardest part for me to understand is the way I feel about you, Lena. I can't believe how much I love you."

She closed her eyes and leaned her forehead against the warm flesh of his back. A surge of pleasure arced through her body, and she was tempted to hug herself. Hearing him speak the words aloud, even in such a disparaging tone, touched the very center of her.

"Rafael," she whispered. "No one has ever made me feel like you do. I think of you constantly when I'm not with you, and when I'm with you all I want is to touch you. You make me crazy and so mad I could hit you. You also make me happier than I've ever been."

"Lena . . ."

She put her arms around his neck and held on while sliding around to sit beside him on the edge of the mattress.

"Be patient with me," she asked when he turned his head to look at her. "Will you? Please, Rafael."

His nostrils flared as he reached for her. He touched his lips to hers and his hands tightened on her ribs until she couldn't breathe. Lena held on to him, and when he groaned against her mouth in what sounded like despair, she opened her lips to deepen the kiss and cradled his bandaged head with her hands as she drew him down to the mattress with her.

He muttered a string of unintelligible words into her ear, and Lena could feel his emotion in his hands and in every part of flesh that was pressed against her. His dark eyes met hers as he pulled away her garments and pushed away his briefs. She gasped and then drew in breath as he drove into her as deeply as he could, as far as her body would allow, and remained there, not moving. She couldn't tear her eyes away from his; all the passion, hope, love, pain, and desire in him was in his eyes as he looked at her. Lena moaned deep in her chest and held on to him with shaking limbs as her body responded to being joined with him, and when he stiffened above her she lifted her head and sought out his mouth with her own. She kissed him until he withdrew from her and pulled away to lay his head on her breast. Lena drew deep breaths and hugged him to her, wishing she could speak. All she could push past her lips was his name. His fingers squeezed her in response, and went on squeezing.

Next door Eugenia was preparing for her early morning visit to the old Hickok place. No one lived there now; she had checked in with the librarian, who also compiled the town directory every year. The place was deserted and dirty and overgrown, she had been informed. Eugenia wasn't worried about getting dirty, but she was concerned about the overcast state of the sky above her head. The morning was a cool one, the first chilly precursor of days to come.

She went to Lena's room to borrow a pair of jeans and a heavy sweatshirt. She had nothing but her loafers to wear on her feet, but they were all right for walking. She had no idea what she was hoping to find that day, no idea what she might encounter, but she was tired of sitting around and waiting for things to happen.

Before she left the house she paused and looked in the direction of the phone. Something told her not to waste her time calling Ross Schweig. Fear made women malleable; it made men aggressive, the entire ugly story of Western civilization: when a man didn't understand something, he feared it, and whatever he feared, he sought to destroy.

Eugenia blinked and hurried out the door, wondering if wearing Lena's clothes meant she was going to begin thinking like her daughter. She glanced next door and thought of stopping in on her way out, but decided against it. She didn't want to intrude.

She got in her car, started the engine, and was backing down the drive when she spied a blue Camaro parked just around the corner. The driver was watching her. Eugenia put the car in gear and drove right up to the Camaro. The driver considered ducking, she could tell, but he changed his mind at the last moment and gave his head a toss as she approached. She stopped beside the car and rolled down her window.

"I know you," she said. "I know who you are."

The blond behind the wheel snorted. "Yeah? What's my name, lady?"

"That doesn't matter," Eugenia told him. "I know who you are inside."

His brows drew together. "Man, Ross was right. You are one nutty bitch."

Eugenia rolled up her window and drove on. She was the one who was right. The blond young man was the same as the aide in her visions. He wanted to do harm not just to Rafael, but to Lena, as well. The knowledge sent a series of shivers down Eugenia's spine as she drove. She considered going to Morales, the detective, and relaying her suspicions, but if Ross Schweig was already telling people she was strange, she couldn't expect much support from the police department.

"Pig," Eugenia muttered under her breath as she considered Ross. Then she shook her head at hearing herself.

She drove to the fort first and sat in the parking lot for fifteen to twenty minutes, waiting to see if any visions would occur. Nothing happened.

Relieved, she started the car and went around the fort, past the old post bakery road, and headed down a dirt path partially obscured by elms and cottonwoods. Anyone not from the area would have driven on by, never noticing that the path was in fact a drive, overgrown with grass and weeds, and hidden in places by dense brush. Eugenia drove as far back as she could; then she stopped the car and got out to walk, hoping the house hadn't been torn down or, if it had, that some foundation still existed.

She walked for ten minutes before she saw the remains of the stone house. It looked much the same as it had when Eugenia was a child: two of the walls were crumbling, the chimney had caved in, the planks of the front porch were warped and rotting. Parts of the gray stones were covered with moss, some of it green, some dead and brown. From somewhere, Eugenia smelled the odor of skunk. She wrinkled her nose and took care where she stepped as she moved closer to the house.

Her eyes took in the surrounding ground as she walked, look-ing for something that would snag her gaze and hold it. The skunk odor grew stronger as she reached the porch, and Eugenia won-dered what had caused the animal to release its offensive spray. She walked around the house once, then tried to focus her mind on the day Martha went missing. She tried to remember where she had been when she first realized Martha was gone. She pictured herself back in the Hall, in the room she shared with the other girls, and attempted to recall the sounds of their voices.

Instead she saw herself the day after. Heard the matron's iron voice in her ear and felt her angry words like slaps against her face.

"Martha," Eugenia breathed. "It was so hard after you were gone. I missed you so much."

She often wondered if things would have turned out differ-ently, if she herself would have turned out differently, had Martha remained there with her at Vandegrift Hall. For all her timidity, there had been a kind of strength in Martha, a calmness and pla-cidity that made anyone near her feel momentarily better about the world. Hopeful, even.

"I wish I could have helped you somehow," Eugenia said to the crumbling stones of the house and the rustling leaves of the trees. She kicked at a clump of earth beneath her feet. "I wish *some*one had helped you that day."

Suddenly a hand touched her arm. Eugenia whirled in shock and clutched at her chest in alarm. An ancient woman with white hair and black, wrinkled skin was standing behind her. The woman was dressed in a bright green polyester jogging suit, and when she saw the expression on Eugenia's face, her lips pursed. "Scared you, I guess."

Eugenia nodded. "Yes, you did. I thought you were Martha."

"Who?"

"Do you live around here?" Eugenia asked.

The old woman pointed to the trees on Eugenia's right. "I live back there."

"There's a house over there?"

"Trailer," said the old woman. "Lived there for years." Her eyes narrowed then. "What you doin' here? Lookin' for rocks? Arrowheads? What?"

"Just . . . looking," Eugenia answered. "I came here a long time ago, when I was a child."

"You run away from the Hall?" asked the old woman, and Eugenia turned to look at her in surprise.

"How did you know?"

The old woman snorted and reached in her pocket for a tissue. "Think you were the first?" she asked, and then she blew her nose. "Someone was runnin' away from that place every other day."

"I never knew you were here," said Eugenia.

The old woman hawked and spit. "Few did." She moved away from Eugenia then. "Don't stay too long, hear? It's gettin' cold out."

"Wait." Eugenia walked after her, but the old woman kept moving.

"Can't do it. Gotta answer nature's call."

"May I come along and wait?" Eugenia asked. "I'd like to talk to you."

"Suit yourself," said the old woman. "You may be here a bit. Things don't happen for me like they used to."

Eugenia smiled politely and followed the old woman through the trees. The tiny mobile home was nearly as old as its owner, and well hidden in the thick copse of trees surrounding it. The screens on the windows were red with rust; plywood patches decorated the outside of the trailer, the original color of which was indistinguishable. Eugenia frowned as she tried to imagine living in such a place.

"Walkin's practically the only thing moves my bowels anymore," said the old woman as she lumbered up the concrete blocks in front of the trailer to open the door.

"You seem very active," said Eugenia, also impressed with the woman's obviously quick mind.

"I'm eighty-six years old. Ain't too damned active no more."

Eugenia cleared her throat as she followed the woman inside her trailer. "My name is Eugenia Fairfax. Could I please know your name?"

"Odaline Burkey," said the woman as she left Eugenia in the tiny living room and disappeared down the dark hall. "Make yourself comfortable, Eugenia. Get some water if you like. Ain't got nothin' else to drink."

Eugenia heard a door slam then, and she assumed Odaline Burkey had gone into her bathroom. She sat down on a throw-covered sofa and looked around herself. Instead of the usual pictures of relatives and friends, there were framed pictures of soap opera stars on top of the television and on various end tables. Eugenia recognized characters from at least four soaps and smiled to herself when she saw a large autographed picture of Bob Barker, the host of "The Price Is Right." She was fascinated and at the same time saddened by Odaline Burkey's living room.

When the old woman finally emerged from the bathroom she looked tired. She entered the living room with feeble movements and took her time sitting down in a faded and cracked wooden rocker beside the television. When she was comfortable, she looked expectantly at Eugenia.

"What you wantin' to know?" she asked. "You ain't one of them social workers, are you?"

"No," Eugenia assured her. "I'm only curious to know if you remember something that happened out here many years ago, Mrs. Burkey."

She smiled. "You already got my memory workin', tryin' to remember when I got married."

"Miss Burkey," Eugenia corrected, and sat forward. "Years ago, when I lived at Vandegrift Hall, there was a girl who lived there with me by the name of Martha Box. One day Martha disappeared, and it was assumed she was one of the girls who got on the train in the middle of the night. I always knew differently in my heart, and yesterday I learned from a local man that I was right.

Some boys took Martha and they brought her here, to the old Hickok place.''

Eugenia paused for breath and looked at Odaline Burkey. The woman's face had become tinged with sadness.

"You know?" Eugenia asked. "You know what I'm talking about?"

Odaline nodded. "They brung more than one out here. Them boys was just no good, you know it? Just no damn good."

Eugenia stared. "You mean they brought girls here and did . . . what they did to Martha?"

One bony shoulder lifted. "Killed just one that I knowed of. My dogs come across her one night, buried 'bout fifty yards in the brush from that stone house yonder. I figured their yappin' must've scared away whoever done it, because she weren't buried very good at all. I went out and got my dogs in and figured to get the sheriff in the mornin'. Din't have no phone then, see. Thing was, when I brought in the police, they couldn't find nothin'. Called me crazy and told me never to trouble 'em again. Got back to my place here and found every one of my dogs layin' dead. Tracks all over, big boots like them boys used to wear. They come back and took her and killed my dogs. That weren't enough, but they left a message on my door."

"What was the message?" Eugenia asked.

"Same old ugly business. A piece of rope all tied up like a noose, left hangin' on my doorknob."

Eugenia swallowed. "You never told anyone else about Mar— the dead girl?"

"I told anybody who asked. You just asked me."

"Who else? Who else asked?"

"The old matron up the hill. The Dutch woman. That one come from a long line of meanness, she did."

Eugenia was surprised. "How did she come to ask you?"

Odaline lifted her shoulder again. "Walked right in here same as you did and asked me if I'd seen a pretty red-haired runaway. I said that girl didn't run nowhere, she was murdered by town boys and buried out yonder. The matron just give me a look and went out. Never saw her again. Always sent someone else after that.''

"Sent someone else?"

"To look for the youngsters that run away. Some of 'em made it out to me. Most didn't. I helped who I could and tried to mind my own business. Sometimes I think it's a bad spot I'm livin' in, like a big open sore on the earth that just keeps fillin' up with pus.''

Eugenia stared at the old woman again. "I think it's a bad spot, too," she murmured.

Odaline gazed at her, her expression vague. "They just keep comin' back, don't they? Like the biggest damn circle you ever saw.''

There was silence in the tiny trailer for several moments. Then Eugenia shook herself and got to her feet.

"Thank you, Miss Burkey, for telling me what you know. I appreciate it.''

"Don't," she said. "I'll never forgive myself for being such a coward about that whole thing. Always thought I shoulda done more.''

Eugenia went to the old woman and grasped her by the shoulders. "You did all you were meant to do. Good-bye, Miss Burkey. I hope we meet again.''

Odaline only nodded. Eugenia let herself out of the trailer and inhaled deeply of the brisk air as she stepped onto the concrete blocks to the ground. She didn't have Martha, but now she knew more than she had known that morning.

TWENTY-ONE

ROSS stumbled back into the brush and fell over a fallen limb when he saw Eugenia coming over the path. He had intended for her not to see him, but the noise of his fall was loud enough to make her steps halt and cause her to peer anxiously in his direction. Ross staggered to his feet and wished he hadn't drunk so much beer the night before. He felt nauseous and light-headed as he stepped out where Eugenia could see him.

"Well?" he said as he watched her shoulders relax.

Her nostrils widened as he approached, and he wondered if he smelled as bad as he looked.

"Go home, Mr. Schweig," said Eugenia, and she moved past him with firm steps. Ross reached out and snagged her by the arm, causing her to bolt back and stare at him in alarm.

"Sorry," he said. "I'm sorry I did that. Just stop a minute and tell me what you found. Anything?"

Eugenia rubbed her arm where he had grabbed it and kept backing away. "I found nothing."

"Okay. That's all you had to say." Ross hated the way she was looking at him, like she was scared and trying not to show it. What the hell was she afraid of? Him?

"Stop looking at me like that, dammit. What do you think I'm going to to do, jump you and drag you back into the brush?"

"No," Eugenia said, stopping suddenly. "You wouldn't do that, because Odaline Burkey would hear me screaming and call the police."

"Oda who?"

"Odaline Burkey, the old woman who lives in a trailer not far from the Hickok place. She's lived there for years."

Ross stared past her up the path. "Her. I forgot about her. The guys—" He paused, then asked, "She's still alive?"

"Very much so. I've just had a chat with her."

Eugenia started walking again, and Ross hurried after her.

"What did you ask her?"

"What do you think, Mr. Schweig?" Eugenia glanced sideways at him. "I don't know what you're so worried about. You've told everyone I'm either mentally ill or teetering on the brink, and just as no one believed Odaline Burkey all those years ago, no one will believe me. That's what you wanted, isn't it? To avoid taking responsibility for what happened to Martha?"

Ross opened his mouth to snarl something at her; then he closed it again. She was right, and it seemed ridiculous in that moment to deny it.

"What did the old woman say?" he asked. "You said no one believed her. About what?"

"Her dogs found Martha's partially buried body. When she went to report it to the sheriff the next day, it disappeared. She returned home and found her dogs dead and a noose over her doorknob."

Ross stumbled over a rock and nearly fell down. Eugenia reached out automatically to steady him. He turned his face away from her and her hand fell away from his arm.

"You knew they killed her," she said in a quiet voice.

"Yeah, I guess." Ross couldn't believe he was crying again. The tears rolled down his cheeks. "I just can't see them doing it. I mean, they were my friends. At least I thought they were. I can't see them burying a dead body.''

"You were drinking that night?''

"We were always drinking. That didn't mean anything.''

"On this occasion it did,'' said Eugenia. "Things went too far and everyone was obviously very afraid. Or just sick.''

"I always thought Sharp and Lewin were sick,'' muttered Ross, and Eugenia stopped again.

"Who?''

Ross took her arm and pushed forward again. "It doesn't matter now. They're both dead.''

Eugenia gently removed her arm from his grasp. "Was there someone else?''

"Just Rad. Rad Lanyard. I've already been to see him. He doesn't remember anything. He's a drunk now.''

One dark brow lifted, giving Eugenia an arch look that reminded Ross of Lena. She was silent, but Ross knew what she was thinking: who's the drunk here?

He told himself he wouldn't touch her again. He hadn't missed the way she pulled her arm out of his hand.

"Eugenia, I'm sorry,'' he told her suddenly. "I'm sorry for everything I said to Lorraine about you. I didn't know what I was doing. I was desperate, and I still am. I thought if I sicced her on you and your daughter, you'd both go away and things would get back to normal. I thought *I* would get back to normal.''

"I understand,'' Eugenia said as they reached her car on the path. "You really should go home now, Ross. You look exhausted.''

"I need to go in and open up the shop. I heard Rafael got beat up last night. Lorraine said Lena helped him.''

Eugenia nodded and opened her car door. "I don't think she'll be persuaded to leave him today.''

Ross looked up in surprise. "Why not?''

Her mouth softened and Eugenia looked quizzically at him. "You really haven't noticed?''

"Noticed what? You're telling me those two are an item?"

"I'm telling you they're deeply in love and struggling with it every inch of the way. Give both of them, and yourself, a break today and let the sandwich shop stay closed."

Ross held on to her car door. "I can't. I can't go home, Eugenia. I can't sleep there. I can't do anything there anymore. I'm beginning to hate my own house, the house my parents lived in, the house I was born in. I can't wait to leave it in the morning."

"Go to Lorraine's place," Eugenia suggested, and Ross saw that her mouth was tight again.

A short, bitter laugh escaped him. "I can't stand her either. No, I'll go in and open up today."

He moved to close her door, but Eugenia put an arm out and held it open. Her face shifted as she spoke, and he could see she was struggling with something herself.

"Come to our place and sleep on the sofa for an hour or two," she said. "I don't believe Martha will come for you while I'm there."

"No," Ross said immediately. "I won't do that."

"You will," said Eugenia. "Don't ask me why I feel compassion for you, Ross Schweig. I don't want to. I just keep remembering something Lena said about you the first time she met you. She said you had kind and gentle eyes, and Lena has never said that about *any* man."

"Sister Superior said that?"

Eugenia looked at him and opened her mouth, then she began to laugh.

Ross watched her and wished suddenly he didn't smell so bad and look so rough.

"Get in," she said to him. "Where is your truck?"

"By the shop."

Ross went around the car and opened the passenger door. He settled in the seat, buckled in, and kept his face straight ahead. He felt Eugenia look at him, and he wanted to tell her he wasn't normally such a mess. Normally he was anyone's idea of a man's man, but circumstances of late had conspired against him and left him feeling less than able.

She understood, he thought, as he dared a quick glance at her. He truly did believe Martha would leave him alone while he was with Eugenia, and much of the resentment and anger he felt toward the Fairfax women slowly began to dissipate as he found himself enjoying a sense of comfort at Eugenia's nearness.

Once at the Lutzes' home she took him inside, showed him to the long, elegant sofa, and went to get him a light blanket and a pillow from one of the beds. Ross sat down on the cushions and took off his shoes. He wished he could take a shower, but he wouldn't ask. Besides, he would still have to put on the same smelly clothes.

"You can shower if you like, and I'll wash your clothes while you sleep," Eugenia offered as she came back with the pillow and blanket.

Ross stared at her. Dumbly, he nodded, and she led the way to the bathroom.

"I'll bring you one of Mr. Lutz's robes to wear."

She left again, and was back a moment later with a blue terry cloth robe. She handed it to him and asked if he was hungry. Ross shook his head.

"Put your clothes in a pile outside the door, and I'll pick them up while you're showering," she told him.

He nodded again and she left him to get started. Ross stripped off his clothes and dumped them outside the door as she requested, taking the time to stick his briefs inside his trousers. He turned on the water and stood for ten minutes beneath the warm spray without moving a muscle.

Finally he picked up a bar of scented soap and began to lather himself.

When he finished, he felt better. He thought he smelled like a goddamned lilac bush, but he felt better.

He toweled off, put on the robe, and was leaving the bathroom door when he heard a phone begin to ring.

"Would you mind getting that?" Eugenia called from some-where within the house.

"Sure," said Ross, "if I knew where it was."

Eventually he located a phone and lifted it to his ear.

"Hello?"

"Ah . . . who is this?" asked a familiar voice.

"Who do you want?" replied Ross.

There was a pause, then, "Lena Fairfax?"

"She's not here right now. Can I take a message?"

"Yes, you can. Tell her Ellen Li called to say her lace curtain is finally ready, and let her know I'm sorry it took so much longer than I said it would."

Ross felt his skin flush. Lorraine's buddy.

"Okay," he said.

"Ross, is that you?"

"Who?"

"Never mind. Thanks."

He hung up the phone and felt guilty all over again for the things he had run and said to Lorraine about Eugenia and Lena. Now Ellen Li was going to run and tattle about Ross being at Lena and Eugenia's house. Christ, what a mess.

"Who was it?" Eugenia came to ask. Her arms were full of folded laundry.

"A seamstress in town said a lace curtain is ready to be picked up."

"Oh, good. Go lie down now, Ross. You look better, but still exhausted."

Ross went to the sofa and did as she said. He was certain he wouldn't be able to sleep, not after Ellen's call, but ten seconds after his head hit the pillow he was on his way to deep, restful slumber.

Radburn Lanyard, known to his few friends as Rad, stumbled out of bed and went to open the medicine cabinet in the tiny, cramped bathroom of his trailer. Last night had been a bad one, with countless shots of tequila on top of half a bottle of Black Jack and at least six beers. He fished around on the shelves for some aspirin and found nothing but a sample package of Tylenol that had come in the mail. He ripped open the package and dumped the contents down his throat. Next he went to the kitchen to open the refrigerator and take out a beer.

He wasn't sleeping for shit. Not since Ross Schweig had come around with his guilty face and wagging fingers.

Rad had completely forgotten about Martha Box. She had been buried away in the part of his mind where he kept all memories that caused guilt, embarrassment, anguish, and suffering. More of her was coming back to him every day, popping up at various times and shocking him with the clarity and intensity of the visuals he was receiving. In response he poured more booze down his pipes, but even that wasn't working. He could still see Martha on the ground, could still feel the softness of her belly when he sank his fist into her for getting blood on his brand-new jeans.

He remembered how the whites of her eyes seemed to glow in the dusk, and how white her thighs looked against the grass.

It was Sharp who killed her. Each of them had taken a turn with her, humping away liked hormone-crazed animals in the trees behind the old stone house. She wasn't the first girl they had taken to the spot, but she was the last, because of what Sharp did. Lewin, who was always laughing, cackled with mirth at watching how sweet Sharp was with her, how helpful he was and the way he kept apologizing to her for doing such a horrible, nasty thing and wondering if she would ever forgive them for cutting her.

Martha said nothing, only looked at him the same way she had looked at him every day for months, as if nothing he ever said or did would matter. Not even this.

Sharp became infuriated and viciously bit into her cheek. When she screamed, he tore away her flesh, and then started hitting her with his fists, pounding at the beautiful face that was soon covered with blood.

Rad remembered shouting, high and soundless, as he watched the blood pour from Martha's nose and cheek. Lewin was still laughing, but hysterically now, and only a brutal kick from Sharp shut him up. Sharp wiped the blood from his slick hands and delivered another kick, this one to Martha's face. Rad rushed forward then and shoved him away.

"Fucking animal! What's wrong with you?"

"What's wrong with you?" Sharp had sneered, his breathing labored.

"You're going to kill her," Rad gasped.

"She's dead," said Lewin from behind them, and Rad looked to see that he was right. Martha was ominously still. Her open eyes stared at nothing.

"What're we gonna do now?" asked Lewin.

"Bury the bitch," said Sharp.

Thirty-five years later, Rad Lanyard was glad to know Sharp was dead. Glad to know he had died a brutal death.

Lewin, too.

But here was Rad with his memories. Ross Schweig was lucky. Goody good boy that he was, it had all been too much for him. Sharp and the others had intended to initiate him that night, to allow him into their little circle and get his first taste of a Vandegrift girl. But Schweig wasn't going for it.

Rad hated him. He hated people who were just naturally good and didn't know any other way to be. It made him sick to think of the way Schweig must look down on him now, the same way he must have looked down on their little group then. He didn't hang out with them after Martha. In fact he avoided them, which pissed off Sharp and Lewin to no end. When news of Martha's disappearance leaked out, the three of them watched Ross carefully, waiting to see if he would say anything to anyone.

They were all relieved when he didn't. And then contemptuous. Coward, they called him. Pussy. Did he think he was too good for the rest of them?

Yeah, Ross told them one day, his face cold and his eyes hard enough to back them down.

Rad and the others did a lot of talking behind Schweig's back after that, but they never spoke to him again, nor he to them. It was just the way things were, for thirty-five years.

Why the hell does he want to know about Martha now? Rad had to wonder. He had to think hard what they did with her. He couldn't remember much after she died, so great was his shock, fear, and horror at witnessing all he had witnessed.

He was sort of hoping he wouldn't remember. He was sort of hoping the whole thing would just go away again, the way it had the first time. It appeared he wasn't going to be lucky enough to die and get away from it the way Sharp and Lewin had.

But then, they were probably in some other kind of hell, custom-made by Martha Box.

TWENTY-TWO

EUGENIA was there when Dixon's aide stole soundlessly into Audrey's tiny room just before dawn and slipped a thin strip of rawhide around the scout's neck. He used a stick to twist and tighten the strip, and in the same motion he dragged the scout off the bed and away from the sleeping Audrey. Though the scout fought viciously and managed to gouge one of the aide's eyes with his thumb, the rawhide was already dislodging his windpipe. Audrey awakened at the sound of the aide's angry cry of pain, and instantly she scrambled for the weapon she kept hidden under her bed.

Her knife was nowhere to be found. The aide had anticipated her action and removed the blade. An anguished scream came from Audrey as she watched the murder of her lover, and the aide threw the blade at her to silence her.

The sharp point struck Audrey in the throat and hung suspended, until her clawing hands yanked out the knife. The metal edge sliced through her carotid and blood sprayed the room. Audrey's slide to the floor was noiseless. The aide shoved the scout away from him and cursed at the still-spurting blood coming from

Audrey's throat. Her eyes were closed, but her heart was still pumping, pushing the blood out through the wound.

It was going to have to be a murder-suicide instead of a double suicide, with the scout killing the laundress and then hanging himself.

It would be the scout's idea to make it look like a double suicide, first hanging his paramour and then himself.

The aide placed a hand to his head when the vision in his eye began to darken. His palm came away covered with blood.

"Son of a bitch," he cursed, and kicked the motionless form of the scout.

A stab of pain accompanied the movement, and the vision in his wounded eye failed completely. The aide cursed again, then began to cry in fear.

Half an hour later he realized he was still sitting in the room with the bodies, and it was getting light outside. He knew that because he could still see with his one good eye. Fearing the commander's wrath, he hastily fixed up the nooses and strung up first the laundress and then the scout, using the rafters and her heavy bedside table to stand on. With the ropes around their necks, the other wounds were virtually hidden, and the aide realized no one need ever know about his bloody blunder. There wasn't much blood on Audrey; most of it was on the bedclothes.

The aide gathered up the sheets and hauled them next door to the laundry. He told the white-haired old woman he had injured his eye, lost his sight, and bled all over his bedclothes. When she stared at the swollen, reddened mess that used to be his eye, he wanted to growl at her, and when she asked him how it had happened he told her it was in the line of duty and to shut up her stupid questions. She did.

Hours later the bodies of Audrey and the scout were discovered, and the entire fort came to a halt as the news spread. The scout was liked by many, as was Audrey, and the truth of their relationship came as a great shock to those who had known them. Annabeth De Peyster Dixon refused to let the bodies be moved until she had gone to Audrey's room to view them for herself. Several thought her behavior ghastly, even ghoulish, but none would admit it aloud.

Annabeth's eyes gleamed as she surveyed the tragic pair, and moments later, outside, she smiled sweetly and clucked her tongue as she happened to catch the eye of her passing husband.

"True love seems ever doomed, doesn't it, dear?"

Her husband made no response, only moved to order some men to go in and cut the two down. The bodies were to be taken outside the walls of the fort and buried without markers. Annabeth demanded it be so.

The stiffened bodies were loaded onto a wagon and taken a half mile from the fort, where they were dumped without ceremony on the ground and buried in a single grave. The burial detail laughed and joked while they dug, and one or two commented on the bandage over the eye of their fellow soldier, the commander's aide.

He smirked and told them he had walked into a bayonet.

Not one of them believed him, and several looked long at the wound in the dead woman's neck, but no words were spoken. Sometimes it was better that way.

Tears slid down Eugenia's cheeks as she watched the dirt cover the faces of Audrey and the scout. A drop rolled off the tip of her nose onto her chin and she opened her eyes to find Ross Schweig lying on the couch and looking at her.

"Does it hurt?" he asked.

"Yes," she said. "It hurts terribly."

He closed his mouth and was silent. Then he said, "When you go where you go, are you still aware of you?"

She blinked. "In a way, yes." She looked at him then. "How did you know, Ross?"

"How did I know what?"

"That I was there, in the past."

He lifted himself on one elbow. "It's hard to explain. Your face just looked . . . different. And I could tell you weren't really asleep, but you weren't here, either. Like that day outside the deli.''

Eugenia nodded. "Yes."

"What were you seeing?"

She drew a deep breath, then slowly exhaled as she seemed to make some decision within herself.

"I was seeing the murder of two people who lived at the fort. An Indian scout and a laundress."

Ross sat all the way up and clutched the blanket with his fingers. "You mean like a long time ago?"

"Yes, that's what I mean."

"Why?" he asked. "I mean, I know you're psychic or something, you have to be, but why are you seeing these things?"

"I don't know, Ross. I wish I knew. I can tell you some of the people in these visions resemble people I know now, and I can also tell you I'm frightened to the point of being terrified for Lena and Rafael, because in my visions they have become the two people I just saw murdered."

Ross went on staring at her, and she grew suddenly uncomfortable. When he realized what he was doing he hastily apologized. Then he looked at his watch. It was exactly two hours since he had lain down and closed his eyes. He felt much better. He felt completely rested.

He stood. "I can't thank you enough for allowing me to come over."

"Have I frightened you?" she asked, her gaze steady.

"Yeah," he admitted, and he began to look around for his clothes.

"They're on the bed in the bedroom," she said. "You can go in there and change."

"Thanks," he said again, and as he left the room Eugenia wondered why his face had not entered her vision as John Dixon this time; and why the aide no longer resembled in any fashion the driver of the blue Camaro.

She began to wonder if she truly was behind the matching of present faces to past circumstances.

Rafael saw Ross and Eugenia leave the house next door and he thought to wake Lena, but she had been resting so comfortably when he left her he was loath to disturb her. To say he was surprised at Ross's presence next door was an understatement. To see him open the door for Eugenia, the driver's door, and then walk around to the passenger door left Rafael dumbfounded. This was not the Ross he had grown accustomed to in the last week. Something had happened.

"What are you looking at?" A yawning Lena walked up behind him and peered out the window in time to see her mother's blue Taurus back down the driveway.

"Is that Ross?" Lena asked.

"Yeah."

"What's he doing with Mom?"

"I don't know. I just saw them come out of the house."

"Ross was in our house?"

"Yeah."

"What did the pig want?"

"Lena," Rafael chided.

"He is a pig. He's mean and temperamental and rude."

Rafael turned to look at her. "And you're not?"

Lena's eyes rounded. "Me? You think I'm—"

His lips on her mouth silenced her. "Let's go find something to eat."

Lena relented under the warmth of his kiss. "Do you have anything in the kitchen?"

"Some eggs." He looked at the clock in the living room. "Guess Ross decided not to open up today. You should have gone in, Lena."

"How could I? I don't have the keys to open up."

"One of us should have gone in."

"You're very prepared, obviously."

"I feel all right."

She smiled at him. "Now you do."

He grabbed a handful of her bottom and pulled her to him. He held her tightly, then released her to tip her head back and kiss her. When he lifted his head he looked seriously into her eyes and said, "I love you, Lena. Get used to hearing it, because I'm going to keep saying it."

Her breath caught in her throat and he said it again.

"I love you."

"Rafael . . ."

"I want to marry you. I want you to be the mother of my children."

"We haven't known each other long enough to—"

"My heart is yours, Lena."

"You said you would be patient with me."

"I said I love you, and love is always patient. Lust is the impatient one."

"Do you want some eggs?"

"I want your eggs, fertilized with my seed."

Lena smacked at him. "Will you stop?"

"I can't. I love you."

He was smiling now, and unable to help herself, Lena was smiling with him.

"Say it," he coaxed. "Tell me what your heart says."

"My heart says listen to my stomach, and my stomach says eat."

Rafael lowered his head and gently kissed her lips, pulling and caressing until she responded to him. Her arms twined around his neck and soon her breath was coming in gasps. She leaned her forehead against him and said, "I can't believe what you do to me."

"Say it," he murmured. "Tell me."

"Rafael, I've never said what you want me to say. I've never said it to anyone."

"I'm glad," he said. "It makes me love you even more."

He went on kissing her, framing her head with her hands and treating her so sweetly it brought sighs from her chest.

"Tell me, baby," he asked. "Please tell me."

A sudden sob from her made him blink and pull away. Her eyes were squeezed shut and her hands came up to cover her mouth.

"I'm sorry," he whispered. "I'm sorry, Lena. I'll stop. I won't ask anymore."

"Rafael," she sobbed, and she repeated his name several times before he was able to calm her. He held her and began to wonder just what he had asked of her. He pulled her head close and whispered again how much he loved her, and that it was all right if she couldn't say it yet. He would be patient. He would wait.

"What if I can't ever say it?" she cried, genuinely distraught. "What if I ruin things between us?"

Rafael looked at her and said, "You can't. I won't let you. And we'll work on the other, because I need you to tell me. I need to hear it from you, Lena."

She nodded her head against his shoulder and he held her even tighter, loving her so fiercely it hurt him deep inside. Her crying tore at his chest like no pain he had ever known. He attempted to smile again. "Come on. We can split a three-egg omelet."

It was several moments before she leaned away. "You have only three eggs?"

"Yeah, I think."

"Let's have French toast, then. Do you have any bread?"

"Not much."

"How about syrup? Do you have any syrup, or powdered sugar?"

"No."

"Forget the French toast. We'll split the omelet."

Rafael smiled and escorted her to the kitchen, where he took the eggs from the refrigerator while she removed a bowl from the cupboard. She cracked the eggs into the bowl and he handed her some milk. Lena threw the shells away and told him his garbage needed to be taken out. Rafael cinched up the trash bag and took it outside to the cart. When he opened the lid he saw the bat that had broken his living room window. He thought the police had taken it with them to check for fingerprints, but Eugenia must have picked it up and tossed it in the trash.

Rafael found himself staring at the brownish stains on the bat and flashing back to a night that seemed a lifetime ago. A night he remembered only vaguely. He saw himself sitting on Roberto Pena's back porch and listening to the sounds of an argument inside the house. Pena's younger siblings were always going at each other, always pulling hair or kicking and shoving. Doors slammed all over the house and Pena started laughing.

"Be glad you ain't got no brothers or sisters, man. Little fuckers are mean."

A light breeze blew away the smoke and the smell of the pipe Rafael was sucking on. He took one last hit on Pena's hash and put his hand up to his face in an attempt to check his breath. Pena watched him and shook his head.

"You were stoned when you got here, Chavez. You goin' t'see that straight little white chick again?"

"Gimme a breath mint," Rafael responded. Pena always carried breath mints. And yeah, he was going to see his girlfriend, who Pena couldn't stand because she was one of the few pretty girls in town who wouldn't even look at him. She liked Rafael.

"Okay." Pena dug in his pocket and took his time unwrapping the package. Rafael frowned as he watched.

"What are you doing?"

"Nothing. Here." He handed over a mint and Rafael put it in his mouth and crunched it up.

"You eat it?" Pena asked.

"Yeah. Why?"

Pena started laughing again, and he informed Rafael he had just slipped him some acid.

"How?"

"How do you think, stupid? It was on that breath mint you just gobbled."

"Goddammit, Pena. Do I ever do that kind of shit to you?"

"Hey, it was a joke, okay? Here, take another mint. You'll be okay for her." Pena fished out another breath mint and Rafael took it and chewed it up while Pena made a terrible face. "Uh-oh. That was the other tab, man. Oh, shit, are you gonna be tripping now, Chavez."

"You did it on purpose," Rafael accused. "You knew I wanted to see my girlfriend, and you did it on purpose. Take me home, you jealous asshole."

Pena laughed. "I gotta go by this house first and pay this guy for something."

"For what? Take me home, Pena. Goddammit, what did you do to me?"

"Relax, okay? I've done two before. This stuff isn't that good. I'll get you home all right."

Pena drove to a house on the other side of town and talked the entire time. After a while, Rafael caught only bits and snatches of what his friend was saying. Rafael was already on his way out. When Pena pulled up outside a house and made a nasty comment about the two fat black widows who lived in the place next door, Rafael found himself staring with round eyes at the two females peering out the window at him. Pena's offhand comment altered Rafael's perception to the point where their eyes appeared huge and red to him, their bodies black and shiny.

He sat in the car what seemed an eternity, waiting for what he couldn't seem to remember. He rolled the window up and then down again, watching the movement of his hand and being freaked-out by the way the cells of his skin appeared to merge with the handle and then with the inside of the door, seemingly disappearing into the upholstery. Then he heard a shout from somewhere, followed by a scream, and suddenly Rafael saw Pena inside the house with the two huge black spiders. Pena was trying to get away from them, but their long legs kept groping and trapping him. They were spinning a web around him, covering his body and finally his scarlet, screaming face. Rafael's arms and legs twitched as he twisted around in the car to search for a weapon, something to carry into battle. His hands closed around an object lying in the backseat and he pulled it out of the car with him as he opened the door and stumbled out.

He didn't remember entering the house, or anything that happened next. All he remembered was the high, keening noise that came from the spiders, and Pena's muffled voice screaming at him . . . from outside the house.

The older Rafael stared at the innocuous-looking piece of wood in his garbage and felt a series of shudders overtake him. Some part of him had always wondered if Pena had not in fact been inside the house when Rafael saw him; possibly to steal from the women. The spiders had come out in therapy, but the memory was too painful, too shocking and all too real to him still, so he shoved it away.

He slammed the lid on the trash cart.

Inside the kitchen, the smell of the omelet Lena was cooking filled his nostrils. She was standing at the stove and holding a spatula, her brown eyes on the contents of the skillet. Rafael looked at her and wondered if he could ever bring himself to tell her about that terrible night, and if it would make any difference in how she felt about him.

He moved to stand behind her. "Smells good."

She smiled as his arms came around her waist. "I'm practically salivating."

Rafael leaned his bandaged head against hers. "I'm glad you stayed with me, Lena."

"Me, too." She turned to look at him then. "You really should buy some groceries."

"I will," he said. "Now."

TWENTY-THREE

DETECTIVE Morales walked around the chair occupied by Lorraine Lake's tall blond son and made a move as if to cuff him on the head. The kid didn't flinch.

"You think we're stupid, Lake?" he asked in irritation. "You think we don't know you're the one after Chavez?"

"Prove it," said Lake.

"I don't have to. You're the only one with any motive to go after him."

Lake laughed. "Tell that to my mom. Her friends might disagree with you."

"Police file photos and bloody bats aren't their style, asshole. They prefer direct intimidation over these prepubescent Tiny Toon terrorist tactics."

"I don't know what you're talking about," said Lake, his unlined face calm.

"No, I guess you wouldn't," said Morales. "You've managed to keep your prints off everything so far, and you used enough sense to wear a stocking cap on your head when you did the chickenshit thing and blindsided him. But lemme tell you something, Lake. Chavez may be dirt, but under the laws of this city, state, and country he still has a few rights. Stop messing around with him, or I'm going to see to it that someone messes with you.''

"Someone besides your daughter, huh?'' said Lake with a hint of a smile. "She's got too many damned moles.''

Morales looked up, but he made no other movement. He wasn't fooled. The stupid shit. Morales's daughter had her heart set on the church. She wasn't going to dirty herself with anyone or anything but the blood of Christ.

Finally he looked at the file before him and set about making some notes.

"What are you writing?'' Lake asked after several minutes.

"Just a few notes for the judge about your sparkling wit and effervescent personality. Tell me, what do your initials stand for? J.D. stands for something, right? Something besides 'jerk-off juvenile dick-faced delinquent'?''

Lake smiled again. "It stands for 'just dandy.' ''

Morales picked up the phone and punched in a number. He spoke to someone, asked them a question, then thanked them and replaced the receiver. He made another notation on the file, writing along the top; then he looked at the young man sitting across from him.

"Get your ass out of here and don't let me see you again.''

Lake winked at him. "Tell your daughter I said hi.''

"Together?'' Eugenia asked as she stared at Ross.

"Yeah,'' he said. "Me and you.''

"Why would you want to go through the fort with me?''

"Not just the fort,'' Ross explained. "Vandegrift Hall. I want to go there.''

"Why?'' Eugenia repeated.

Ross finished unlocking the door of the deli. "Maybe Martha will come to you while we're there. Maybe she'll tell you what she wants from me.''

"You don't know?''

"No.''

"How about justice? Maybe she'd like a little of that."

"From who, Eugenia? Sharp and Lewin are dead now, and the only other guy who was there is a drunk who might as well be dead."

"And there's you, Ross," Eugenia reminded him.

His look for her was hard. "You're not going to let me forget it, either, are you?"

"No more than she, apparently."

"Which is exactly why I want you to go with me," said Ross as he gestured for Eugenia to go into the shop ahead of him. "The two of you obviously think alike. You said she wouldn't come for me while I was sleeping on your couch, but who knows what could happen if we walk through the fort."

"Ross . . ."

"Eugenia, please. It's just for an hour or so. I won't let anything happen to you, I promise, even if you go into one of your catatonic things."

"It's more of a hypnagogic state," she informed him.

"Yeah, okay, whatever."

"You said you'd worked in a state hospital once."

"Only for a summer. The patients spooked me." He shook his head. "But they don't spook me anything like Martha."

A flashing reflection of sunlight on metal caught Eugenia's eye, and she looked out the window to see Lorraine Lake emerge from a dark green Bonneville. Lorraine looked up and saw Eugenia at the same moment, and the two women eyed each other through the glass of the sandwich shop.

"Shit," Ross said under his breath when he saw Lorraine. Her blue eyes were cool as she opened the door and walked inside. She fished a notebook out of her purse and opened it up before taking out a pen.

"Just the person I was hoping to see," she said to Eugenia.

"Me?" Eugenia's fine dark brows rose.

"Yes. I'm doing a story on you. I hear you're something of a psychic—but only in Fort Grant. I've checked with your friends

and business associates in Eugene, and they all seemed very surprised to hear about your abilities. In fact, I'd say they were
shocked."

Eugenia's eyes were round as she stared. "You called Eugene?"

"Of course. Ross here said you were worth checking out. One
woman, your neighbor, I believe, swears you are normally the
sweetest, most intelligent woman she's ever known, but she says
you *have* been having some problems since the death of your husband. She was really very worried about you."

"Why are you doing this?" Eugenia asked. "Because I defended Rafael Chavez? Because I made his business my business?"

Lorraine ignored her. "Tell me about the ghosts at the fort. I
hear you go into trances of some sort and speak with the dead.
Would you call yourself a medium?"

Eugenia looked helplessly at Ross.

Ross swallowed guiltily and looked at his feet.

"Lorraine," he said slowly, "would you please just go away?
Forget I ever said anything. Forget I ever came by, would you?"

"You've got to be kidding me," she said with a smile. "This is
farfetched, but it's still a good story. Now, Eugenia, did you discover these psychic abilities as a child, or did they come to you
only after the death of that husband your neighbor referred to?"

Eugenia fought to maintain control; she struggled to shield
herself from the woman's antipathy and antagonism, but in Lorraine Lake's voice she was hearing a voice from the past, a voice
that told her over and over again she was nothing but trash, nothing but useless, worthless human refuse to be dealt with in the only
way society saw fit.

"I have nothing to say to you," she said in a voice that cracked.

"Excuse me?" Lorraine put a hand to her ear.

"Get out," said Ross. "Get out now, Lorraine."

"Oh, what's wrong? Don't you need me anymore, Ross? Aren't
you still tired and ashamed of running away from the closeness

you said you experienced with me?'' She turned to Eugenia. ''Has he said any of this to you yet?''

Eugenia looked away from her.

Lorraine smiled again. ''Well, I suppose your response is going to be 'no comment.' I'll just write that down now, shall I?''

''Don't do it, Lorraine,'' said Ross, and he took a step forward.

''Is that a plea or a threat?''

''It's both. I have friends in this town, too, you know.''

Lorraine opened her mouth and began to laugh. She was still laughing as she flipped closed her notebook and put away her pen. The complete and utter amusement in her face appeared purely evil to Eugenia. She was reminded of Annabeth De Peyster Dixon's face the day she went in to look at the bodies of the laundress and the scout.

No one would dare to thwart Annabeth De Peyster Dixon in her aims and desires, and it appeared Lorraine Lake enjoyed the same distinction.

When the dark green Bonneville was gone, Ross turned to Eugenia.

''I'm sorry. I can't tell you how sorry I am. I'm embarrassed and ashamed of myself for ever approaching that woman. Hell, I'm embarrassed to have ever touched her, let alone talked to her about you.''

Eugenia didn't look at him. ''I'm going now.''

''Eugenia, wait. Please.''

''For what?'' She wheeled suddenly and poked a hard finger in Ross's chest. ''Just what sort of man are you, Ross? What kind of life have you led, never marrying, only sleeping with women you can't stand, and telling yourself you're still a good person. You're *not*. As far as I'm concerned, you're the lowest kind of man, a man who watches and sees but keeps his mouth shut, not just about Martha Box, but about everything going on in this town, including Lorraine's little terrorist group, the CBFG. The most galling thing about you is the way you expect me to help you. You expect it, and I haven't disappointed you thus far, have I? Little Eugenia is still doing things to please the townsfolk who look down on her. She's still hoping to be accepted in some way and begging for some small measure of affection." Eugenia paused and removed her finger. "I'm not that little girl anymore. I don't have to do anything for you, and I don't have to put up with the likes of Lorraine Lake."

Before Ross could open his mouth, she twisted on her heel and stalked away. He went after her as she yanked open the door, but no sounds came from his mouth. Eugenia got into her car and drove away, without giving him another glance.

At home she went next door and nearly burst into tears while telling Lena and Rafael about Lorraine Lake. Her hands were shaking as she finished, and Lena put down her fork to rise and place her arms around her mother. Rafael stood also and came to sit on the other side of her.

"It's just a story, Eugenia," he said in an attempt to console her. "She's been writing stories about me for years."

"It's not just a story," Eugenia argued. "It's my life we're talking about. She's calling people in Eugene and asking these horrible leading questions. How can I ever go home and face them?"

"Mom," Lena said gently, "if Dad were here, he would tell you it doesn't make any difference what anyone else thinks. How *you* think is what's important."

"Yes, I know that. I know. Lena, Rafael, you can't understand what it's like to hear all those old voices again and feel the old feelings. I was like some frightened, pathetic animal, trapped and cornered."

"I do know," Rafael said. "I do know how you feel, Eugenia. Remember?"

She drew a deep breath and looked at each of their faces while she attempted to calm herself.

"Yes, I do remember. I'm sorry." She looked at Lena then. "I know I shouldn't say this now, not now, but I am ready to go home. I don't want to stay here anymore."

Rafael's gaze swiftly lifted to meet Lena's.

Lena swallowed. "You're probably feeling the need to go home and defend yourself, don't you think?"

"It's more than that," Eugenia insisted. "It's the sense that I've done all I came here to do, and if I stay any longer I'm going to start regressing. Do you understand?"

"No, I don't," Lena told her. "You said before if we left now you'd feel like we were leaving three-quarters of the way through the movie."

Eugenia gripped her daughter by the shoulders and squeezed. "Lena, I've already seen how this movie ends. Please, please believe me."

Lena looked past her to Rafael, and Eugenia turned to see him sitting on the edge of his seat, his face tense, his hands clenched.

"Don't take her from me," he said when Eugenia looked at him. "Please don't take her away now."

"I'm sorry, Rafael."

"Maybe . . . maybe I could put you on a plane," Lena suggested.

"How would I get around at home?" Eugenia asked.

"I don't know. We could ask someone to drive the car to Eugene. People take out ads in the paper all the time."

"Are you telling me to find another partner for the business? Are you saying you're in love with Rafael and you want to live here with him?"

Rafael waited, his dark eyes glued to Lena's face, and Eugenia waited, her breathing still shallow. Lena looked at her hands and said nothing.

"Lena," Eugenia said finally, "you're part of the reason we need to go. It's something I've seen in the visions that frightens me. I don't want to worry you, or Rafael, but there is a person here who means to do both of you great harm."

Lena and Rafael glanced at each other.

"We know that, Mother. He's already harmed Rafael."

"He's not finished yet. It's the boy in the blue Camaro, the one who sits and watches the house."

"Boy?" said Rafael.

"He's probably eighteen or so," said Eugenia, "but he's very big for his age. Tall, with broad shoulders."

"Is his hair blond?" asked Rafael.

"Yes."

"Who is it?" asked Lena.

"The jerk who kicked that poor kid in the head. The one Morales asked me about. At first I thought it was because he believed I could identify him. Now I don't think he cares whether I can identify him or not. Who's going to give a damn what happens to me?"

"I do," Lena murmured.

"And so do I," said Eugenia, "but Lena is my daughter and my main priority. I don't want anything to happen to her."

"So you want me to come with you and leave Rafael here?" Lena asked.

"Rafael has to stay here until he finishes his parole, Lena. You know that."

"How many more months?" Lena asked him.

Rafael shook his head. "Not months, baby. Years."

He and Lena looked at each other, and Eugenia's heart wanted to break at what she was doing to them. She ought to know better, she told herself. More than anyone, she should know how little control a person actually had over fate. What was she hoping to change by running away? Lorraine's article would still be written and read by everyone in Fort Grant. The blond boy in the Camaro would still seek to brutalize Rafael, and Ross Schweig would still be living his nightmare with Martha Box. The absence of Eugenia Fairfax would have no bearing on any of these matters.

"We were going to leave in another ten days anyway," Eugenia said. "Did you remember that, Lena?"

She was still looking at Rafael. "Yes."

"We'll stay the ten days."

Lena blinked and looked at her mother. "Until the Lutzes come home?"

"Yes."

Rather than make Lena and Rafael happy, as she had expected, Eugenia's announcement caused both of them to swallow and look away from each other as if in pain.

Eugenia had forgotten how it was with love.

TWENTY-FOUR

ROSS didn't open the sandwich shop. He sat at one of the tables by the window and stared through the glass at the fort, his thoughts echoing all Eugenia had said to him and his mind cringing before the truth. He had indeed spent his entire life avoiding himself. Because he was scared. He was scared of admitting what Eugenia knew, that he was a coward who wanted only to blend in with everyone else and preferred things to go on just the way they were, without change. He had never allowed himself to go near a woman he was genuinely attracted to, always turning the relationship into a combative one to avoid actually caring.

He had never really wondered why. Now he thought he knew. It was because of Martha, because he had been half in love with her and had stood by and watched and done nothing but run away. The hatred he subconsciously maintained for himself refused to allow him to care for anyone else as punishment for his sin of silence. He saw it all clearly, having it laid out for him by the trembling yet defiant Eugenia, who didn't know him at all, but saw all these things with a clarity that was shocking and painful and highly disturbing. Ross didn't know who he was anymore.

Or, rather, he *did* know who he was, but the facts were so unpleasant he wanted to disown himself.

He didn't know what to do. He felt like selling the shop, selling his parents' house, pulling up stakes, and leaving town. Go some place where people didn't know him or what he had done. Or what he hadn't done.

Ross wanted to hate Eugenia. He wanted so badly to hate her for slicing him open and showing him the color of his insides, for taking his cowardice from him and holding it up for all to see. He wanted to, but he couldn't. He had seen the quivering of her limbs when Lorraine spoke. He had sensed the rush of adrenaline in her, the fight or flight response. For a moment he had seen the little girl she spoke of, the one who was timid and afraid and needed affection and reassurance. Ross couldn't hate Eugenia Fairfax. She frightened him, awed him, and aggravated him, but he genuinely admired her.

He also believed he might achieve a sense of absolution with her. He wasn't certain how, but feelings were all he had to go on lately.

There was another feeling he had. The feeling that he had to find Martha, or what was left of her. He had to know where she was.

Without further thought, he rose from the table by the window and left the shop. He was going to see Rad Lanyard again.

"Oh, Christ, what do you want?" asked a smelly, stubble-faced Rad when he saw Ross standing on the rickety steps of his trailer.

"You know what I want," said Ross. "I want to know if you remember anything more."

Rad blinked in the light and backed into his dark living room. "It's too bright out. Come inside."

Ross didn't want to—the air outside was much healthier—but he followed the wispy-haired Rad in.

"Find a place to sit," mumbled his host.

"No, thanks." Ross stayed near the door. "What about it, Rad? Anything else you can tell me about that night?"

Rad reclined on the couch and put an arm over his face.

"Just the stuff you don't want to hear about. You think you been havin' a bad time of it? I can't tell you how bad this has been eatin' at me since you came over. I'd like to kick the shit out of you for ever comin' here in the first place."

Ross inhaled. "What about the old woman? The one in the trailer? You remember anything about some dogs?"

Rad removed his arm. "Dogs?"

"Yeah," said Ross. "Dogs. The ones that started barking while you were burying Martha."

Rad's eyes came wide-open. He sat up and looked at Ross. "What are you talking about? Who told you that?"

"It came by way of the old woman."

"You talked to her? She's still alive?"

"I didn't talk to her," was all Ross said.

"Jesus." Rad's gaze went far away, and since he appeared to be thinking, or remembering, Ross let the silence lengthen. Finally he could stand it no more.

"Well?"

"No," Rad said, and he shook his head. "Nothing. I still can't remember anything."

"You don't remember burying her? Or trying to?"

"No, man, I told you, I can't remember anything."

Anger rose in Ross, but he forced it down. "You look sick, Rad. You still working?"

"Yeah. Barely."

"What's wrong with you? Have you been to a doctor?"

Rad shook his head again. "I haven't thought about that old woman in years, you know? Hell, we thought she was ancient back then, so she must be gettin' up there now. That damned Sharp liked to mess with her." He laughed then. "Sharp liked to mess with everybody, fine son of a bitch that he was."

Ross looked at him without saying anything, and Rad became suddenly angry.

"Why'd you come here, Schweig? Why'd you ever show up to rub my face in this? You needin' to feel good about yourself, or just better'n somebody else?"

A single noise of renewed irritation came from Ross's throat. He wanted to hit Rad. He wanted to hit him hard and pay him back for ever punching Martha that night. But he thought if he started hitting him, he might not be able to stop; he might just keep going, until Rad's face was as red as the blood that had stained his new jeans and made him sink his fist into a terrified girl's belly, a girl who didn't escape with just a blow to the gut.

Before he could do something that would make him even more ashamed, Ross made himself twist the knob behind him and leave the filthy trailer. He could hear Rad screaming at him as he left, calling him names and saying all the things he and Sharp and Lewin had said thirty-five years ago. They were just as true now as they were then, Ross realized, and the knowledge compounded the amount of guano falling on his head that day.

Martha came to sit beside him in the truck on the way home, and Ross looked at everything but her. He thought he could feel her smiling, and something told him he had only just begun to squirm.

Rad stopped yelling when he heard the noise of Ross's truck die away. He cried hard for a few minutes and fought the strings of mucus that trailed from his nose and chin; then he went into his kitchen for a shot of whiskey. As he drank from the bottle he thought of the dogs and the old woman and all he remembered after that. He remembered everything. In the flash of a nanosecond the entire rest of the evening had come back to him, and now his stomach was rumbling with the threat of sending back the precious whiskey he had sent its way.

He cringed at the vision of Lewin trying to get her underpants back on. The deadweight of her legs. The elastic that tore and made Rad think of his own mother's underpants hanging on the clothesline, pink and blue with faded and stretched gray elastic.

The humiliation of watching Martha's humiliation. Telling himself she was a bad girl, a whore's daughter, and she would have ended up a whore anyway. Telling himself it didn't matter what had happened, he really didn't have that big a part in it, hadn't really hurt her or done any of the really bad stuff to her.

Telling himself he was never going to tell anyone what they had done, and agreeing with the others that she had probably done something to deserve it, otherwise it never would have happened.

That was the way things worked, right?

And then there was the rest. Digging and digging and getting the piss scared out of them by the dogs, who barked their particular bark that said something was amiss, beings were about who did not belong.

Scrambling to get away unobserved; hearing the old woman call her dogs off; and then watching her come to see what the hubbub was about. She moved pretty well for someone so old, he remembered thinking.

Her going then, and them running hard to get away before she could call the cops. Until Sharp got to looking around and realized there were no telephone wires leading to her place. No wires of any kind from any direction. That meant she had no phone. Rad was ready to keep going, just get away, but Sharp insisted the three of them go back and get Martha's body. They had to, he said. Someone might have seen Martha in the car with them.

Rad saw them skulking back to get Martha, the three of them shaking now with fear and a grisly kind of excitement. Sharp took her head, while Lewin and Rad carried her legs. He couldn't believe how heavy she was. The three of them carried her clumsily out of the brush and down the path to the car, each boy eyeing every blade of grass that moved as if it were a fully armed policeman ready to jump out and shout they were under arrest.

Sharp took off Martha's blouse and wrapped it around the

bloody leg and foot, so no mess would be made inside Rad's car. Lewin rode in the front seat with Rad, and once they were driving he poked Rad in the side and made a furtive gesture toward the backseat. Rad glanced in the rearview mirror and saw Sharp bending over Martha's body. Unable to see, he turned his head and looked in the backseat. He saw Sharp kneading Martha's breast beneath her bra with one hand and unfastening his jeans with the other.

Lewin and Rad kept their eyes straight ahead while Sharp did what he did. The sounds he made sickened Rad. He couldn't believe where he was and what was happening. He couldn't believe the things he had witnessed and was still witnessing.

But these were his friends, and that's what he kept telling himself that night, over and over. These were his friends, and if they went down, they would all go down together.

In a sense they had, he guessed. Rad had never made himself into the famous singer he intended to be. He had never found a wife, or had any children, or done any of the things someone with a normal life did. Someone who hadn't collaborated in the murder of a young woman.

That night had changed things for all of them. Rad stopped believing he was as good as everyone told him he was, and he started seeing himself as maybe just okay, or at least not as bad as some people, like Charles Manson or the guy who shot John Lennon.

But even that was hard to believe anymore. The booze didn't make anything go away or change things for the better. His trailer was still a dump, his car was still a piece of shit. He was about to lose his job at the lounge for showing up drunk once too often and singing too many Bob Dylan songs.

And then there was Martha, and that long, long drive around the outskirts of town while they listened to Sharp doing what he did and tried to decide what they were going to do with her.

Rad shut off his thinking then. He shut off everything as he walked into the bedroom and took the .38 revolver from his nightstand. He was tired of it. He was tired and sorry and sick of being Radburn Lanyard, lounge singer and drunk. It was time to be something else. He sat down on the bed, put the gun in his mouth, and calmly pulled the trigger.

TWENTY-FIVE

JOHN Dixon Lake did some checking on things before going home to kill his mother. Once he was finished with his surveillance, he happily realized that at least four people who hated his mother's guts would be without an alibi. Rafael Chavez was alone in his house while his girlfriend was out running. His girlfriend's mother was alone at home, and Ross Schweig was getting drunk in the empty lot in front of his sandwich shop. His mom was still at work, but she would be coming home soon, and her loving son would be there to greet her.

He couldn't say exactly when he decided to kill her, but the plan he would use had been taking shape since his talk with Morales. He had to admit it wasn't foolproof, and if he screwed up he'd go down as an adult on murder one. But he didn't intend to screw up. He had established his alibi already, making sure everyone in study hall saw him head back to a private corner of the library, the place serious students went to study undisturbed. There was no other exit but the door, the one leading past everyone again. On his way in, J.D. dropped a fat brown spider at the empty end of a table filled with girls. Once the spider began moving he was counting on their screams to cover his exit, and he was not disappointed. One girl screamed, then another, and the third leaped from her chair, drawing the eyes of everyone in the library as the chair fell over behind her. J.D. watched to see if anyone noticed him leaving. No one did. They were all watching the girls in their battle with the intruder. To return, he would use the oldest trick in the world: back in the door as if he were just leaving the room and shake his head in self-derision. *Forgot my pen.*

It was so simple J.D. knew it would work. And so far it had. He had escaped the library undetected, he had checked out his mother's newest enemies, and now he was going home. On foot. He wasn't overly worried about the neighbors, because most of them worked and were gone during the day. But there was never any way to tell who might be watching, or who might look out the window in a random moment and see J.D.'s Camaro out front. He would have to sneak in the house, kill her when she came home, and sneak out again.

He felt anxious and excited all at once at the thought of actually killing his mom. It wouldn't be like kicking his buddy in the head, or doing Chavez. This would be different. But he had to do it. One reason was to draw some of Morales's heat away from himself, and another reason was to draw sympathy from the community. A poor boy who had lost his best friend and his mother all in one month deserved sympathy. And he might end up with a mutual fund and some money in the bargain.

Besides that, his mom was starting to piss him off, always asking where he was and what he was doing, and forever slipping condoms into his jeans pockets and wallet while he was in the shower. He didn't mind her snooping when it was directed toward other people, but when she turned her antenna on him it was like she became obsessed and even jealous—and how weird was that? A mother jealous of her son.

J.D. had always wondered about her, thought she was a little too loving with her motherly caresses. He had read it was the son who was supposed to fantasize about sleeping with the mother, but this thing was seriously twisted the opposite direction, he believed.

It hadn't been so bad when Ross was around, but J.D. hated Ross and was glad to see him take his sandwich-fixing ass on down the road. Ross got all he wanted. J.D. couldn't believe his mom had been so stupid about the guy. But he guessed she wasn't that stupid; she didn't take him back when Ross came begging.

That Eugenia lady *was* weird, though. She spooked J.D. when she said what she did to him, about knowing who he was inside. He didn't know what the hell it meant, but it made him want to smack her.

He was still thinking about her as he pried the screen off his mother's bedroom window and undid the latch on the window with his penknife. He left the window as it was for the police to find and slipped through the house to the garage. He removed a large claw hammer from his dad's old toolbox and then stole back into the house to wait for his mother.

J.D. was named after his great-great-great-grandfather on his mother's side. Lorraine used to tell how John Dixon had been an exalted commander of the fort, and how for generations afterward the Dixons had enjoyed positions of wealth and influence in the community. J.D. wanted to know why all this wealth and influence had stopped with his mom. Lorraine slapped him and didn't talk about it again.

For that slap, J.D. told himself, and all the others he had been dealt. For all her uppity, snotty bullshit and all her icy looks—that was why he was doing this.

As if he needed a reason.

The last thought made him smile, and he was still smiling when he heard his mother open the front door. His first thought was to keep hiding and leap out behind her. His second thought was what a letdown that would be, not to see the shock and surprise in her face. He wanted to see that. His third thought was to wonder why she was the only reporter on the paper able to leave at three o'clock, when everyone else had to stay until at least five or six. She must have done it with someone who counted, J.D.

thought to himself as he switched the hammer back and forth between his hands.

From his position behind a big wing chair he watched her remove her jacket and toss it over the arm of the sofa. She was humming to herself. From her briefcase she removed her laptop computer, and he could see she was going to finish some work she had started that day. She looked entirely too happy, and J.D. sensed she was anticipating the crucifixion of someone. She always got happy when she did that.

It was probably the article about the Eugenia woman. J.D. had listened to his mother making phone calls out West and heard her asking her nosy-assed questions.

This made things look even better, J.D. realized. Here was his mom, working away on her article about the crazy lady, when either the crazy lady, her daughter, her daughter's boyfriend, or her own ex-boyfriend shows up to murder her.

J.D. rose from behind the chair and sauntered over to the table. "Hi, Mom."

Lorraine gave a start and emitted a tiny shriek of alarm. Then she grew furious.

"Damn you, don't you ever scare me like that."

"Okay," said J.D., and he twisted around to swing the claw hammer like a baseball bat, putting the weight of his body behind the motion.

He glimpsed a look of incredulity in his mother's blue eyes before the hammer made impact with her forehead. Her glasses flew off, her head snapped back, and her body tipped over backward in the chair she was sitting in. She crashed to the floor, still wearing the same look of incredulity below the huge purple dent directly above her nose. He was surprised the thing hadn't sunk right into her brain, he had hit her so hard. She twitched once, just once, and then was still. J.D. bent over her and looked down. Her eyes were still open, but they weren't blinking or anything. The dent in her head was filling with blood underneath the skin.

J.D. stood back and exhaled. That had almost been too easy.

He went into the kitchen and grabbed the sponge on the sink to wipe his prints off the hammer. Any of the possible murderers would do the same thing, he told himself. He dropped the hammer by his mother's body on the way out.

It was okay that his prints were on the toolbox in the garage and everywhere else in the house. Just not on that hammer.

He hoofed it back to school as quickly as he could without calling attention to himself, and on the way he practiced crying.

He cursed in anger when several students he knew saw him hurrying into the school, but he told himself it wouldn't matter. They didn't know shit.

J.D. made his backwards entrance into the library and saw that the place had practically emptied out since he left. That meant the spider was still on the loose. He walked back to the table he had occupied, pretended to pick up something, then swung back toward the door again.

"Wait," a voice said, and J.D. froze. Then he forced himself to relax and turn around to look at the school librarian. She bent over to pick up a piece of paper that had slipped out of his notebook and fallen to the floor.

"This is yours," she said.

"Thanks," he managed. Then a new idea struck him, the idea that a form of insurance might be necessary. Not that he was worried or anything, but after thinking about it a few seconds he realized how clever it would be to add a new character to the play. He looked around for someone in study hall he could take home with him; someone who had been there the whole time and knew that J.D. had been there the whole time, too.

"Hey, Jared," he said to a kid gathering up his books and preparing to leave.

Jared nodded and looked mildly surprised. He had played baseball with J.D., but never socialized with him.

"What're you doin' after school?" J.D. asked him. "Anything?"

"Nah, not really. Why?"

J.D. lifted a shoulder. "I'se just thinkin' maybe you'd wanna come over and play some video or something."

"Ah . . ." Jared was shocked now.

"Mike used to come over after school all the time," J.D. said, and put on his most mournful face. "Man, he used to kick my ass on *Street Fighter II.*"

Jared looked down at the mention of Mike, their fallen comrade and lost pitcher. "Yeah, sure, I guess. For a while, anyway. I gotta call my mom, okay?"

"Sure," said J.D. "I'll go get my car and meet you out front."

TWENTY-SIX

WHILE John Dixon Lake was busy killing his mother, Eugenia was watching the death of his great, great, great-grandmother. It came to Eugenia while she was hanging the repaired lace curtain Lena had picked up before her run. Eugenia stood frozen on the stepladder while the scene unfolded across her vision. She saw Annabeth giving painful birth, her porcelain face contorting in agony as she worked to push out the baby inside her. Annabeth hated the child already, hated the man who had given her the child even more. She had intended to remain childless and avoid motherhood, but her husband's latest infatuation convinced her something had to be done. It was conceivable he could change his ways entirely if he had a child to dote upon, and Annabeth would no longer need to worry about the shame that would come to her should anyone find out about the latest accident he had arranged, fatally injuring his personal aide. Annabeth was tired of his nonsense and ready for something different from her husband. A child, she believed, might bring about the desired changes that her charm, wit, and money had failed so far to deliver. She was also tired of the other women of the fort giving her their looks when she got up and walked away from conversations about babies and children. It was all boring drivel to her; why should she stay when she had no interest? Now she would stay and look down her nose at them, for she would have a nanny for her child. She would take the old laundress and let her striker do the fort's laundry until a new laundress could be found.

As another pain ripped through her abdomen, Annabeth found herself remembering the face of the laundress in the grave. Annabeth had hated her red hair and perfect teeth, the sweet shyness of her.

Eugenia frowned and began to wobble precariously on the stepladder.

No. That's Martha's face you're remembering, Annabeth. Not Audrey's.

Annabeth gritted her teeth and growled her way through the pain. The next time she thought of Audrey, it was Lena's face Annabeth was seeing. The white-haired old laundress hurried into the room then, her arms full of fresh white linens. Her face grew pinched with worry and poorly disguised irritation when she looked at Annabeth.

"Yer lookin' peaked, Missus."

"I'm giving birth," Annabeth said in a cold, but weak voice.

"I know that, I do. Come, let's have a look and see how yer progressin'."

She moved to the end of the bed and lifted the sheet over Annabeth's legs. The old laundress frowned.

"The babe's tryin' to crown, Missus. Can ye push?"

"What do you think I've been doing?"

"Ye'll have to push harder then, and it's important that ye start doin' it right now."

"I can't push any harder. I'm doing all I can."

"Missus, if ye want this babe to live, then ye better start pushin'."

Annabeth wanted to come off the bed and sink her teeth into the old woman's ugly, ruddy face. Instead she gave a tremendous heave and put all her energy into pushing out the beast inside her.

She felt horrible pain as her flesh ripped and tore, and she screamed as she pushed out the head. The old woman was smiling and nodding, urging her to go on, just one more.

Why did I do this? Annabeth asked herself, her thoughts close to delirium. *What did I hope to achieve?*

Besides the respect and adoration of her husband, who before her pregnancy had only ever looked at her with contempt.

What besides that? Security. Stability. Perhaps even a small amount of revenge, and a thumb to her nose, saying *just try and get rid of me now.*

"Dirty, filthy scoundrel," she seethed between her teeth. "Lying, cheating infidel. Monster of men."

"Ssh," said the old laundress. "He'll hear ye, Missus. He's in the next room."

The door opened before the old laundress could close her mouth. John Dixon entered the room and walked over to the bed where his wife lay writhing in pain.

"One more good push, sir, and ye'll have yer babe," said the old woman.

"Well?" Dixon looked at Annabeth, and beneath the benign smile and warm glow of his features, Annabeth saw something that made her squeeze her eyes shut in terror.

She had made a mistake in judgment and badly erred. Annabeth wondered how she could possibly have been so stupid. Her husband was going to kill her. She had given him all he needed. While she remained childless he had no opportunity to construct a "natural" death, and any accident would be investigated thoroughly by her parents. Now he had facts on his side: out West, death during childbirth, or shortly thereafter, was a common occurrence.

Annabeth moaned and forced herself to stop pushing. She wasn't going to have this baby. She was going to keep it inside of her and stay alive.

"One more, Missus," the old laundress kept repeating, and Annabeth wanted to cover her ears, because her body wanted to push, push, push it out of her and get it over with, but there was her husband standing over her with his glistening eyes and feral smile.

"I can't," she cried. "I can't do it."

"Yes, you can," her husband said in a gentle voice.

"Don't kill me," Annabeth begged, and she opened her eyes wide to look at him. "Don't kill me, John."

Dixon picked up her hand and patted it. "Whatever are you talking about, my dear?"

"It's the pain, sir," said the laundress. "It makes women crazy, it does. Best ye be goin' out now so we can get this babe born. I'll call ye when it's time."

Annabeth watched her husband give an absent nod and leave the room. When he was gone, she whispered fiercely to the old woman. "He's going to kill me. Once the baby is born, he's going to find some way for me to die."

"Nonsense," said the laundress. "Get to yer pushin' now, Missus, or you will be dyin'. Yer soakin' this bed with blood as it is, and that ain't so good."

Annabeth opened her mouth to reply, but a dreadful pain in her lower body, accompanied by a heavy gushing of fresh red blood, rendered her speechless. The laundress saw what was happening, saw that the highborn lady was not going to make a mother after all, and so took a small blade from the pocket of her apron and bent down to help the babe the rest of the way out. Annabeth screamed in agony at the sawing of her flesh and bled to death in her bed while she watched the white-haired laundress slice through the umbilical cord and then swaddle and coo over the dark wet head of the red-cheeked baby.

When Eugenia saw lace in front of her face rather than bloody linen, she realized she was holding on with a death grip to the frame of the window. She climbed unsteadily down the ladder and went to sit on the sofa while she digested all she had seen. She could not help but feel pity for Annabeth and the cruelty of her death. But other elements of the vision were even more disturbing to Eugenia.

Why had Annabeth seen first Martha's face and then Lena's as Audrey? Was it Eugenia's own self intruding upon the vision? It had to be. Both Martha and Lena could not have been Audrey. Unless Audrey had come back in Martha, and Martha had come back in . . .

Eugenia blinked. No. Too much. It was too much even to consider.

It didn't mean anything that Ross didn't start seeing Martha until Lena went to work for him. And it was of little consequence that Lena's lifelong aversion to males could be explained by a past life and death as someone like Martha Box.

They just keep comin' back, don't they? Like a big damned circle.

Eugenia shook her head and left the sofa to go and look at the calendar. Only nine and a half days left before she got out. The question was, would she truly get away?

Next door Rafael leaned his forehead on one hand while he held the phone to his ear with the other. His counselor was furious.

"Didn't I tell you to avoid this woman? Good God, Rafael, what makes you think you of all people would be able to relocate your parole?"

"You're saying it's impossible?"

"In this lifetime, yes. There's no way in hell you're going to Oregon or anywhere else. You stay right where you are and find yourself a good job."

"The job I have is the only one I could get. These people won't allow me anything. Only Lena and her mother treat me like I'm a human being."

"Which is probably why you're so infatuated with her. I guarantee you, Rafael, you will get over it. Trust me, I know what I'm talking about. You think you're the first con ever to get out and fall in love right away? All you guys do this. You all want to jump out and start families.''

"Please tell me who else I can talk to," Rafael asked, ignoring everything else.

"About what? Oregon? I'm telling you to forget it. It's not going to happen. If this girl is the one for you, then how come she's leaving, Rafael? Think about it.''

"It's complicated," he said.

"It always is. She's probably got a sick mother or father who needs her at home, right?''

Rafael was silent.

"I thought so. She'll be gone two weeks and you'll find someone else. That's the way it happens. And after that particular someone, or maybe after the next someone, you might find *the* someone. Stop trying to rush things. You're a young man yet, with plenty of time to get your life in order before you go looking for a wife.''

Rafael remained silent. There was nothing he could say to make this person understand. At the moment he felt utterly hopeless. Lena was going to walk out of his life again, but this time she was getting in a car to drive across the country, and Rafael knew in his heart if he let her get in that car, he would never see her again. She would find a hundred different excuses and rationalizations for the feelings she had for him. She would go back to her old job and her old ways and do her best to forget about him. She told him herself she would ruin things between them.

For a sick, frightening moment he almost wished something would happen to Eugenia, so Lena would have to stay.

Then he heard his counselor saying, "Don't do anything stupid, Rafael. You're too close to complete freedom and independence to throw it all away over some woman. You stay put and keep reporting in to your p.o. when you should. Hear me?''

"I hear you. Thanks for talking with me.''

"That's what I'm here for. Call me again, Rafael, and let me know how you're doing.''

"I will. Good-bye."

Rafael replaced the receiver, and for the first time in years he wished he had something to put in his mouth and wash down his throat; something that would make the hurt go away and make him not care.

It would be easy to find. If Pena knew where to find a whore, then he would know where to find—

He brought a fist to the side of his head and hit himself hard. The pain made his vision momentarily darken. He hit himself again, causing nausea to rise in his throat.

He would not go back. Would *not*. He would deal with this like a man and take the pain of losing without blunting the edges. Once she was gone he would be grateful for ever having had her at all. He would get his ass out the door every morning and go to work. He wouldn't think about her, wouldn't call her or write her; he would do as his counselor suggested and get on with his fucking life.

A knock at his door drew him out of his thoughts and made him instantly alert. Lena would not knock. Eugenia would.

He slipped through the room and saw the object of his thinking standing on his porch.

"Hey, Chavez," Bob Pena said with a wide grin for his friend.

Rafael had spent at least ten of his years in prison hating Roberto Pena. He blamed Pena for slipping him the acid in the first place, blamed him for the second tab, blamed him for leaving him alone in the car and for taking off and running away after he saw what Rafael had done.

Pena said he couldn't blame him, and he did all he could to help Rafael's mother while Rafael was incarcerated. He shoveled snow off her walks and kept her grass cut and did everything he could to make it up to Rafael, because he, too, blamed himself for what had happened. It was his fault, he wrote in numerous letters. He *was* jealous of Rafael's girlfriend, and it was out of spite that he gave Rafael what he did.

Faced with such honesty, Rafael could not help but relent.

Pena sent him packages at Christmas and on his birthday, and he promised to do all he could to help Rafael when he got out. It didn't matter that his help had fallen through, Rafael guessed. Good intentions counted for something.

"Hey, Pena. You're not working today?" Rafael asked.

"Took off early to come by and see how you're doing. Can I come in?"

"Sure." Rafael stepped aside to let his friend enter the living room. "Sit down. You want a beer?"

"Yeah, okay." Pena sat down on the sofa.

Rafael got two beers and brought them into the living room. He handed one to Pena and sat down in a nearby chair. Pena was looking at his bandaged head.

"Heard someone jumped you. Any ideas?"

"Yeah, I know who it was. How'd you hear?"

"Kid at school told my kids. You know how it is. Can't hide much in a town where everyone knows everyone else."

"And I'm still news," said Rafael.

Pena nodded. "Yeah. I don't have to tell you how freaked I was when the Ruanda Beker thing happened. I was thinking you must have the worst goddamn luck in the world."

"I was thinking the same thing," said Rafael.

"I'm glad they got that shit all straightened out. My wife was telling me to stay away from you and keep you away from the house. She doesn't know you like I do, so she was kinda worried."

"I understand."

"So does this guy have a grudge against you for something, or is he just one of the town assholes?"

"Both."

"Huh. Sure he's not hot after that girl you been seeing? The one at the sandwich shop?"

Rafael frowned. "Your kids told you about that?"

"Kids didn't have to. You know people are watching you. They're saying the only reason she's with you is because she's not from around here and doesn't know what you did."

"She does now," Rafael informed him, and he told Pena about the police file photos and the bloody bat tossed through his window.

Pena's brows met. "This guy is seriously twisted. If you know who he is, how come you're not pressing charges against him?"

"There's no proof it's him."

"Then how do you know?"

"Because he sits in a blue Camaro and watches my house every night. Because he has the same blond hair as the guy who kicked that kid to brain death and because he thinks he's going to trap me into doing something to him and get my ass sent back to jail. That's all he and the rest of these assholes want, is me back in a cell."

Pena was nodding. "Blue Camaro, huh? That's J.D. Lake, one of the little bastards arrested for Ruanda's murder. He's the son of Lorraine Lake, the reporter."

"J.D. Lake," Rafael repeated, and his mind matched the information with what he already knew to come up with confirmation of his initial impression: Lake didn't care who knew because he believed his CBFG ass was covered.

Pena took a drink of beer and asked about Lena.

"What about her?" said Rafael.

"What does she think?"

"She's leaving soon. Going back to Oregon with her mother."

Rafael could feel Pena's dark eyes on his face. He lifted his beer and drank.

"You pissed she's leaving?"

Rafael swallowed and shook his head. "I knew she wasn't staying."

Pena laughed. "Took all you needed, right?"

Rafael said nothing.

"Well, hey, listen . . ." Pena stood up and put his beer on the end table. "I'm supposed to stop and pick up some milk on the way home. I'd better get going. You take care, Rafael, and watch out for yourself, okay?"

"I will." Rafael stood and walked him to the door. "Thanks for stopping by."

"De nada, amigo. See you later."

As he watched his friend walk out to his car, Rafael saw Lena walking up the street still dressed in her running clothes. Pena shook his head and turned to wink at Rafael. Rafael ignored him.

So did Lena. She was looking at Rafael. She lifted her hand in a small wave and he nodded at her before turning and going back inside the house.

Just looking at her hurt.

TWENTY-SEVEN

DETECTIVE Morales and the other men in the room wore grim faces as they followed procedure over the body of Lorraine Lake. Her kids were next door with the neighbor. The ten-year-old girl had a pass to leave school early that day to prepare for a Girl Scout function; she walked in the house an hour ago and found her mother dead.

Morales and his team were already there by the time J.D. and his friend came storming in to see what was happening. J.D.'s cry of anguish looked and sounded like the real thing. His face went white and he puked all over the dining room. He asked what had happened about a thousand times, until someone finally pulled him out of the room and took him next door. Then he tried to leave and go after Rafael Chavez. Chavez had done it, J.D. claimed. Him or his crazy damned girlfriend's mother.

It was something Morales intended to ask him about later, once he finished up with the body. The attack had obviously been a surprise, judging from the expression in the victim's eyes. And since she had been attacked face on, instead of from behind, the perpetrator was probably someone whom she knew.

The killer wanted to make it look like the work of Chavez,

doing the head-bashing bit, but not even Chavez would be this stupid, Morales told himself. Sure, Lorraine Lake was his worst enemy, but Lorraine Lake figured as the "worst enemy" for dozens of people, most of them victims of some article or another. Practically everyone Morales knew hated what she said and did but were nice to Lorraine's face because of what she could do to them. This had been going on for years, starting in high school, when Lorraine was editor of the school paper. It had somehow come out that Lorraine's mother, Letty Dixon, got pregnant when she was sixteen and gave birth to a boy she gave up for adoption. The baby stayed in Fort Grant, and his name was Donnie Sharp.

Lorraine had a fit when she found out, and she went crazy when she actually heard people gossiping about it. Donnie Sharp, her half brother, was crude, disgusting, and a deviant. She began a smear campaign that covered nearly everyone in the community, digging up every unmentionable act she could find and making subtle references to it in church and at school and every other place people gathered. Soon the same people who had been talking about her were trying to be her friend in order to spare themselves any public embarrassment. Lorraine welcomed them to her, and using the same tactics, had been making friends ever since.

The list of people who had cause to bash in her sly, calculating brain probably had its own waiting list.

Still, Morales had to start somewhere, and he guessed it was going to be with her bonehead son. Find out what he thought he knew.

Morales had already pulled aside the kid with J.D. and asked him the smart-ass's whereabouts that afternoon. The kid said J.D. was in the library; he knew, because he was there himself. Were they good friends? Morales wanted to know, and the kid shook his head and said he didn't have any reason to lie for Lake. Today was the first time he had ever hung with him outside of school.

That was interesting in itself, Morales thought, but he couldn't immediately say why. He suspected J.D. Lake as a matter of principle; that, and because he hated the smug young son of a bitch.

There was little sympathy in the detective's face when he walked next door to question Lake. J.D. looked up and blew his nose loudly when Morales entered the living room. Morales took J.D. by the arm and quietly escorted him to the kitchen, where they could talk.

Lake drew himself up to his full height and looked Morales in the eye, daring him to question his grief.

"What makes you think Chavez did your mom?" asked Morales, sparing the kid nothing.

J.D. blinked. "She was trying to get rid of him, send him back to jail. She made everyone in town hate him."

"Everyone in town already hated him. He knows that. Nothing she did to him was any different than what he's already used to."

"Yeah, but she was working on a story about his girlfriend's mom, the one Ross Schweig came to tell my mom about. Ross says she's crazy, and my mom did some calling around to ask people about her. She was getting ready to write a story about her. I think it's still in her computer. Did you check?"

"We will," said Morales. "You're telling me the motive for murder was to keep a story from being printed? A story about a visiting woman who doesn't even live here?"

"Hey, I don't know," snapped J.D. "I'm only guessing. How the hell am I supposed to know?"

"You were quick enough to judge. You were ready to go and beat the shit out of Chavez . . . again."

"I don't know what you're talking about."

The smugness was back. Morales curled his upper lip and walked out of the kitchen. The kid was such a dick. Morales laid odds with himself that J.D. Lake would never make it past the age of twenty. If somebody else didn't pop his sorry ass before then, maybe he'd do it himself.

"Hey," Lake called after him. "You better find out who did this to my mom. If you don't, I will."

Make that nineteen, Morales thought to himself, and he kept walking. Next door he found himself staring in irritated amazement as a uniformed officer informed him about a call that just came in from downtown. Radburn Lanyard, the lounge singer, had been found dead in his trailer by a cocktail waitress. The new body required Morales's attention, when he could spare a minute.

Morales sighed and looked around himself at the crime scene in Lorraine Lake's house. He could spare a minute. Lorraine Lake wasn't going anywhere.

When Ross couldn't drink enough to make himself drunk enough to forget why he was drinking, he drove to Eugenia's house and left the truck at the curb while he weaved his way across the street. He tripped on the first step and banged his knee hard on the third when he tried to catch himself. Lena heard his curse and came to the door. She made a face when she saw him. He opened his mouth and vomited when he saw her.

"God, how disgusting," she said. "Mom, come and help me. Ross is here, and he's getting sick all over the porch."

Eugenia hurried up behind Lena and made a face of her own. "Go get Rafael. We'll need his help."

Lena was only too happy to have an excuse to run next door. She came back seconds later with Rafael, and the three of them who were sober looked with derision and pity at the one who was not. Ross looked back at them and told them all to go to hell. All he needed was the sofa.

"After another shower," said Eugenia. "Your clothes are soiled."

"You're not letting him come in again?" said Lena in surprise.

"Do you want to let him drive home in this condition?"

"No, but why should he stay with us?"

"He's no trouble when he's sober, Lena."

"I know that, Mother. I work for him."

"No, you don't," said Ross, his voice slurring the words. "You're both fired. Both you and your mother."

"I don't work for you," said Eugenia as she came to put an arm beneath him.

"Well, you should. I'm a nice guy. I'm a good boss. Tell 'em, Rafael. Tell 'em what a decent guy I am."

Rafael said what Ross wanted to hear and bent to help Eugenia get him into the house. Lena was left with the task of cleaning up the vomit.

She walked around the house and turned on the hose to spray the offensive substance from the painted boards. When she was finished she went inside in time to find Rafael shoving Ross into the bathroom. Eugenia held a robe in her hands and was waiting to hand it to Rafael.

Lena shook her head and went into the kitchen to see about dinner. A pot of water was boiling on the stove and she dumped in enough spaghetti to feed the four of them. Then she went about preparing meatballs. When the meatballs were simmering on the stove she went to check on Ross's progress. He was being led out of the bathroom and into the hall. Eugenia held his soiled clothing in her hands and went past Lena to put them in the washing machine. Rafael put Ross on the couch and asked Lena for a blanket. Lena took a throw off a chair and handed it over. Rafael thanked her and covered the already-snoring Ross. Then he turned and looked at Lena.

"Stay for dinner," she said. "I'm making spaghetti and meatballs."

When he hesitated, she added, "Please." When he still hesitated, she went to him and clasped his hands in hers.

"Don't punish me because I have to leave. You know I can't let her go by herself."

His dark eyes bored into hers. "Do you want to go?"

Lena met his gaze. "No."

He lifted his arms around her and pulled her to him.

"I'm going crazy, Lena. I'm going crazy trying to figure out how to keep you with me. I can't go with you, I've already asked about it. They say I have to stay here."

"I'll come back to you," Lena told him. "Once she's settled and finds another associate, I'll come back."

Rafael closed his eyes and leaned his forehead against hers. "Why don't I believe you?"

"I don't know," she said. "Why don't you?"

"Because I know you. Once you get home things will be different. You'll tell yourself it was the water here, or some other kind of bullshit. You won't want to think about me."

"That's not true," Lena said, and she squeezed a handful of his flesh. "Rafael, you mean too much to me."

His hands came up to frame her face. He forced her to meet his gaze again. "Do I, Lena?"

"Yes," she breathed, and she moved forward to brush his lips. "Please believe me."

"I have to," he said. "I love you."

She made a noise in her throat and kissed him again, harder this time, with more feeling. He held her and kissed her back, and when she pulled away to draw breath he told her he was going to love her so good before she left she would never forget him.

"Yes," she said again, her voice a whisper. "I want you to."

They didn't hear Eugenia enter the room. Only when she loudly cleared her throat did they lift their heads and pull apart.

"Your meatballs are burning," Eugenia said to Lena.

Her face colored and Lena excused herself to go to the kitchen. Unwilling to let go of Rafael, she pulled him along behind her. He came willingly, his eyes still dark with passion.

Lena looked at him, and for the first time she could imagine herself as his wife. She could imagine being round with his child and laughing and arguing and loving him in every way. She could see him as a good, loyal husband and a proud, caring father. She could see herself living with him the rest of her days, sharing in his life, whatever that life may be.

Her lips trembled with the urge to say all she was feeling, the need to tell him. He could see she was on the brink of speaking, and the hope in his face suddenly strangled her and rendered her incapable of speech. She gave him a weak smile and turned to the stove to check on the meatballs.

"It's okay," he whispered against her hair, and Lena's eyes grew moist as he reached around her to squeeze her waist. They stood together that way, her turning the meatballs, him holding her, until the ring of the doorbell made them look at each other.

A moment later Eugenia called to them. Lena walked into the foyer, followed by Rafael, and they saw a familiar face waiting to greet them.

"Chavez," said Detective Morales. "Miss Fairfax."

Lena nodded. Rafael said nothing.

"I have some news for all of you, could be good or bad depending on your point of view," began Morales. "Lorraine Lake was found murdered in her home this afternoon."

Lena, Eugenia, and Rafael looked at each other. Then a snorting sound from behind them made them turn to look at Ross on the sofa in the living room.

Morales stepped inside and glanced into the living room with an expression of surprise. "How long has he been here?"

"Not long," said Eugenia. "Half an hour."

"Where was he before? Did he say?"

"No, he didn't. He's been drinking."

"Why did he come here?"

Eugenia blinked. "It's rather a long story, Detective Morales."

"Condense it for me, would you?"

"Well," she looked at Lena and Rafael for help. "I don't quite know how to explain."

"Try." Morales's face was grim.

Eugenia cleared her throat. "Ross tells me he thinks I can protect him. He claims he can't sleep at home anymore, and that's why he came here."

Morales lifted his dark brows. "Protect him from what?"

"I . . . well, from something that happened a long time ago. He's been having nightmares about it, and he seems to think I can help."

"Why would he think that?"

"I'm not sure," Eugenia said. "It's all so complicated. I have to ask, do you think Ross did something to Ms. Lake?"

Morales lifted a shoulder. "That's what I'm trying to find out, Mrs. Fairfax. I need to know where he was today. For that matter, and just for kicks shall we say, I need to know where all of you were today. Okay?"

Eugenia's eyes rounded, and Lena stepped forward.

"You're saying my mother and I are suspects?"

Rafael put a hand on Lena's arm. "No, he's saying I'm a suspect. Again."

Morales took a piece of paper from his pocket. "I'm saying Lorraine Lake was writing a story about Mrs. Fairfax and her alleged psychic abilities. She's got all kinds of quotes from the folks back home in Oregon, and I'm guessing, Eugenia, that you knew about this and were pretty upset about the whole thing. The part I'm having trouble with is figuring how the guy who put her onto you in the first place comes to be snoozing on your sofa. And now you're telling me it's because he thinks you can protect him. Somebody better start telling me something that makes sense, and I mean—"

"What's going on?" Ross staggered into the room and looked at everyone through bleary, red-rimmed eyes. "What's all the yelling about?"

Rafael moved behind Ross to steady him. "Lorraine Lake is dead, Ross. Murdered. Morales came here to question us."

Ross's mouth dropped open. He stared in disbelief at Morales. "What happened? Who did it?"

Morales looked Ross over and ran a tired hand over his face. "Can I get a cup of coffee?"

Eugenia nodded. "Come in and sit down."

Morales walked into the living room, followed by Lena, Rafael, and the still-unsteady Ross. Eugenia turned off the meatballs, made some coffee, and brought Morales a cup. The room was silent when she entered, with everyone looking at each other and saying nothing.

The detective thanked Eugenia for the coffee, and took a sip. Then he turned to Rafael.

"Where were you this afternoon, Chavez?"

"At home."

"Any visitors? Anyone besides your neighbors here who can back you up?"

"Bob Pena came by around three-thirty."

"Stay long?"

"Just a few minutes."

"Talk to anybody before that? Anyone?"

Rafael looked at Lena. "I called my counselor."

"Your counselor?"

"Yeah."

"Don't you mean your therapist?"

"I mean my counselor."

"Okay, okay. I'll get the number and check it out later." Morales turned to Lena then. "What about you?"

"I picked up a lace curtain in town and then I went out running," Lena informed him in an icy voice. "Only several dozen people saw me."

"Think they'll remember?"

"The males will," said Rafael, and Lena silenced him with a look.

Morales smiled and looked at Eugenia. "Mrs. Fairfax?"

Eugenia opened her hands. "I was home alone most of the day and saw no one but my daughter, Rafael, and Ross."

The detective nodded. He turned to Ross.

"What time did you start drinking today?"

Ross's mouth came open; then he shook his head. "I don't know. I couldn't say. This afternoon, I guess."

"That's a shame. Alcohol does terrible things to your memory, doesn't it? A big guy at Radburn Lanyard's trailer park gave me the tag number off your truck and said you'd been by to visit Lanyard a couple times in the last week. You remember that?"

"Yeah," said Ross.

"Good. A friend of his found him dead in his bed this morning, shot with his own gun."

Ross's breathing dipped and then stopped. He stared at Morales and waited.

"And today your ex-ladyfriend is murdered in her home, and her little girl tells me all about how Ross came and begged her mom to take him back, but she wouldn't do it. He told her all sorts of stuff about this woman, this Eugenia person, and then he got mad at her mom and left. The little girl was in the bedroom and heard the whole thing."

"I didn't do anything," Ross said in a hoarse voice.

"Lorraine left the paper at three o'clock today, Ross. She would have gotten home about three-ten or so. Her daughter found her at three-thirty. That gave someone twenty whole minutes to come in, kill her, and leave. Can you tell me where you were during those twenty minutes, Ross?"

Ross was shaking his head. "Parked in front of my shop. I didn't go in. I sat out in the truck all afternoon, drinking beer. I wouldn't hurt Lorraine. I wouldn't hurt anyone. I went to see Rad Lanyard because . . . because . . ."

His voice trailed off and he looked at his hands.

"He was the third?" Eugenia whispered.

"The third what?" Morales asked, his tone impatient. Then he stood. "Enough of this. I'm tired and I want to go home. Ross, you come with me. I'm going to hold you until I get some answers from someone."

"You don't have to go," Rafael said. "He doesn't have just cause."

"The jailhouse lawyer speaks," sneered Morales. "I've got enough to satisfy a judge. C'mon, Schweig. I'll ask you ladies to stay in Fort Grant until you hear something from me. I don't have to worry about you, do I, Chavez?"

Rafael ignored him. "You have a lawyer, Ross?"

Ross shook his head.

"Do you want us to call someone?"

He nodded. "I didn't do anything."

"We know," said Rafael, and he was looking at Morales as he said it.

Eugenia remained silent and unmoving as she watched the detective lead Ross out to his car. Lena felt her mother looking at her and she turned.

"What is it?"

"Nothing."

"Nothing? You were looking at me as if it were something."

"No . . . I . . . was just thinking that sometimes your hair has a reddish cast to it in the sunlight."

Lena frowned at her and at the strangeness of the response. Rafael interrupted the exchange by asking for a phone book. Lena led him into the house and away from her mother's probing eyes.

TWENTY-EIGHT

MORALES looked at Ross as they drove away from the house. "What the hell is going on with you? What was that woman talking about back there?"

Ross's chin was on his chest. He was thinking about Rad Lanyard. The fool had killed himself. Ross was seriously considering something like it himself, maybe jumping from the car in the middle of a busy intersection. Morales hadn't cuffed him or anything; it would be easy to do. The detective nudged him on the arm, hard.

"Ross, talk to me. Lanyard was the third what? What did she mean by asking you that?"

"Rad shot himself, didn't he?" Ross said. "You didn't say suicide, but that's what it was, wasn't it?"

"What makes you say so?" Morales asked.

Ross looked at his hands. "I think I made him remember something he didn't want to remember. Something he thought he'd never have to think about again."

Morales snorted. "I'm getting tired of this bullshit. Kindly explain to me just what the hell you're talking about. Why were you going to see him?"

Ross drew a deep breath and filled his lungs with air. He was surprised Martha wasn't there with him, laughing at his predicament. He wondered if she had been to see Rad last night. Maybe she was finished now, he thought with a sudden spurt of hope. Maybe she had accomplished everything she meant to accomplish, driving Ross to visit Rad and causing Rad to do what he did. Maybe now she would leave him alone.

"Schweig?"

"I heard you," Ross said. "If I told you, you'd think I was crazy, and since you already think I killed two people, I'd just as soon keep my mouth shut."

"Fine," said Morales. "Was that the equivalent of asking for a lawyer?"

"Yeah, I guess. You didn't read me my rights."

"You know your rights, don't you?"

"Yeah. Am I under arrest?"

"Unless you start talking to me you are."

"You mean if I talk to you, you won't arrest me?"

Morales looked at him in frustration. "I need some help here, Ross. Two people you knew are dead. I can put you with both of them under questionable if not incriminating circumstances. Help me out, would you?"

"I don't know what to tell you," said Ross. "I've already said where I was and what I was doing this afternoon."

The detective glowered at him. There was silence in the car for several tense moments, then Morales took a card from his jacket pocket and held it on top the steering wheel to read Ross his rights.

Ross stared out the windshield at the familiar streets of town and wished Rad had left a note telling him what they had done with Martha. This was justice in a way, he supposed. He had never done time for Martha's murder, but he might do time for one he didn't commit. Which led him to wonder who had killed Lorraine, how it was done, and why.

Then he stopped wondering and realized he didn't give a shit.

Then he felt bad for not giving a shit.

He couldn't see Eugenia, or Lena, or even Rafael killing Lorraine any more than he could see himself doing it. Maybe it was Martha. Maybe Martha did it.

Ross snickered. Then he began to laugh, and soon he couldn't stop. He felt Morales staring at him, heard him saying some smart-aleck shit, but he couldn't stop laughing. He laughed until he cried, and then he couldn't stop that either. By the time they reached the station, Ross was blubbering into his hands. Morales hauled him out of the car and led him inside the building, all the while telling him to buck up. Ross couldn't do it. He couldn't stop until he was sitting in a jail cell by himself and Martha came to sit beside him on the cot.

He wiped his nose on his sleeve and closed his eyes. It was going to be a long night.

Eugenia thought so, too. She had closed her eyes for only seconds, or what felt like it, and witnessed the death of the white-haired laundress at the gloved hands of John Dixon. Two women, both younger and more attractive, had arrived at the fort with their husbands, and John Dixon set his romantic sights on the prettiest of the two and decided he would have her as nanny for his child. He arranged for both husbands to accompany the laundress on a mission to barter and trade for goods with a nearby encampment of Cherokee Indians. If the old laundress was along, he explained, then the men of the Cherokee camp would know immediately there was no danger and not be alarmed.

John Dixon ambushed the three of them himself from the top of a ridge covered with a sparse growth of cottonwood trees. Three Indians out hunting witnessed the slaughter, and knowing they would be blamed for the attack, took John Dixon captive. As any coward would, he immediately began to beg for his life. The Indians turned the horses of the slain back toward the fort and sent them off. Dixon's horse they kept. The bodies of the dead were taken back to camp and burned; Dixon was held prisoner while the men decided what to do with him. The last Eugenia saw of John Dixon, he was being poked in the ribs with a sharp stick by a beautiful, smiling black-eyed little girl.

Next she saw a man she knew to be the son of John Dixon, fighting and dying in a battle with other men. There were dead and wounded everywhere, most of them white men, few of them Indians.

Then she saw a child, and this child she recognized. It was the child felled by the bucket. The one who would not stop when the stern, harsh-voiced matron called. He was orphaned by the man who died fighting Indians, and he was the grandson of John Dixon.

She saw the bucket fly again, saw the blood soaking the ground around the head of the child, and for the first time in her visions she saw the child lift his head. The surge of joy Eugenia experienced was quickly dispelled by the look of pure hatred in the eyes of the young boy. When his gaze landed on Eugenia there was a queasy feeling in the pit of her stomach, and she knew this boy did not die after all. He had lived to sire children of his own, children who carried the same sickness and misery in their souls as the first Dixon in Kansas, commander of the fort.

When Eugenia opened her eyes she knew with sudden perfect clarity what she had been sent to Fort Grant to do. She was to stop the cycle. She was chosen as a child and had been given the horrible preliminaries. Now she knew why. The cycle had been temporarily interrupted with the birth of girl children. Lorraine Lake was dangerous and as vicious as any of her ancestors, but she drew blood with words instead of weapons. Her son, the boy in the blue Camaro, Rafael had said, was brimming with the bloodlust of his great-great-great-grandfather, with none of the romanticism.

Eugenia thought she should have seen the resemblance the day she confronted him. His eyes were the same chilling blue as his mother's, whose were the same as John Dixon's. Even the shape of the mouth and the length of the nose were the same. Eugenia didn't know why she hadn't seen it before. Perhaps because she hadn't been looking. Because she had been so wrapped up in Ross and his trouble with Martha that she was sidetracked.

Ross. Eugenia thought of him sitting in jail and felt sympathy for his plight. She knew now who had killed Lorraine Lake, knew it in her very soul. But who would believe her? Who would take seriously what she had to say, based on a few visions? Would a boy actually kill his own mother for no other reason than because it suited his purposes?

Rafael would believe her, she knew, and Lena, but only because, like her, they knew Ross could not have committed the murder.

She left her bed and walked through the house to the kitchen. Lena was next door, having been nearly carried there by Rafael. The transformation in Lena was nothing short of miraculous. Her combative nature and wry sense of humor had softened, along with every other part of her. Seeing her cling to Rafael that day had deeply touched Eugenia. This, too, had been meant to happen, she felt.

Eugenia paused. She examined her last thought and wondered why she no longer thought it was crazy, why she no longer questioned the validity of any of the impressions she received. Because she wasn't the only one who felt it? Because there never was and never had been any such thing as coincidence?

Briefly she considered taking Lena to visit with Odaline Burkey. She wondered if being near the scene of Martha's death might affect Lena in some way, in a manner that visiting the fort had not.

She poured herself a tall glass of milk then and sat down at the table to peel a banana. Rather than being sidetracked with Martha again, she needed to be thinking of what to do about the Lake boy. She had no idea how to go about stopping the cycle. She didn't think she could harm anyone, and the idea of doing so caused her to shiver. How else to stop him?

Seeing him sent to prison would not work. He was a young

man, and he would be out in plenty of time to sire children, if he had not sired any already.

Eugenia doubted he had. His mother was not the type to permit such lapses. In fact she could see Lorraine Lake doing everything within her power to prevent such a social embarrassment.

She shook her head. She was at a complete loss as to know what to do, now that she thought she knew why she was here. There was no way she could see herself contributing to the taking of a life.

She paused then as a fleeting memory pricked at her mind. Fire. Searing heat. Roaring flames.

Eugenia closed her eyes. She guessed she had at one time contributed to the taking of life. Two lives. When she was six years old she set fire to her house by putting a wet washcloth over a large lightbulb. The bulb exploded and the room was set aflame. Her father heard her screams and came running. Eugenia's clothes were on fire and he quickly threw her down and extinguished the flames before dragging her outside. She refused to let go of him, still screaming and crying, but he pried himself loose and went back in the house after his wife. A neighbor held Eugenia while she cried and listened to her father shouting hoarsely for her mother. Neither came out of the burning house. Both succumbed to smoke inhalation.

When no relatives came forth to claim her, Eugenia was sent sixty miles away to the nearest orphanage with available space, where she was no longer Eugenia Scavino, cherished and adored daughter of Italian immigrants; she became a lowly little ''wop'' whom nobody wanted and no one in the world cared about. She was to keep her mouth shut and her face and clothes clean, because if she didn't, then it was to the kitchen she would go, where the steam and the heat would curl her hair and sear her young cheeks.

Some of the children from the orphanage were adopted out, boys who could work, and girls who were blond. Others, like the ethnic-looking Eugenia and the red-haired Martha, were passed over. Redheads were scorned and laughed at in those days, called "carrot top" and "red" and generally thought of as in some way freakish because of their coloring. It was the same for Eugenia, whose dark eyes, hair, and olive skin set her apart and made her different, and thus unwanted. These were the children who were treated the worst by the matron and by the people in town. They were the underclass of the underclass, the seedlings who would grow into lowly weeds and someday require extirpation.

Funny how hardy some of those weeds could turn out to be, Eugenia thought, her mouth crooked. Funny how the being who created the garden didn't discriminate, but picked the best person for the job.

Me, Eugenia told herself. *I'm the one who has been chosen.*

The memories she had evoked made her stronger rather than diminishing her will. She did have the strength to do whatever needed to be done; she must have, or she would not have been chosen.

She would be told what to do, she knew suddenly. In the same way the visions came to her, the solution to the problem would come to her.

Eugenia was certain of it.

TWENTY-NINE

LENA was dreaming. She was in the dark interior of a car with laughing, jeering men with green, dashboard-lit faces. She was lying in the backseat and hurting from deep within. These men had done harm to her, and she could do nothing to help herself. Each time she struck out at them her arms passed through their flesh as if they were ghosts. They didn't look like ghosts, and they didn't feel like ghosts since they were able to poke and prod her at will. Their laughter caused Lena's terror to pass and become anger. She hated them. She hated them with a white-hot fury that lifted her understanding to a peak of complete awareness. She willed each one of them dead for what they had done to her. Soon the nervous laughter changed and the attention of the two men in the front seat became focused ahead, their faces suddenly grim.

Another invasion came, more degrading yet, and causing even deeper pain, with the white-hot hatred filling her and overflowing onto the groping, slobbering being above her.

Then she grew terrified all over again, because the car was stopping and everyone was getting out. She was dragged from the backseat and lifted from the car. The men carried her to what looked like a pit and awkwardly tossed her into it. Without knowing how she knew, she realized they were in a dump, a place where the people from town went to burn their trash. She began to scream as one of the men brought a gas can from the car and poured its contents over her. Her screams went unheard, and no matter how hard she tried to climb out of the pit, she could not move her arms or legs. Nothing would move. She was going to burn. They were going to burn her.

The first match landed on her face.

She screamed again and again, and soon she felt her arms moving. She clawed at her face to remove the match, and then she felt hands grip her by the arms. They were trying to shove her back down. Lena fought like a demon, hitting, biting, and scratching, all the while shrieking her hatred for the men who attacked her. From far away she heard a voice shouting a name, vaguely familiar, and she paused in her struggle to listen. When she opened her eyes she saw Rafael, long red marks on his face, neck, and arms where she had attempted to scratch him with her bitten-down nails. He was breathing hard and looking at her with a pained, incredulous expression.

Lena's mouth dropped open. She felt perspiration on her skin; her hair was damp at the scalp. She stared at her arms and hands and wiggled her fingers just to see them move.

"I . . . it . . . was awful," she whispered. "I've never had a dream like that, ever. It was so real."

"I couldn't reach you," said Rafael. "I yelled at you for five minutes and couldn't get through to you."

"I wasn't . . ." She had started to say, *I wasn't me,* but that sounded too strange to her. For a moment she was reminded of another dream, a dream of horses and soldiers and the feeling then, too, that she was herself but not herself. Never in her life had she had such dreams.

"What happened?" Rafael asked, and she looked at him in incomprehension until he said, "In the dream."

Lena told him all she remembered, starting with the car ride and the green faces and the deep, deep hurt that went somehow deeper than physical pain. When she finished, he was silent for a long time. Finally he said, "You said you hated me. You said I was a filthy, disgusting pig and I deserved to die for what I did."

"I wasn't talking to you," she told him. "It was those men, the three men in the dream."

"You've said that to me before," Rafael responded.

"No, I didn't. I never said anything like that to you."

Rafael remained unconvinced. "You're still afraid of me, aren't you? This is your way of telling me you still can't deal with what I did, no matter what you say to me while you're awake. Or maybe you were awake just now, I don't know."

Lena sat up in bed. "Rafael, it was a *dream*. It had nothing to do with us. Those men were going to set my body on fire. They were going to burn me."

"And that doesn't strike you as symbolic in any way? Did you feel you needed to remind yourself how much you hate men?"

She couldn't believe he was saying these things to her. She couldn't believe he was serious.

"I don't hate men. I've never hated men."

He gave a short laugh. "Right. And I've never liked women."

"Rafael—"

"Have you ever thought about why you can't tell me you love me?" he asked. "Has it ever occurred to you to wonder why something so simple is so difficult for you?"

"Yes, I've thought about it," she admitted. "I'm not altogether certain, but—"

"It's not because of any superiority bullshit; it goes deeper than that. What went wrong, Lena? Did Daddy stroke you the wrong way, or didn't he stroke you enough?"

"Rafael, please stop," she begged him. "How can I tell you what I don't know myself? I've always thought I didn't need the same things as other people, and yes, it had something to do with all the attention my father gave to my mother. But I never begrudged her that attention. I was never jealous or heartbroken. I just don't know how to love a man. With mother it was never love, though I'm sure she did love my father. With her it was always need, and I swore to myself I would never need a man the way she did."

Rafael studied her in silence for several moments, his eyes searching hers to confirm the veracity of her statements. Finally he said, "You know how to love. I've never felt so loved. And you do need me. You're a part of me now, and we need each other."

Lena looked at him and slowly nodded. "You're a part of me, too. I can't imagine being without you."

He put his hands on her arms again, gently this time. His voice was earnest. "Don't be without me. Say you'll stay, or marry me before you go, so I know you'll come back to me."

Her lashes fluttered. "Marry you?"

"Please, baby. Please say yes."

Lena stared into his face. His eyes were moist with intent; his hands squeezed her flesh.

"I . . . I don't hate any part of you, Rafael, you know that."

"Marry me."

"The dream was just a dream. I'm not looking for any excuses to stay away from you."

"Then say you'll be my wife."

She swallowed. "I will come back to you. I've said I would, and I will."

He emptied his lungs and gave her arms a final squeeze before removing his hands.

"I'm sorry, Lena. I keep pressuring you. I don't want to. I see the fear in your eyes, and I hate myself for putting it there. Blame it on my passionate nature, or my ignorance."

Lena drew in the air he expelled. She looked at his bent head and marveled over how black his hair was. Deep blue-black and silky rather than coarse. It would be nice to see it long again, she thought, and gently combed the length with her fingers. She felt herself reaching out to him, extending more than her hand, and it was frightening, almost terrifying, to inch out so far along the precipice. Her breath went shallow and she forced herself to focus on him. Rafael lifted his head to look at her.

"I don't suppose there'll be any doubt about the color of our children's eyes," she said, "but I hope they have your hair."

His gaze fixed on her. His brows met.

"I'll have the Norplant removed while I'm in Oregon," she continued, her voice soft. "And contrary to what you believe, I won't be disappointed with a boy."

Rafael closed his eyes. His chest rose and fell with emotion. "I want both," he said. Then he opened his eyes and looked at her. "Will you marry me?"

She nodded. "Yes."

He took her in his arms and held her so tightly against him she had trouble breathing. She held him just as tightly and wiped furtively at the tears rolling down her cheeks, until she felt the wetness on his.

"Let's tell Eugenia," he said. "She's probably awake."

Lena held fast. "No. Hold me. Just keep holding me, Rafael. I don't want this feeling to end yet."

Rafael buried his face against her neck. "I'll be good to you," he promised. "I'll do my best for you, always, and try to make you proud of me."

"I'm already proud of you," she told him. "The way you held your temper with Morales today, and the way you helped Ross. If it hadn't been for you, I'd have been a yelling, screaming mess."

"Ready to protect all of us?" Rafael said with a smile, and he kissed her neck.

"If need be, yes."

He pulled back to look at her. "The dream, Lena. Do you think it could have been suggested in some way by your mother? I mean, maybe these visions she's been having have affected you, and you don't realize it. Maybe the two of you have some kind of psychic connection. It's not unheard of."

She gave her head a small shake. "Most of my mother's visions take place in another century. My dream was definitely in this century.''

''Just a thought,'' said Rafael. Then he looked at her. ''What century?''

''The last one, dealing with people who used to live at the fort when it was first built.''

Rafael lifted his brows. ''Really? When I was in prison my mother sent me a picture she found in an old book. It was a drawing of some of the first dragoons and a scout. She thought I looked so much like the scout she had to take a copy of the picture and send it to me.''

Lena looked at him. ''Well?''

''What?''

''Did you look like him?''

''No, it was actually kind of strange, because I saw no resemblance whatsoever, aside from both of us having black hair and dark eyes. My mom swore to it, though.''

Lena faintly remembered her mother mentioning a scout, but she couldn't recall any of the details, save for the fact that she thought he was murdered.

''Do you believe we live again?'' she asked Rafael.

''You mean reincarnation?''

She nodded.

''I think something must live again,'' he answered. ''Maybe some weird strand of DNA that occasionally repeats itself.''

Lena cocked her head. ''Huh?''

''Gene memory, hell I don't know. Does your mom believe she's been reincarnated as someone from the fort?''

''No, I didn't say that. All I said was that she has visions of people who lived at the fort. She had them even as a child at the orphanage.''

''Bad stuff?''

''Horrible, like murders and things. It really tears her up when it happens.''

''There must be a reason for it,'' said Rafael, frowning.

"That's what we think."

"But you don't know yet. And you're leaving anyway."

"Because Mom wants to. I think she's tired of waiting and making herself sick over it. I'm not sure if she believes our leaving will end it, but it may serve as some sort of catalyst."

"Has she tried to identify any of the people in her visions?" Rafael asked.

"I think so, yes. I know she's been to the library."

"You don't know? Doesn't she talk to you?"

Lena shook her head and made herself comfortable in the crook of his arm. "No. She started to once, and I made some comment she took the wrong way. She shut up and hasn't told me anything since. I know the visions are pretty involved. You heard her before, when she said what she did about having seen the end of the movie. I think she's drawing a parallel with what's happening in the visions to what's been happening with us. That's why she thinks we're in such terrible danger; she thinks history is going to repeat itself."

"It could," said Rafael. "Half the people in this town claim ancestors who served at the fort. Bob Pena's ancestors, and supposedly my long-lost father's ancestors intermarried with the Indians who roamed the territory long before the whites came to build their fort. Thinking about it now I wonder if that's why I felt so comfortable with them the night they invited me to dance. There was a weird sort of kinship there, really heartfelt. Maybe blood recognized blood."

"What about your mother?" Lena asked. "Where did her people come from?"

"California, originally, for centuries back. Then New Mexico. My mother left there when she was very young."

"You know all the dates of birth and death and everything?" Lena asked, envying his knowledge of his past.

"It's all written down in my mom's Bible. Just names on paper. I never had any grandparents to visit, or aunts, uncles, and cousins. It was always just me and my mother."

Lena touched his face. "I had one set of grandparents, my father's people, but they died when I was little. My father was an only child, and my mother was an orphan, so I had no aunts, uncles, or cousins either."

Rafael kissed her fingers and said, "We'll make our own family, Lena. I'll be counting the days until you come back without those things in your arm."

She curled her fingers around his hand. "It could be weeks, Rafael. Or even months."

His lids lifted. "Months? You mean to get pregnant?"

"No, I mean before I come back. My mother has to find someone to take my place. That won't be easy. We work as a team, each with her own special training."

Rafael sat up. "You've agreed to marry me, and you're sitting here telling me you could be gone from me for months?"

The phone beside the bed rang before Lena could answer. They both turned to stare at the offensive object, neither moving to answer. It was the middle of the night, and nothing good ever came of a phone call in the middle of the night.

Finally Rafael extended an arm to pick up the receiver. After saying hello he listened in silence for several moments, and then he looked briefly at Lena before thanking the caller and hanging up.

"What?" she asked. "Who was it?"

"The lawyer I talked to earlier. He said the police just called him. Ross tried to hang himself in his cell."

Morales hung up the phone for the second time and cursed aloud before apologizing to his sleepy wife and telling her to try and go back to sleep. Ross Schweig had as good as convicted himself by attempting suicide. Who but a guilty man would try to hang himself and avoid the condemnation of the people he had lived among all his life?

Never mind the Martha Box business. Morales doubted he would get anyone to listen to him about her. There had been only seconds to digest the information from the first call before the call from the jailer came.

Lorraine Lake's daughter had phoned him, just as she had promised to if she remembered anything else. No matter that it was two in the morning. The girl said she couldn't sleep anyway. J.D. had opted to stay with a friend rather than relatives, and he left, leaving her by herself with an aunt who snored too loudly, and she'd been thinking and remembering just as Morales had told her to do. Lorraine's daughter, who wasn't her daughter at all, but the daughter of the man Lorraine had been married to before his death, remembered more of the conversation between Ross and her stepmother. She knew it wasn't nice to eavesdrop, but it was hard not to listen since her bedroom was right over the family room and all the sounds from the family room came up through the heater vent into her bedroom.

Ross told Lorraine something that happened a long, long time ago, to a girl named Martha Box. The daughter remembered the name because Ross kept repeating it. He said some guys had grabbed Martha Box off the street and they wanted him to come along, but he ran away. Martha Box was a girl from some kind of hall, the daughter told Morales, and the detective knew instinctively she was referring to the orphanage. She said Ross kept telling her mother how this Eugenia person must have done something to him, because he suddenly couldn't stop thinking about Martha Box and seeing her in his head. She was dead, he figured, and for most of his life he had tried and been successful in forgetting about her and that long-ago night, until Eugenia Fairfax and her daughter came to town. He wanted Lorraine to do something about them, to help him somehow, and that's when Lorraine told him to go and Ross got mad at her for not taking him back.

Morales had thanked the girl and hung up more confused than ever. Why would Ross ask Lorraine to help him when he believed Eugenia was the one who could protect him? Did he think she could protect him against his own memories or guilt?

Then the other call had come. Ross was found hanging in his cell and he was now on his way to the hospital, unconscious and "pretty much blue all over," the jailer had said.

Radburn Lanyard, Morales thought suddenly, and he remembered the whisper in Eugenia Fairfax's voice as she asked, *"He was the third?"*

The third what? The third guy who was in on whatever happened to Martha Box? What the hell *had* happened to her, and how had this managed to stay covered up for thirty-odd years? People always talked about murders. Always. Whoever committed one couldn't help telling someone else, and that someone had to tell someone, who had to tell someone, and on and on until somebody finally called the cops. It bugged the shit out of Morales to know that no one had talked this time. No one.

He was sleepy, and bone tired, but he couldn't stand it. He couldn't figure out what the hell was going on and it was driving him crazy.

He reached for his pants and quietly dressed without waking his wife. Eugenia Fairfax was the one he was going to wake up, after he did some snooping through the old county records. Morales wanted some answers and he was going to get them that night, one way or another.

THIRTY

THE milk and the banana succeeded in making Eugenia sleepy and she had just dozed off when she heard the sound of the door opening downstairs. Her brows puckered slightly; she hoped Lena and Rafael hadn't argued again. She was going to have to speak to Lena about getting along with men. It was the simplest thing in the world if a woman could only learn to keep half the things she wanted to say to herself and say them aloud only after the man was out of earshot. Eugenia had learned the technique in the orphanage and used it successfully in her own marriage. Arguments between her and Leonard were virtually nonexistent.

Lena was so proud and stubborn and convinced of her superior intelligence, it would take some doing to teach her how to keep a man's ego inflated, the true key to a successful relationship, Eugenia felt.

She considered getting up and going down to talk to Lena, who was probably rummaging in the kitchen by now for something to salve her wounded and suffering self. Then she heard light footsteps on the stairs.

"Lena?" she called.

The footsteps paused.

"It's all right," Eugenia said. "I was already up. You didn't wake me."

She sat up in bed and reached for her robe. She crossed the room and had passed through the doorway when she was suddenly grabbed by the throat and shoved back inside. Eugenia landed on her backside on the floor and rolled instinctively to her right, avoiding the lunge of her assailant and causing him to crash into the wooden frame at the foot of the bed. Eugenia was up in a second and scrambling for the door, but she was caught by the foot and dragged backward. She grabbed for the dresser and pulled herself in the other direction, her hands scrabbling madly through the tiny perfume atomizers and sterling silver brush and comb set on top to find a weapon. Her hands closed around the heavy hand mirror and she turned to smash it with all her might into the face of her attacker.

The mirror shattered, but the blow did little to deter him, and his strong hands reached to close around her neck.

Eugenia knew who it was. All her instincts told her who it was, and she was shocked, because she never believed things would turn out this way.

She struggled on, her fingers clawing and her legs kicking at his middle. She couldn't let this happen. She could not let him win. She gave up clawing at the hands tightening around her throat and felt for anything around her on the floor. Her left hand found a shoe, a low black pump and she smashed this, too, into his face with all her strength, causing him to cry out in pain and momentarily loosen his hold on her neck. Her throat was too damaged to scream, so she did the only other thing she could think of and threw the shoe at the nearest window.

The pump bounced off the glass and fell to the floor.

Eugenia moaned as a fist struck her across the face and caused her vision to darken. He hit her again, and again, and then he resumed strangling her. She felt something warm course down her cheeks and knew it was blood from her nose.

In the dimness of her room she believed she could see his face, the gritting of his teeth, the manic gleam in the icy blue eyes. He knew she had come to stop him, she told herself as tiny bursting sparks flamed and then extinguished themselves in her rapidly dwindling consciousness. He had no other reason to kill her.

As if reading her thoughts, he said, "Maybe Chavez'll get blamed for you, you crazy bitch. You know me, huh? You know who I am inside? Findin' out now, aren't you? You think I'd let you slide? You think I'd let you get away from me?"

Eugenia's gorge rose. She wished she had never confronted him that day, never spoken to him. If not for that mistake, she might have emerged the victor.

His grip on her throat grew tighter still and she gave up and closed her eyes. Her throat and chest burned and she saw herself years earlier, standing over the steaming pots and searing heat of the stoves in the orphanage kitchen. Her mind played an array of such scenes as her limbs grew increasingly numb.

Seconds later, some part of her still groping for continued consciousness, she felt him remove his hands and lift himself off of her.

He thought it was finished. He thought she was dead.

Eugenia fought to withhold any audible intake of air. She remained as still as possible, her lungs screaming for breath, and she felt him kick her in the thigh. The pain made her want to cry out, but she was motionless. Finally, after what seemed forever, he left the room and walked down the hall.

The gun, was Eugenia's first thought after sucking in a huge breath of sweet, sweet air. She fought to keep herself from gulping over the fire and swelling in her throat. She felt as if a hand was still clamped around her neck. As quietly as possible she lifted herself off the floor. For several seconds she clung dizzily to the bed frame and prayed hard for her head to clear and for no boards to creak beneath her feet.

A surge of adrenaline helped bring things into focus as she

heard the breaking of glass downstairs. Was her would-be murderer trying to make it look like a robbery gone bad?

She used the noise to mask swift movement out of the room and down the hall to the bedroom Lena used. She quietly opened the drawer in the night table and felt inside with her fingers.

Eugenia did something she normally did not do and cursed softly.

The gun was gone.

Then she spotted the phone. She picked it up and ordered her shaking fingers to press the right buttons. She heard a ring, then another, and then a voice answered.

Before Eugenia could utter a sound, there was a click on the line and she heard the unmistakable sound of another phone in the house being picked up.

She jabbed her finger to depress the button and hang up, but she pushed the wrong button, because she clearly heard the voice on the other end of the line repeat itself and ask if there was an emergency.

"No, I hit the emergency button by mistake," said a male voice very loud in Eugenia's ear. "Sorry."

"No problem," came the response. "Thanks for not hanging up."

"Wait," said Eugenia on her end, struggling to push coherent sound past her bruised and dangerously swollen throat. "Please . . ."

"Too late," said the voice on the extension. "They already hung up. Don't you go anywhere. I'm on my way."

Eugenia picked up the phone and threw it out the nearest window, shattering the glass and causing shards and splinters to fly everywhere. Then she ran into the hall and dashed for the bathroom, where the door was heavy, and the lock was good.

Panic brought a screeching noise from her damaged throat when she saw him come barreling up the stairs right behind her. In his hands was a knife from the kitchen, long and thin and sharp. Eugenia felt the tip of it catch her robe and she whirled to kick him. Her foot connected with his crotch, but the knife was pointed at her and he shoved as he fell forward against her. The blade sank into Eugenia's groin and penetrated deeply, causing her knees to buckle and her breath to cease.

Agony kept her from feeling anything when she saw Rafael appear behind her attacker and stare in shock before hitting the mask-covered head from behind. The blow stunned the wheezing boy, but not enough to keep him from ripping the knife out of Eugenia and savagely twisting to thrust it at Rafael. Eugenia slid to the floor as she watched the length of the blade pass through the bare flesh of Rafael's hard waist and come out the other side. Rafael roared in pain and lunged, knocking the attacker into Eugenia's room and out of her sight. There was the sound of a skull being slammed against the hardwood floor, and then she heard nothing but grunts and the ugly splat of fists repeatedly striking flesh, accompanied by the foulest language she had ever heard coming from Rafael's mouth as he spewed with rage.

Eugenia hoped he killed him. She hoped Rafael did not stop, but completed the job she had been sent here to do.

She looked at the blood on the floor around her and pulled up her robe and gown to look at the wound. Eugenia blanched and balled up the robe to try and stanch the steady flow. Then she thought of Rafael again.

"No," she croaked, as loud as she could. "Rafael, stop. Don't kill him. They'll kill you. Stop."

She was gratified when he emerged from the bedroom and came to lean over her. "Oh, God, Eugenia, I thought you were dead. I thought he'd killed you."

Her lips parted and she looked at his side, where the knife was still laced through his flesh. "I think he did. You should take that out."

He looked down and seemed surprised to see it there. He uttered another expletive and yanked the blade out.

The light in the hall came on, illuminating the blood and the ashen faces of both Eugenia and Rafael.

"I heard glass break . . ." Lena was saying, but she stopped talking as she topped the stairs and saw the blood on the floor around her mother and the knife in Rafael's hands.

Rafael saw the expression on her face, saw the pain and fury and misunderstanding in her eyes, the utter disbelief, and he saw the gun in her hands. He lifted a palm.

"Lena, no—"

It was too late. Lena saw nothing but betrayal. She saw her own selfishness and foolishness and gullibility in the form of her fallen mother. She had trusted him. She had believed in him. When he left her to come next door and talk to Eugenia about Ross, he had been so sincere. *"You get dressed and I'll be back with your mom in a minute."*

He was going to find her dead, Lena guessed in those insane seconds. He was going to kill her, then find her dead, leaving Lena conveniently free to stay in Fort Grant with no attachments.

She was such a fool.

Hatred, liquid hot and shrieking like a freight train, roared through Lena's gut and lifted her arms with the momentum. She pointed the pistol at Rafael's chest and fired, hitting him just below the collarbone. Reflex made her squeeze the trigger again, and she hit him in the shoulder as he fell.

Her arms lowered then, and she saw the round oh of dismay on her mother's face. Lena blinked and stared as the ringing of the shots sang in her ears. Her mother was shaking her head, mouthing the word, "no."

Movement out of the corner of her eye drew Lena's attention, and instinctively her arms came up. The gun was knocked out of her hands and sent spinning down the stairs. A tall figure with a blood-covered face stood smiling at her.

Dread filled Lena. She glanced once at Rafael, slumped over next to her mother, and then back to the black-clad blond before her. A cry of anguish erupted from her and curled her hands into claws. She launched herself in a frenzied attack against the blood-covered youth and fought hard for several seconds before suffering a blow to her middle that robbed her of air and left her gasping. He stood over her and grabbed a handful of her hair to yank her up. He struck her with his free hand, knocking her down again, and then stepped back for a kick to the head.

His foot never connected. Eugenia had picked up the knife Rafael discarded and dragged herself up to a sitting position. From there she used the bathroom door to pull herself up, and then the wall. She hurled her body forward and buried the blade as deeply as she could in the back of the blond boy and then sank to her knees as he growled and wheeled and used his arms and hands to try to reach the thing sticking out of his back. She couldn't believe it when he leaped over Lena and ran down the stairs. She couldn't believe he wasn't going to die.

"Mom," Lena whimpered as she crawled to her white-faced mother. Her eyes were fixed on Rafael. "What did I do? What did I do?"

"We need an ambulance," Eugenia told her in a hoarse whisper.

"Rafael," Lena moaned, and she began to sob.

"Ambulance," Eugenia repeated, and she gave her daughter a nudge. "He may still be alive."

Lena lifted her head; her face was hopeful. She ran in search of a phone and ended up leaving the house because the phones wouldn't work. Outside she nearly stumbled over the body of the youth. He was lying prone in the drive, the blade sticking out of his back. The slam of a car door made Lena look up and she saw Detective Morales headed toward her. She pointed to the body and in a high, frantic voice said, "He tried to kill us. We need an ambulance, please. My mother and Rafael."

Having said this, she turned to run back inside the house. Morales tried to stop her and ask questions, but she ignored him and kept running. Upstairs she found her mother looking even paler. She kissed her, told her an ambulance was coming, and then she moved cautiously to approach the inert Rafael. The pain and guilt she felt overwhelmed her and were made worse when she spied what appeared to be a stab wound in his side.

And the terrible bullet holes.

She jumped up to grab towels from the bathroom to stop the flow of blood. If he was still bleeding, then it meant his heart must still be beating, she told herself. She bent down close to his face and pressed her lips against his cheek.

"I know you'll never forgive me," she whispered, and fought back a sob. "I know you'll hate me for what I've done, but I'm so sorry, Rafael. I'm so sorry. Please don't die. Please hold on."

There was no movement from him, no response of any kind and Lena could find no trace of a pulse. She lay down on the floor next to him and put her arms around him while she sobbed.

"Tell him," said Eugenia in a thready whisper. "Tell him, Lena."

Lena clutched him to her and put her mouth above his ear. Tears from her cheeks fell onto his face and rolled down his skin while she whispered into his ear.

"Don't leave me, Rafael. I love you. I love you so much, and I'll never love anyone again, so please don't leave me. I swear I love you. I love you more than anything and I want us to get married and have babies and be together always. Please, please, don't leave me."

Eugenia wanted to smile, listening to her daughter. She had long dreamed of Lena falling in love with a man, marrying, and having children of her own. It was the sweetest thing she could have wished to hear before she closed her eyes.

She was so tired. She would have been cold, but the numbness was back and quickly taking over. All she wanted to do now was sleep while she waited for the ambulance. She was faintly annoyed at the idea she would have to find the boy and battle him again. He should have died. The knife she plunged into his back should have killed John Dixon Lake, the last of an abominable seed.

A vision prodded at her consciousness, and she saw herself standing outside and looking at Rafael, who was moving down the steps and away from her. She called him back and they proceeded to engage in heated conversation, with Rafael tossing his long black hair and gesturing in sadness to blood on his buckskin shirt.

Their conversation was an important one, but Eugenia couldn't for the life of her make sense of what was going on or what either of them were saying to each other.

She finished their brief talk by giving him a gentle hug and turning to walk away from him. Of all people, she saw Odaline Burkey waving to her from the end of the sidewalk. The old woman was smiling from ear to ear and nodding her white head as Eugenia went to join her.

The vision made no sense to Eugenia, but she was suddenly warmer than she had been, and incredibly, vibrantly happy.

Lena stopped sobbing and lifted her head when she heard a choking noise deep in Rafael's chest. She stared hard at him for several seconds and swore she saw him take a breath. She clasped his hand in hers and told him all over again how much she loved him, how desperately she needed him, and how sorry she was for hurting him. A hitching sound came from him then, and Lena shouted for joy as several ambulance attendants came charging up the stairs. Two of them stopped at her mother and bent over her; the other attendant and Detective Morales came to see about Rafael.

"He's still alive," Lena cried. "Help him, please."

The attendant quickly checked Rafael over and after a moment he made a noise with his tongue. "Judging from the blood on the floor, this guy should have bled to death ten minutes ago."

"The lady did," said one of the other attendants, and Lena blinked and felt shock momentarily stop her heart before she locked gazes with the harried-looking Detective Morales.

"What did he say?" she whispered. "What did that man just say?"

Morales looked over his shoulder, his mouth curving down,

and Lena followed his glance to see the attendants leaving her mother and coming to see if they could help with Rafael.

"Mother?" she cried, her voice cracking on the last syllable.

Her mother's face was still and white. Her lids remained closed. One of the attendants looked at Lena and gently shook his head. "I'm sorry. She was already gone. There was nothing we could do for her."

Lena came to her feet in one swift motion. Her mouth fell open and she screamed. The sound of it echoed through the house and caused expressions of pain on the faces of the men near her. They glanced at one another as she screamed again, and again, and when her voice went hoarse they all turned to look at her. Lena took a step toward her mother, then she fell to the floor in a dead faint.

Epilogue

IT took Ross nearly six weeks to recover from his attempted suicide at the jail. He offered no excuse and was given no apology by Detective Morales when he was released. After J.D. Lake's death, one of his neighbors suddenly remembered seeing the boy breaking a window of his own house one day, the same day his mother was found dead, it turned out. He thought it was funny, but didn't consider it anything of importance until news of the boy's murderous intent was released in the papers. Teenage boys did some crazy stuff, but never anything this crazy, and certainly not in a town like Fort Grant.

Detective Morales kept close company with Ross anyway, pumping him about Martha Box and the guys who had abducted her. He had looked through the county records and found mention of her disappearance, but nothing else. Morales wanted to know the whole story, and he bugged Ross about it until Ross agreed to tell him. All the principal characters were dead, and no one but Ross would be hurt, so Ross went ahead and told what he knew to the police, causing the file to be reopened, retyped, and then refiled again, only with different information this time. Morales saw to that. He remembered his father, also a policeman, telling him about a hermitlike black woman calling them out to her trailer by the old Hickok place one day, said she'd found the body of a young woman out there the night before. The police found no sign of a body, Morales remembered his father saying, and officially the woman was written off as a nut, but a few of the officers suspected foul play.

On a whim, Morales went to see if the woman was still alive, and he found the long-dead corpse of Odaline Burkey, who had apparently died in her sleep and lain undiscovered until Morales's arrival.

Without telling Ross why he believed him, Morales changed the official cause of Martha Box's disappearance, with the immediate effect of ending her visitations to Ross.

Ross didn't realize it for several days, but one morning it finally came to him that he hadn't seen Martha in a while. Not since he had told her story to Morales.

It should have made Ross happy, but it made him think only of Eugenia Fairfax and the terrible things he had caused to happen to her. After Eugenia's death, Lena took her mother back to Oregon for burial in the plot beside her husband. While recuperating in the hospital, Ross heard Rafael was a patient, and he went to visit him daily, not saying much because of his damaged larynx, but keeping him company until Lena came back.

She wasn't gone long. She stayed long enough to take care of her mother's affairs and put the house up for sale before hurrying back. Ross couldn't believe the change in her. While near Rafael she touched him constantly, always holding him and kissing him and murmuring in his ear how much she loved him. Rafael would close his eyes and squeeze her, then he would lean back and look at her, and when he looked at her a certain way Ross knew it was time to get up and leave them.

They were married a week after Rafael left the hospital, and Ross was never so shocked as when Rafael asked him to be his best man. He assumed the honor would go to Roberto Pena, but Rafael said he wanted Ross. He stood at the altar with them and felt happy and sad at the same time, knowing there would soon be children, and realizing there would be no grandmothers or grandfathers to play with or spoil those children. Ross wondered if they might allow him to fill that role in some way.

The owner of the local paper, after reading all that was written about Rafael and his part in attempting to thwart Eugenia's murder, called to offer him a job. Half the employees protested and threatened to quit, but the owner told them to go right ahead; he'd bring in people from out of town to fill their jobs. Common sense and a general knowledge of local economics caused many of the employees to rescind their threat to terminate. Rafael went to work in the advertising department and was given a salary, health insurance, paid sick leave, and retirement benefits, just like everyone else.

Lena still worked for Ross, just for something to keep her busy until she decided what she wanted to do. She confided to him one morning she didn't feel good about leaving him alone, and that was why she wasn't trying too hard to find a more permanent job. Ross told her she could work for him as long as she liked, so long as she didn't feel sorry for him, and she smiled and gave him a kiss on the cheek.

Ross went in the bathroom and had to fight to keep his eyes dry. There was no cause for Lena Fairfax to care about him, but he was glad she did. He felt a warmth and a closeness to her he would never be able to explain to himself, particularly after the animosity he had directed toward her during those first weeks. He hoped Lena decided to stay there and work with him even after she got pregnant and started having kids. He wanted to be involved and remain a part of her life. With Rafael, and with Lena, he felt young and almost pure again. Eugenia had granted him absolution, but Lena had brought him hope. For some reason she made him believe in second, third, and even fourth chances to get it right. Whatever it was.

Author's Note

I borrowed the concept of an orphanage built inside the remains of an old fort from the Goodlander Home, in Fort Scott, Kansas, which housed children from 1892 until 1958. No other relationship between the orphanage in the book and the Goodlander Home exists, and none should be inferred.